LIAM LIVINGS

Kieran's Pride

Kieran Book 2

Kieran's Pride © 2014 Liam Livings (Previously published as Best Friends Perfect, Book 2)

Second edition

Editing by Val Hughes
Cover art by Ethereal Designs

This book was professionally typeset on Reedsy.
Find out more at reedsy.com

Contents

Acknowledgement

A few people deserve thanking for helping make this book happen:

Chris Quinton who suggested the great new titles for this series.

Rhys for making a wonderful new cover.

Val Hughes for being a splendid editor and teaching me so much.

The beta readers: Nick G, Tim, Nick W, Julian, Adam, Hannah, Sara, Hayley, Jenny, Ian, Alex and Clare.

Thanks to Hayley and Ford, who are my real life Hannah and Grace. Who both kept my chin up when I did my little trip around Oz in my first planned gap year, and also kept me occupied in my *unintentional second unplanned* gap year when the wheels somewhat fell off my life.

Thanks to my readers, I hope you enjoy spending time in Kieran's world,

Lots of love and light,

Liam Livings xx

One

February 1999

*T*he twenty three hour flight felt much longer because my headphones didn't work, so I couldn't watch the endless round of second rate films, and my over-head lights had broken, so I couldn't read my book for most of the time either. Short of taking some of Jo's magic tablets, which seemed to knock him out from Europe to Asia, I didn't have much to take my mind off the endless time stretching in front of me.

I looked to my side and Jo was dead to the world. I moved in my chair, knocking him gently, hoping he'd wake, but nothing. The magic pills had certainly done their work. Good job I was here with him, or anything could have happened. I've saved him again. Jo's hair was squashed where he lay against the seat. Occasionally he moved and chewed his cheek; a little bit of spit accumulated in the corner of his mouth. I wiped it with a tissue and he turned away, still asleep. He could have done with a shave. I brushed his cheek with my hand gently. I remembered staring at Ben, in bed together, as I propped myself up on one elbow, watching him sleep next to me. But this was Jo. This was completely different. Ben and I were over, and I wasn't going to spoil this trip on a crappy ex-boyfriend.

Part way through the flight I summoned the courage to ask a female flight attendant if I could move seats. Before, I'd have just suffered in silence, but now I felt more assertive. Jo wouldn't put up with it, so why should I? After a short time reading she asked me if I'd been to Australia before and I explained I was travelling with my family, but that eventually it would be just me and Jo.

"Are you two friends?" she asked.

"Best friends—he rescued me. I couldn't have gone if he hadn't come with me, and he wanted a year out before going to drama school, so I suppose we rescued each other really."

She smiled, and I returned to my book, aware of my slight over-share, but still smiling.

After a long time, lost in my book's glorious campness, the flight attendant tapped me and told me I'd have to return to my seat for landing. I closed the book and she said, "Good was it?"

I nodded as I made my way back to Jo. *Not as good as what's about to happen when we land.*

Jo was starting to stretch and turn in his seat as I sat next to him.

During the landing, Jo woke enough to hold my hand. He knew landings and take offs were my most hated part of flying, ever since I'd read in one of Dad's magazines they were the likeliest times for accidents to happen. Thanks, Dad. He squeezed my hand as we hit the tarmac and looked at me when we finally stopped moving, all in one piece, with no broken bits of wings, or emergency landings.

Jo waved his hand in the air vaguely, his head rolling around on the headrest. "Can you get my thinggummy from the thing?"

"Bag? Overhead locker?"

He nodded, then his head rolled about a bit more.

When it was our turn to file out, along the aisle, I had to apologise to other passengers, as Jo's legs weren't working quite as before. After a few attempts, he eventually stood and I led him out by the hand, mine and his bags under my arms.

Paul and I took one side of Jo each, and walked him to Customs. Paul had seen me struggling with two bags and Jo, and offered to help with a shrug. A whole plane of people were sorted by four Customs desks. The queue snaked up and down the terminal, slowly shuffling past the desks. At Customs, Jo and I weren't allowed to the desk together since we weren't family. Jo's "How about sisters?" was met with a shaken head and a waved hand. Jo couldn't remember the address where he was staying at first, since it was my uncle's place, and he was barely able to stay upright, and tried a few times to rest his head on his arm on the desk, like a pillow, until the Customs official told him off. In the end I shouted the address to him from the other side and Jo nodded. The Customs man handed his passport over and waved him through, shaking his head.

We all met at the baggage reclaim carousel. Paul and I left Jo at a seat facing the carousel while we searched for our bags.

Mum stood nearby, watching proceedings carefully. "You mustn't get someone else's bag, just because it looks like yours. Make sure you check the tag. Or did you put an extra strap or ribbon on it. The girls at work said use a ribbon. I meant to get some tinsel, but I forgot."

And I was back to the *how on earth am I going to stand this for weeks on end? Why did I agree to this? We've not even left the airport yet and already I am ready to scream.*

Paul reached for his bag. "Mum, we're fine. Don't worry. Dad'll get yours. Kieran, get a trolley, and get yours and Jo's bags."

We tried pushing Jo on a trolley as he was still pretty wobbly on his feet, until a smiling woman in a red suit and hat explained they weren't designed for people, it breached health and safety, and we did understand didn't we? Before taking the trolley off us.

Mum counted everyone and their two bags each then said, her hand at her brow, "There's meant to be five of us, and ten bags and there's only four, but still ten bags. I don't know what's going on here." She started to count again until Dad pointed out she'd not counted herself yet.

Uncle Colin and his two children, my cousins, Colin and James, met us at the airport. We left the air-conditioned terminal with its red LED thermometer showing thirty eight Celsius in the shade, to be hit by a wall of hot air which tasted like sand. Mum leant against the luggage trolley and fanned herself with the luxury sunglasses brochure. "I hope it's not like this at night, or I'm not gonna sleep the whole time we're here. I can't handle that."

Paul leant against the trolley and said, "Fuck me, it's hot!"

Mum clipped him round the ear. "Language. Don't swear around your cousins, they'll pick up bad habits."

February in Sydney was going to be very different from February in the New Forest.

Mum turned from Paul, apologised for his language then

said, "This is Kieran's friend Jo, who he's travelling with after we leave."

Uncle Colin shook our hands firmly.

"Alright? How was the flight?" Colin asked, his English accent long faded into an Australian twang.

Jo replied, "I slept for most of it, I've got these fabulous little tablets, they just knock you out. Last thing I remember, we were somewhere over Europe and next thing I'm here. Someone must have collected my bag from the carousel, the kind soul. Perfect."

Yawning, I said, "Long, but it's nice to be here now, even if it is one o'clock in the morning for us." I stretched my arms over my head, then rubbed my eyes too much for public viewing; I was more than ready for bed.

Colin looked at everyone in turn. "You've gotta stop thinking about what time it is in the UK, you're here now, and its two o'clock in the arvo. Time for us to get back to mine and have something to eat, alright everyone?" He looked at his watch and tutted, making it clear there would be no sneaking off for a nap.

Uncle Colin shook Dad's hand, they had the same dark hair, dark eyes and slight build, Colin was much more tanned and wore shorts and T shirt to Dad's jeans and shirt. Colin kissed Mum's cheek. He introduced my cousins to us, who I'd never met. Two dark haired boys, of five and six, Colin and James, stood behind Uncle Colin, smiled at me and waved as I introduced myself. They wore matching white and blue T shirts, shorts and flip flops and peered from under adult sized wide brimmed hats. Without corks, I was disappointed to note.

We drove in Uncle Colin's air conditioned Aussie people

carrier, which made a British terraced house look small. After about half an hour through suburbs which all looked roughly similar to the previous one–large one storey houses with pools and gardens with small low rise shops and schools. We eventually arrived at Uncle Colin's house, a large one storey house with a pool and huge garden. I hadn't noticed the shops or school but felt sure they'd not be far away.

"So welcome to our place, make yourself at home," Colin proclaimed as we pulled up in the drive. "We'll have a barbie later, I've got some roo burgers if you want."

He showed us our rooms, Mum and Dad shared a room, roughly twice the size of the master bedroom in a medium sized UK house. Paul, Jo and I had a twin and double room to fight over. Paul immediately said he wasn't sharing with anyone which left Jo and I sharing the twin. We had single beds on opposite walls, separated by a wooden bedside cabinet with a night light. This *guest room* was almost twice the size of our living room back home.

I looked at my watch, two a.m. UK time. *I wonder if I could get away with a little sleepy sleep now. Away from Colin and his strictness.* "Do you think he's joking about the kangaroo burgers, or what?" I asked Jo as I unpacked my backpack. I had visions of Skippy, skewered with bits of pepper and onion and thrown on the barbie. I had never felt less hungry in living memory.

I'd deliberated for a long time about what to take and what not to take for this trip. I'd packed what I described as a capsule wardrobe—everything matched and could be layered to deal with everything from Kings Canyon dry forty degree heat to the cold spring of Melbourne. Hannah had laughed at my capsule wardrobe concept and pointed out that after four months away with my dark roots showing from my hair, having not shaved or slept in the same bed more than two nights running, I'd probably not give a shit about whether my hoodie matched my T shirt. Probably true, but as far as I was concerned, there were standards to be kept.

"I don't know him well enough to say yet. Let's see how the evening works out, eh?" Jo replied.

"What about...you know?" I asked.

"What do you mean, do you want us to come out dressed in drag, or have you got some leather arseless trousers you could pop on just so he gets the message?" He sat on his bed smiling, legs crossed, one hand at his hip.

"OK, but how shall we tell them? I don't think Mum's said anything, and Dad definitely won't have said."

"I intend to do exactly as I would normally." He uncrossed his legs and changed hand hip combinations. "I'm not changing anything for anyone. It took me years to be OK with myself, and now I am I don't give a shit what other people think. If he's too small minded to understand, that's his problem, I'm not forcing him to be gay. I don't mind if he's straight, it doesn't bother me one bit."

We walked to the enormous, could have been used for ballroom dancing, living room together, and found that everyone else was already there, listening to Colin's grand tour of the house.

"Out the back we've got a pool and sports pitches, the garden's big enough so we can play football, or soccer as we call it here, and cricket. Do you boys want to have a kick about later before we eat?"

"I would, I doubt they will," replied Paul.

"Not at the moment thanks," I replied. *Just a little snooze.*

7

Can't do any harm can it? A teeny weeny forty winks. He'll never know.

"Do I look like someone who plays soccer? In these shoes, you must be joking…" Jo fingered the material of his shorts.

Colin looked at us three and then looked at Dad for help. Dad shrugged and smiled.

Mum looked at the patio doors and said, "Yes well, these look nice, Colin, did you have them put in, or were they here when you moved in?"

Colin continued his tour of his estate, never missing an opportunity to boast about how much more space he had here than in the UK. He finished in the kitchen. "Do you want a beer? I've got some stubbies in the fridge." He looked at me, Paul and Jo. Paul nodded quickly.

Before I had a chance to say anything Jo said, "Do you have any Malibu and coke, or Archers and lemonade? Anything like that."

I rubbed my eyes then looked at my watch. "I might go to bed for a bit, I'm really tired, and it's now four o'clock in the morning at home."

Colin replied, "There's no point thinking about the UK time, you're here now, worst thing you can do is have a sleep, and you'll never get onto Oz time that way. What was it, lemonade? see what I've got for you, Jo." He walked out to the garage in search of the drinks and returned with some bottles. "What have you got planned while you're in Sydney? Oz is great for sports and outdoor stuff, there's nothing like it in the UK. Wide open spaces, hardly anyone around, you could walk for days and not see another person. Can't do that back home can you eh? You boys are going to love it, perfect for young men like you two. Wish I could have travelled like you are when I was

8

your age." He paused to think about this for a moment. "Do you want to go swimming in the sea? We could drive up to the Blue Mountains and spend a few nights trekking, hunting for food, camping under the stars, that sort of thing. What do you reckon?" He handed us our drinks–two small bottles of beer.

Jo raised an eyebrow at me. "About the camping; that's not the sort we're…"

I jumped in, shaking my head at Jo. "Mum and Dad want to see all the usual touristy stuff, the opera house, the ferry to Manly." Jo knocked my shoulder. I didn't look at him and continued. "A day trip to Canberra, that sort of thing. I'm sure the mountains are lovely, but I'm not sure we'll have time while they're here, you see."

Mum joined in, "And I'm not leaving without a picture of me in front of the opera house and bridge, I'm not coming all this way without that. And someone told me there's this special shell you have here, which you can get on a ring, I want one of those. And Kieran and Jo are taking us to this, parade. What's it called, boys?"

"It's called Mardi Gras, Pamela," Jo replied with a smile.

Uncle Colin spat his beer over the floor and looked at Dad, then Mum with raised eyebrows. "Boys, go to your room. Now!" The two boys left the room slowly, looking at the floor, shoulders hunched.

Mum snapped her fingers and looked at Jo. "That's it, Jo yes, we're looking forward to that aren't we boys? Well Paul and Dad aren't sure if they're coming, but me and the boys are going and we're all getting dressed up. They're hiring costumes, and everything,"

You could have heard a pin drop.

Mum rescued the silence, diving in head first a big smile

9

on her face: "Does anyone need a top up, my drink's all gone, must be the heat, it's so hot here isn't it? I don't know how you do it, must be air-conditioning I suppose. Not sure if I could handle it, with my feet, they swell up with the heat you see, don't they?" She looked at Dad, who nodded.

Dad looked at his brother. "I probably won't go to this Mardi Gras, thought I'd spend some time with me ol' brother, haven't seen you in so long, almost forgot what you look like. Leave these to do their own thing, I'm sure they can tell us all about it later."

Colin looked at his brother, wanting to test if it really was his brother and his nephew, he clung onto familiar territory: "What sports do you do back home? They must have you in some teams for school or college."

"I was at drama college, so we didn't do sports, but I do take an interest in the Olympics when it's on." Jo carefully picked a bit of lint off his jeans.

"Oh right, what bits?" Colin asked, getting excited at this glimmer of hope.

"Men's Olympic diving, or men's gymnastics mainly." Jo smiled.

Colin looked at Mum and Dad for help. Mum looked back, smiled and shrugged her shoulders in a "what can you do" gesture.

"I'll help you with the barbie, where's your charcoal Col?" Dad said, walking outside, leading Colin with him.

He *was* serious about the kangaroo burgers. I tried one after much persuasion from Paul and Dad. Turned out it's a bit like venison, but much cheaper. We discussed plans for the next day and agreed to have a family trip to Sydney Opera House and one on the Manly ferry to visit the beach. Jo couldn't resist the offer of going somewhere called Manly. He told everyone we'd be going to Oxford Street, in Sydney's Soho, for some shopping in preparation for the march. Colin almost choked on his burger, but I was pleased at Jo's modest description of our plans for the afternoon. He could have described it as going to pick up some frocks for the gay Mardi Gras march, but he chose not to, and I was grateful for that.

"I'm off to bed, I can't keep my eyes open." I yawned and stretched. We both thanked Uncle Colin for the barbecue and went to our room.

***

"How was that?" Jo asked, winking as he undressed.

"You're terrible Muriel, you did it deliberately to wind him up." I found myself fascinated by the door knob rather than allowing myself to catch a glimpse at Jo, then felt the door knob wasn't really helping matters so settled on a fixed stare at the bin.

"He makes it so easy though, I can't help myself, all that stuff about the great outdoors, it's just like you said the GAP year interview was. What is it with Australian men and sports?"

"He's British, but I get your point."

"What was it you said to Bruce, they can stick their sport up their arses, and leave us with the diving."

We climbed into our beds, leaving our boxer shorts on.

"I can't believe we did it, didn't we Jo, we're here?"

"I know Kieran, we really did it, we're here. The rest is just bollocks isn't it? Where's Mrs. Colin?"

11

"You know those secrets families don't talk about?"

He sat up and leant forward licking his lips in anticipation. "Yeah."

"It's one of those."

"Nothing, not a clue?" He settled back down the bed.

"If I knew I'd tell you, but nothing. One minute she's here, next she's not - no explanation."

There was a pause, then Jo said, "He thinks we're a couple, you know that?"

"I know, great isn't it? I'm going to sleep, we've got some serious touristing to do tomorrow. Night."

"Night."

***

We got up at seven-thirty-of-the-earlier-than-I-expected-while-on-holiday-o'clock, but as Mum pointed out to me, we didn't want to "waste the day, lying in bed" did we?

Dad and Uncle Colin had constructed an itinerary with military precision, with breaks, travel and including more than enough sightseeing for one day. We started with a picture outside Sydney Opera House, then a ferry to Manly beach, which lived up to its name as it was filled with men and women gorgeous enough to be the face, or crotch of an underwear campaign, all cavorting around the beach, playing volley ball and sunbathing. Jo and I kept ourselves in check, only subtly staring at the men, as we were aware this was a family day trip, and didn't want to *cause a scene*. We saw the harbour bridge, which took us to North Sydney, had lunch in Hyde

Park after looking at the Anzac war memorial, looked at the ducks hanging in the shop windows and waving cats in China Town. Every time we stopped, Mum took pictures of everyone posed in front of the latest building/bridge/waving Chinese cat statue, and we all smiled obediently.

As Dad was about to suggest we go to Sydney Aquarium I realised I'd had enough. "That's me, I'm done. No more tourist sites for me today."

"Me too, I'm done here." Jo held his hand in the air.

"But we've still got all these things to see," Dad said, showing us a piece of paper with a long list of locations not yet ticked off in his neat handwriting.

Jo gently pushed the paper away, smiling at Dad. "We're going to Oxford Street to look at costumes for Mardi Gras."

Mum put her hand on Dad's arm. "If that's what they want to do, let them do it. You two will be alright getting back to Uncle Colin's won't you?"

Dad's face couldn't hide his disappointment. "That's right, you two go and do your own thing, we'll see you tonight."

"I've got the address, we'll be fine, see you later." I kissed Mum on the cheek, and we were gone.

Oxford Street had rainbow flags bunting between the streetlights, rainbow flags hanging from every shop front and rainbow posters with details of parties after the parade stuck to shop and cafe windows. The pavement was filled with a colourful mix of wide-eyed tourists, gay couples happily holding hands, and a generous smattering of people giving their Mardi Gras costumes an early airing.

I looked at Jo. "How did you know to come here?"

"Someone from drama college went last year, when I told everyone at college I was going, he gave me a list of the places to go."

"Nice, I can see what you did there. Where are we going to start?"

"Start at one end of the street and work our way up? But first, I want a coffee and a sit down. Here?" Jo nodded to a cafe we were standing outside, a large rainbow awning covered us from the shade.

It made my and Grace's cafe in Gosport look like a doctor's waiting room. The staff were all out of work actors or models, not one vertical surface was uncovered with something rainbow or pink, and the walls were covered in pictures of campy gay icons—Bette Davies, Judy Garland, Lisa Minnelli, Rock Hudson. We sat next to Guy Pearce, dressed as Felicia from the film, *Priscilla*.

Jo best-friended the barista as soon as we sat down. "Yes, we're both *from London*, just visiting and we need to buy something to wear for Mardi Gras." He smiled at the toned and tanned barista who wore a white vest and black jeans with a tiny white apron round his waist. "Any suggestions for shops?" Jo said, exaggerating his English accent as the barista finally got round to taking our drinks order.

We finished our coffee and, both armed with some local info, and Jo with the barista's phone number on the back of a black and white picture of his perfect for TV face, we headed for the costume shop.

"You're not getting another angel are you?" I asked as we walked into the shop.

"Done that, needs to be something spectacular, I want everyone to look at me." He strode into the middle of the shop and started to look around.

"How can I help you two?" asked the drag queen behind the

till. "I'm Shirley, and what shall I call you?" She folded her arms on the mirrored table, the back of her enormous red wig and blue sequinned dress visible in the mirror behind her.

Jo introduced us. "We're going to Mardi Gras and want something special to wear. I want everyone to look at *me*. I'm studying drama and I want it to be quite theatrical, a show. Think Guy Pearce in *Priscilla Queen of the Desert*, think a scene from *Les Mis*—which I've been in as well. We're staying with his family at the moment, but once they go, we can do whatever we like. It's his first big Pride—I've been to loads before though. Kieran doesn't mind what he wears, do you?"

"I've been to Brighton Pride. And, I thought you liked my family?" I looked at Jo, shocked.

"They're fine Kieran. Anyway we haven't got all day, so what have you got?" Jo looked at Shirley.

Shirley pointed at us both. "Do you want two costumes which go together, because you're together, or separate?"

"Oh, no, we're not *together*, together, we're just friends." I put my hand over my mouth to emphasise how repugnant the thought was.

"*Best* friends, it's more like sisters." Jo looked at me, then Shirley.

"Or brothers…"

Shirley nodded. "Yes, I can see that. I think I've got something for you, which will be perfect. I'll be back in a few minutes." She walked into the back of the shop.

We waited and took in our surroundings: wall to wall costumes hanging in themed areas on all four walls. They would never have anything like this in Southampton. When the first African hair specialist had opened there, it had caused a flood of letters in the local paper, so this was miles off.

15

Shirley returned pushing a wheel chair with blonde and brown wigs, a white frilly dress, a dark grey pinafore style dress, a makeup pallet and a blue hair bow.

"Tadah, what do you think?" She laid bits of it onto the mirrored table.

"What is it?" Jo picked up the bow and stroked its shinyness.

"*Whatever Happened to Baby Jane?*" Joan Crawford and Bette Davies—the film from the 60s? Haven't you heard of it?"

Smiling to myself, I said, "I've seen pictures of the actresses, but didn't really know what they'd done; it's an old film isn't it?" I shrugged and looked at Jo.

Shirley tutted, rolling her eyes, in an "I've got tights older than you" gesture and said, "From the 60s, so if that's old for you, then it is an old film. Look, I've got a picture of them in the film here." She reached into her enormous handbag and fished out a notebook, with pieces of paper sticking out of it. She showed us the iconic picture of the two sisters in a room together, the dark haired sister in a wheelchair, cowering her face away from the blonde sister after she had just slapped her face.

"It's Blanche and Jane Hudson, characters played by only the biggest gay icons of the twentieth century. It's dark, it's camp, they're sisters, it's perfect." Shirley persevered. "They're trapped in a relationship together as Bette Davis, the blonde one, has to look after her sister played by Joan Crawford in the wheelchair. Both of them are bitter that their acting careers aren't what they used to be, and they take it out on each other by being vile to each other."

"Like what?" Jo put the bow back and started to handle the frilly dress.

"She gives her disabled sister a rat for dinner." She put her hands on her hips. "Do you want the costumes or not? I'll show you how to do the makeup."

We tried the costumes on, Jo wheeled me into the middle of the shop and did a twirl. He'd insisted on being Bette Davis as it would involve more acting than me just sitting in the chair. I wasn't bothered as I hadn't heard of the characters before, and it seemed a good option to get out of walking all day in the parade.

"Do you think people will get it? Will they know who we're supposed to be when we're in the parade? Will they *know* I'm Bette Davis?" Jo was stroking the blonde wig now.

Shirley rolled her eyes and put her hands on her hips once again. "It's one of the most iconic gay cult films of the last 40 years, it's been used in thousands of cabaret shows here and in the UK. Sweetheart, they will know *exactly* who you are meant to be."

"Fabulous, we'll have it, won't we Kieran?" He looked at me, smiling and with a familiar twinkle in his eyes.

Shirley showed us how to do the face makeup for full dramatic effect. We arranged to leave the wheelchair in the shop until the day of the march when we would collect it to complete the costumes. I paid: Jo hadn't managed to arrange for his Australian bank account to be open yet, so he had to use his home account, which had high bank charges. I didn't want him to waste his money so it made sense for me to pay and he would pay me back later.

Mum pounced on us when we returned that evening. She held my hand tightly. "What have you two got there? Are you going to show us all?"

"Don't think everyone will be interested, Mum, it's our costumes for Mardi Gras," I replied, trying to get to our room before anyone else took an interest.

Mum reached into our bags as we walked past, and picked out a wig and dress. She looked puzzled but couldn't leave it at that. She needed to understand more, especially if she was going to join us on the parade as she had promised.

"What did you get?" She held the dark wig. "They look nice, don't they Dad?" She showed Dad the costume, he looked on in interest from afar.

"It's from *"Whatever Happened to Baby Jane?"* and we're the two sisters. "One's in a wheelchair, and the other one is Bette Davis." Jo picked the frilly dress from the bag.

"Yes, and who's in the wheelchair?" Mum put the dark wig back in the bag.

I looked at her, optimistically smiling, willing her to smile back. "Me, it means I don't have to walk on the parade, not bad eh. He's got to push me all the way."

"Bit much isn't it? It's not exactly a comedy that film." She bit her lip and wrung her hands "Definitely not a comedy from what I remember."

"I'm Bette Davis, and everyone will know it." Jo did a twirl and stopped, facing Mum, smiling.

Mum smiled at Jo then looked at both of us. "I'm sure it'll be lovely, I can't hardly wait to see you in them, when we go on the parade. I've got an extra film for my camera for the pictures. Bought it in Boots before I came out, it's cheaper than here I was told by whatsit at work. What should me and your brother wear, do you think? I've not had chance to think about it. What do the families wear? Is there a flag we should be waving, or something? Anyway, plenty of time for that yet. Well, I'll let you boys pack it away in your room. Hope you're hungry, dinner's ready in about half an hour."

Dad looked up from his car magazine. "Me and Col will be by the barbie. When you're ready grab a beer and join us."

***

March 1999

On the day of Mardi Gras, we were up at seven, putting on our costumes and makeup. We left our room and walked into the kitchen as Jane and Kate Hudson. I pushed a few stray hairs from the dark wig away from my eyes and walked around the kitchen getting used to the feel of the pinafore dress. Wearing a dress was one thing—so different from trousers or shorts, but wearing a dress with full face makeup and a wig took it to another level. Strangely I'd found the dress on its own more odd than the whole costume. Wearing the dress on its own I felt like just that: me wearing a dress. Once Jo put my makeup on and helped me adjust the wig, I didn't feel like myself any longer—I was Joan Crawford as Blanche Hudson. So by the time I walked into the kitchen for Mum to see me for the first time like this, I no longer felt worried about her seeing me in a dress, because I wasn't in a dress. I was Joan Crawford. Jo's method acting skills were definitely rubbing off on me, or something...

"Very realistic, I think I've got a red lipstick which would go." Mum peered closely at Jo's face. "Isn't it realistic Paul?"

"I don't know what it's meant to be, so how am I supposed to know?" Paul replied. "Why do we have to get up this early?"

I adjusted my wig. "Jo said we have to get a good space near the front of the crowd, so we can join in at the end of the main parade, didn't you Jo?"

Jo nodded. "If you've got that lipstick Pamela, that would be great, this one we got from the shop is a bit crap. I don't think it's going to last all day."

Mum rushed off to collect the lipstick and returned proudly holding it. "Here, we'd better get going, or we'll miss our place, and we don't want to wake Dad and Uncle Colin do we?"

"What are they doing today, Mum?"

"Dad said he'll watch it on the telly, you know he don't like crowds. They want to spend some time alone, it's been years since they did that. Your Uncle Colin has some work thing he can't get out of so…"

"Mum, it's Saturday," Paul said.

"Shall we go then everyone?" Mum looked around the room at us all. Paul wore his cut off jeans, big red Doctor Marten boots, socks hidden from sight—Jo and I had had quite a conversation with Paul about that one—and a white T shirt with *My Brother's The Gay One* on the front and *I'm Proud Of My Gay Brother* in black marker pen on the back. He'd insisted on black, despite our suggestions of rainbow colours, but as Mum said, "It's the words what count."

Mum fluffed out her green tutu, that she'd sewn onto a rainbow coloured tie dye T shirt then put on her matching green feathery eye mask. She waved a rainbow flag on which she'd written—with some help from us on spelling—*Straight Mum Proud Of My Gay Son*—we all felt quite proud how it sort of rhymed, if we did the aural equivilant of squinting as Grace would have said.

***

Jo insisted that we push right to the front of the crowd so we could clearly see the parade floats as they passed. "I've not gone to all this effort with the costumes to be stuck at the back where no-one can see us."

We rushed to Oxford Street to collect the wheelchair and Jo used this as a reason for us to be at the front of the crowd. The parade passed along Oxford Street, so we felt in familiar surroundings. The fact that I wasn't actually disabled didn't seem to matter. Jo secured us a space just behind the police barrier, with a clear view to the road where the parade passed.

I looked up from my wheelchair and saw Mum and Paul waving rainbow flags and taking pictures of the parade as it passed. Paul also enthusiastically and liberally used a whistle, which he hung around his neck for the whole day. *He's not dragging his feet now is he? Handy to have a trendy gay brother isn't it?*

"Look at those women on bikes, they must be hot in the leather, I'm getting a picture of that. They won't believe this back home when I tell them if I've not got a picture." Paul jumped up and down as the dykes on bikes passed.

Next, were a group of topless line-dancing cowboys. As well as white cowboy hats, they wore white leather trousers, white boots with silver spurs at the back, glinting in the bright sun. The Steps song "five, six, seven, eight" blared out as they passed. I started to join in with my hands to the prescribed dance steps.

Jo enjoyed the life-guards as they formation danced past, all tanned in tiny red Speedos, yellow and red swimming caps, holding yellow and red feathers to wave in time to the music.

"Just like me at the Duke?" Jo looked at me.

I smiled back at him: it seemed like a lifetime ago.

My favourite part came as a buff man passed us wearing a blue and silver shimmering peacock's tail on his back like a rucksack. He didn't need his own music, his little silver trunks and smile were enough. As I noticed his silver boots with silver wings, I took a photo to remember the moment.

A group of leather clad bears passed: a sea of leather waistcoats, trousers and hairy chests. One wearing a leather kilt stopped to pose as Jo took a photo.

Paul stared, open-mouthed as a group of women in black leotards jumped through hoops and cavorted in front of us. A couple of them held a banner that read Lesbians In Leotards—Because Why Not? Paul looked at me and before he even asked the question I just nodded and said, "Not everyone's one of your neat little stereotypes."

A float drove past slowly full of superheroes: Superman kissed Robin while Wonder Woman smiled down at us, adjusting her tiara. Mum tapped me on the shoulder. "I remember Wonder Woman—always thought she had a nice belt. Have you seen the size of Robin's underpants?"

Mum noticed a man wearing a white cape and underpants with *"Butt Man"* across his chest and asked what it meant. I distracted her and avoided total mortification, by pointing to a man wearing a blue and gold pharaoh head-dress and gold chest, part of an ancient Egypt float blaring out *Walk Like an Egyptian* by The Bangles.

As we saw the end of the parade pass, Jo prepared us to join. He wheeled me in the chair and we were flanked by Mum and

Paul.

"Very good girls, where's the rat?" a passing drag queen asked Jo.

"She's eaten it! I gave it to her, I'm Bette Davies you see." Jo beamed and looked from side to side as he pushed the wheelchair.

The drag queen smiled and walked past.

We stopped a few times for people to take photos, every time asking where we'd got the idea for the costume to which we both said we were massive fans of the film, without missing a beat.

Mum waved her rainbow flag. "These are my two sons. And this one's of the family too."

Paul blew his whistle loudly and continued walking next to the wheelchair. I waved at the crowds and smiled through my caked on makeup.

I looked round to Jo. "Aren't wigs hot? I'm glad I'm sitting down."

Jo waved reverentially at the crowds and smiled down at me.

We reached the end of the procession and wandered into Hyde Park, which was covered in groups of people having their own version of a picnic. Some had a table and chairs with champagne glasses and dainty sandwiches with the crusts cut off. Others lay on the ground on a blanket drinking wine from plastic cups or sometimes the bottle. Some groups danced, waving their arms in the air, and rolling their heads about their shoulders with their eyes closed—these people didn't seem too bothered about eating it seemed.

We sat under a tree overlooking a fountain where some of the more enthusiastic revellers were splashing around in very little clothes. Mum struck up a conversation with a group of men about my age sat under another tree. We wanted to get something to eat for our own picnic and Mum was the person who wanted to get it. She walked back.

"They said come over and have some of theirs. Plenty of it. They got potato salad, smoked salmon sandwiches, cold rosé wine, no rubbish." She picked up her flag and walked back to the group of men.

I started to object, "What if they're…"

Jo said, "It's broad daylight. Middle of a city. Everyone's in a party mood. Come on."

Paul tapped my back. "Don't you think Mum's got a pretty good weirdo sensor from working at the salon?"

So we joined the group of six men under their tree and soon we were comfortably mixed with their group.

Paul was talking cars with a spikey haired man in a pair of dungarees with nothing else underneath. He complimented Paul on his T shirt, then went back to transmission tunnels and cylinders.

I found myself sharing a scotch egg with one half of a couple, as Tony, an animated and drunk, ginger haired, A & E nurse, in a pink fairy outfit, told me about how he'd persuaded Ben—blond, centre parting, sailor's outfit—who did something to do with computers and money, to move to Australia from the UK after they'd met backpacking the year before.

Ben left Tony and me deep in conversation about nurses in the UK and nurses in Oz. He turned up later with a box of rosé wine, some tissues and a white hoodie. "Anyone want some more?" He offered the wine around then handed Tony the hoodie. "He can't stand the cold. Soon as the sun's down he's complaining about it being like bloody Coober Pedy. Not that he's ever been to Coober Pedy."

"So you went all the way back to your place to get his hoodie?" My heart melted and I debated whether to grab his hand and run for the hills, claiming him for my own while I had half a chance.

"I don't think so, that's an hour and a half round trip. I bought him one from the CBD, it's over there." He pointed. "Not far."

"CBD?"

"It's what they call the city centre over here, you'll get used to it."

Mum was giving three of the guys some hair tips about how you shouldn't really wash your hair more than once or twice a week, then some ideas for new styles as they all seemed to fancy a change. "What do you do after this, or is this it? Seems a bit of a waste to get this dressed up and that's it."

One of the men, floppy dark curtains haircut, bow tie, black shorts and not much more said, "Mardi Gras Party."

"What's that when it's at home?" Mum said.

He explained, twenty thousand tickets are sold for a big after the parade party. When he said Danni Minogue was performing I heard Jo squeal.

"We can't come all this way and miss out on seeing a real live Minogue in her native habitat. We must get tickets. What do I have to do to get tickets? Who do I need to persuade and peruse, and perhaps even a little bit more?" He traced his finger down the Butler Curtains Man's glistening chest.

We all sat in silence, waiting for Jo to kiss him.

The butler guy pushed Jo's hand away. "Sorry, darling, I'm off men at the moment. But I've got a coupla spare tix if that's any good."

Mum clapped. "I thought they was gonnna kiss then. I think

25

they'd make a lovely couple, don't you?" She turned to one of the hairdressing clan men who explained Jo wasn't the butler's type, but he did like the young one in the funny T shirt.

"Paul!" Mum shouted then sipped her wine. "You got an admirer here!"

The rest of the night passed in a bit of a blur. I remember getting to the party, via someone's flat, not far from where we'd met the group. Some people changed, others just had a quick flick and put on a bit more eau de toilette and hair gel. We dropped the wheelchair off at the costume shop. There was a nightclub and a lot of dancing, and at one point, Mum was lifted up on the dance floor by two very large, very butch drag queens. Paul got an awful lot of attention and kept pointing to the wording on his T shirt.

Two

Chapter 2

M um, Paul, Jo and I had come back to the house at about six o'clock the next morning all feeling very tired and looking more than a bit worse for wear. Our makeup was smudged, our flags long since lost, our wigs squashed into Mum's bag. By the time we got back we'd danced and walked most of the alcohol out of our systems so we weren't drunk. Gradually we emerged around midday to a house devoid of Uncle Colin and my cousins.

That evening Uncle Colin sat in the living room staring at me, Mum and Jo when we arrived from an afternoon of sunbathing and sleeping in the back garden. He stood in the middle of the floor, his arms stubbornly folded across his chest. "Is this what you want to do while you're here in Oz?" he spat. "Get *dressed up*, stay out all night and get drunk in some *gay bars?*"

Mum put her bag on the floor and looked at Colin. "Come

on Col, it's just a bit of fun. We had a couple of drinks. We're not doing anyone any harm. We left quietly yesterday morning, so we wouldn't wake anyone. I did call the house to say we'd be back late. I left a message so you wouldn't worry. You said you'd watch it on telly with Dad."

"Dad?"

"Michael."

"No Pamela, I didn't. I had to work and Michael said *he'd* watch it on the telly. Only because he thought he *had to*. I don't understand why though. And what about these…things they were wearing. What about them?" He pointed at Jo and me. "I've seen the wigs and dresses and Christ knows what else in their room."

Mum looked at me and Jo stood next to her. "It's Baby Jane—a film from the sixties. Everyone got it, they all knew who they were. And the boys we met at the park, I could've taken 'em all home with me. They was lovely. I was so proud of my Kieran and Jo, proudly on the march with me and his brother. What's wrong with that?"

Exasperated, Uncle Colin stuttered and spat before finally getting his words out: "*Dresses*, they're wearing *dresses* Pamela. My nephew, a young man, wearing a dress, with his *gay* friend, both in dresses, both parading themselves through Sydney like it's nothing. Don't you worry Pamela?"

"I'm going to bed." Paul walked across the room towards his bedroom.

"Probably best he doesn't hear this anyway." Colin looked at Paul as he walked past.

"You stay if you want Paul." Mum held his arm.

"I'm knackered, night everyone." Paul shrugged Mum off and left the room.

Chapter 2

Mum walked towards Colin and stared him straight in the eyes. "Worry? I'll tell you about worry if you want Colin. When you have a son who cries in his room and won't go to school cos he's being bullied, that's worry. A son who watches his friends go into couples, but don't know what he's meant to do, that's worry. A son who don't go out but just watches hours and hours of some American TV programme instead, that's worry. So don't tell me about worry Colin, cos I know all about it. I've watched him grow up and a mother knows there's something different. I might not have a degree or any of them A levels or O levels, but I'm not stupid you know. I'm a state registered hairdresser and I've worked in salons during the eighties. I used to know lots of gays then. Most of them are gone now. I went to see them in hospital you know. I've never seen anything so sad, watching the life go out of 'em when they'd always been so full of life and I've seen that film with Julia Roberts when she dies, something about Magnolias. Now *that's* a sad film. Well, this was worse than that."

Dad appeared from their room, his hands in his pockets, staring at the floor as Mum continued, still staring at Uncle Colin, not breaking the eye contact.

"Since he met Jo and his other friends he's been completely different. Ok so it's all a bit new to us, friends turning up in dresses, kissing each other when he says hello to the boys, but I've never seen him more happier. And yes, when he brings a boyfriend home, it's gonna be a bit strange, but no more strange really, than when Paul brought his girlfriend home the first time. It's my little boys growing up into men, and that's always gonna be hard. Don't matter what they're doing, as long as they're happy and safe, that's all *I* care about. All I can do is be here to help when he falls over, like I've always done.

That's all you can ever do as a parent. Thought you'd know that Col. When Colin and James grow up you'll know what I mean. They're still little kids now, you wait until they come to you when they're grown up, their little hearts broken, but you don't know what for, that's when it's difficult. Look, we won't make a big thing in front of them, but do you think they'd care? It's on the TV now, songs, you can't hide them forever." She paused, looking around the room as everyone took in what she'd just said. "Right, I'm going to bed, me feet are killing me. Should've brought my walking boots for the parade. Night boys, get a good night's sleep, no staying up talking. It's full on tomorrow." She kissed me, then Jo. "Dad, didn't see you there, coming to bed? Night Colin, see you in the morning."

Dad slowly walked with Mum to their room, his arm around her waist.

***

The next day, I diligently wrapped the sandwiches in Bacofoil and handed them to Mum to put in the cool box, keen to distract myself from last night's scene.

"Thanks Mum. Glad you enjoyed Mardi Gras."

"Yes and today's going to be the same. Dad's been going on about Canberra since we said we'd come out here. God knows why, can't see the big excitement myself, but equally if that's what he's interested in, it's his holiday too."

We put on sun cream and hats. As it was due to be over 35 degrees I thought it warranted getting my legs out for the day. Jo had persuaded me to buy some shorts for the holiday before we left. It was a rare occasion for me to show off that much skin in public.

"You can't spend that long in Oz wearing jeans and jumpers,"Jo had said. He'd helped me choose some shorts, a new addition to my wardrobe.

Jo chose his shorts for the trip to Canberra, a pair of cut down combat trousers in shades of blue. We'd both brought the same ones because Jo had said they were the latest thing and we had to have them. Today was his turn to wear them, because we didn't want to both wear them, looking like some mad twins did we? Jo said that I could wear my pair next time.

We put our backpacks in the boot. We weren't coming back to Sydney as we planned to continue onto our next stop. We piled into Colin's people carrier, I sat in the middle back seat. Jo said he got travel sick if he didn't sit near a window, so I moved over to the middle seat. Colin sat my cousins in the back row of seats—little white hats with flaps covering their necks, smudges of suncream on their faces and big smiles on their faces—then looked me and Jo up and down as we left the house, taking in our outfits: coloured T shirts (no Steps logos), shorts and trainers.

"Is that all you're wearing today?" Paul looked us up and down incredulously.

Jo rolled his eyes, then held onto Paul's hand like he was a small child. "Now, Paul, it's not like we wear clothes like that all the time, we can just wear normal things you know Paul. They were *costumes*, for a *parade*, this is just a *trip* to, where is it?"

"Canberra, the capital of Australia," Dad said, turning round from the front seat.

"Feels like Sydney's the capital, anyway. Those costumes

would've been a bit over the top for today don't you think, Paul?"

"Some people would say they were OTT for the parade." Paul removed his hand from Jo's.

Mum clapped. "That's enough, has everyone got everything, sunglasses, sun cream, Walkmans, books for the journey? Jo, Kieran did you pack all your stuff? We've got to go now or we'll never get there."

"It's not like we'd wear them around the house, Paul" I added, determined not to let Paul or Mum have the last word.

"They *were* fun for the parade" Mum said. "I'll drop them back after you're gone. All the stuff is in a bag in your room isn't it boys?"

"Did I tell you they were my idea?" Jo looked around the car. "We did the play in one of my classes at drama college, and I knew the characters. I thought it would be perfect when I knew Kieran was coming with me on the parade. We were lucky they had the costumes. Mind you, I think we could have made something up with some old wigs and dresses don't you think?"

"Ready? Let's go." Uncle Colin started the engine.

We spent an interesting day in Canberra, which reminded me of a cross between Basingstoke and Milton Keynes: endless roundabouts, lots of trees, no litter, no building older looking than my uncle's house. Their version of the House of Commons and Houses of Parliament were like a modern version of what I'd seen of our system on the TV. They used the same red and green colours to show the difference between each house. I felt like I was in Doctor Who's TARDIS while walking around the parliament buildings, a mixture of glass, stone and light. Dad and Colin were fascinated and took the audio guides

eagerly as we paid our entrance fee. I was happy to just absorb
the atmosphere and listen to a nearby tour guide as she moved
around the building shepherding groups of visitors from room
to room, explaining everything as she went. Mum looked after
cousins Colin and James, making sure they didn't disappear
and taking them by the hand when it was time to move on.
Paul milled around looking totally unimpressed as was his
usual approach.

I couldn't believe I was really in Australia, with my family,
and my gay best friend. After today it would be just Jo and
me on our own. No more parents, no more Uncles. We
could do whatever we wanted together. Overall it hadn't
been too mortifying. Overall I'd enjoyed the time with my
family. Surprisingly Paul had been mostly easy to get along
with—varying from being unimpressed to being properly
enthusiastic at some of the most surprising things. Who'd
have thought Paul would go to a gay pride march with me,
and enjoy it so much? It must have been all the attention he
got from the men—flattery is flattery whichever sex it comes
from, I suppose.

After the light picnic, that evening Uncle Colin took us to an
outdoor food hall to mark the end of the family holiday as Jo
and I made our own way. The central area had shaded outdoor
tables and chairs, with food outlets around the edge, so the
whole family could pick the type of food they wanted, but all
still eat together.

We all went to collect our meals while Mum saved the table
we'd secured. We returned gradually with our food choices, all
waiting until we were all sat with our food before we started

to eat.

Colin banged the table with his fork and we all looked up from our food. "Don't worry I'm not going to make a big speech, I can see you're all hungry. I just wanted to say it's been great to have you at mine this past few weeks. Sightseeing in Sydney, going to the beautiful beaches we have here, hanging around at my place, it's been bloody ripper. And even that festival some of you went to, if that's your thing, then that's your thing." He paused and looked around the table. "It's not all been perfect, but that's families. We're all here now, eating together aren't we? Good luck to Kieran and Jo with your trip around the rest of Oz, and make sure you don't leave it so long next time before you come to visit again. A toast, Kieran and Jo."

Everyone joined in the toast. Mum looked at us and said, "And make sure you look after each other, I don't want your Mum calling me cos she's worried about you."

Obviously affected by the emotion and beer, Dad added, "You never know, next time maybe we'll see you at the parade thing in person, not just on the telly."

I noticed Mum squeeze Dad"s hand under the table.

Colin dropped us at Canberra's YHA youth hostel, a short drive from the centre, on the edge of the bush surrounding the town. Mum cried as she hugged me goodbye. The others gave me a manly hug and slapped Jo's shoulder. I watched the car disappear and looked at my four foot tall, blue and black backpack at my feet. *This is it, all I have, thousands of miles from home. This bag and this friend.*

"We'll check in and see what it's like at night in this town," Jo said and winked at me.

Not bad as it turned out. Canberra's gay scene was like a

small provincial town in the UK, with better tans and more opportunities for partying outdoors. We crept to our beds at four in the morning. Unfortunately one of the disadvantages of sharing a very cheap dorm with ten other men is that as soon as the first one wakes up, you do too. Someone had to get up at a joyous eight-of-the-early-morning-for-work-o'clock. We struggled to sleep after that, but didn't do well as the light streamed in through the useless blinds hanging in the windows. Between that and the constant coming and going of guests we gave up at ten and lay in the shaded grounds under a tree on a blanket.

After a few hours we felt human again and went to the hostel's large kitchen, to make some lunch. It had metal work tops, a bank of enormous fridges, cupboards for guests' food and three large wooden table with benches either side, like in a school canteen. During the tour the receptionist explained that each youth hostel had cooking facilities for guests to make their own meals—it helped keep costs down when travelling around for long periods of time, like we were. We certainly didn't have enough money to eat out all the time. Guests stored their food in bags scrawled with their name, to prevent others stealing their food.

I was stood in the kitchen making myself a sandwich and Ed, one of the people we'd met last night, walked in. He shouted my name across the kitchen. We chatted about what we'd done today to minimise the effects of last night, I was mildly interested until he mentioned he was travelling with an Italian guy Fabio.

"Oh him, just someone I met on my travels," Ed replied. "Straight, I keep him around for aesthetic reasons. He's got a car and needed someone to help pay for petrol—his friend got home-sick and flew back to Italy."

Fabio walked into the kitchen and I had to make a conscious effort not to stare too much: a perfect smooth muscled chest with a cute knot of hair around his belly button, his bottom was well defined through his shorts, all rounded off by the most angelic face you could imagine, dark brown eyes. He had peroxided his dark hair so he had blond ends, which he styled aggressively into spikes. He introduced himself and warmly shook my hand.

"We will have a swim to cool. Will you come too?" Fabio asked in a thick Italian accent.

"Not this soon after eating, no. I mustn't get a stitch, but I might come out in a bit." I was still holding his hand.

I ate my sandwich while looking out to the pool. Fabio quickly stripped down to his itsy bitsy teeny weeny red Speedos and I couldn't believe my eyes. Fabio and Ed played a small game of water polo. After they had exhausted themselves they sat in the sun to dry. I had just finished eating so I took this perfect opportunity to make two cups of tea, one for Jo too, and then I would go and sit in the shade gazing at Fabio's body through my mirrored sunglasses.

"Where are you going?" Jo looked at the poolside entertainment and smiled.

I sat by the pool for twenty minutes as Fabio lifted his arms and opened his legs to ensure every nook and cranny was dried. I stared in wonderment, sipping my tea.

Once completely dry, they left to explore what Canberra had to offer during the day. Jo blew a few kisses at Ed and Fabio. Ed turned around to reciprocate mockingly. I blew a kiss to Fabio who responded with a shy smile.

I spent the rest of the afternoon reading by the pool,

occasionally I went to the kitchen to make myself and Jo a snack.

**

I noticed Fabio and Ed had changed to go out later that night. Fabio wore a pair of very tight and flattering jeans, a Dolce and Gabanna T-shirt, which hung perfectly on his frame, complimenting his chest, and a bright orange jacket.

"Oi, where are you going dressed like that?" I shouted from my sun lounger.

Fabio walked over to me and replied, "Hungry Jacks. Then a bar. Ed?" Ed shrugged.

"Teach me some Italian." I leant forward so I could see my reflection in his sunglasses.

"What you want to say?" Fabio asked and sat on a chair next to mine.

Ed rolled his eyes and looked at Jo who smiled.

"The proper stuff, get to the smut, don't worry about the rest. I want to know how to swear. I want the smut."

"Ok, I have one. Farmi un bocchino. It means to—you know." He pointed to his groin and then his mouth.

I nodded. "Farme un bocchino." I looked at Fabio when I said it.

"I will do it for two of your little biscuits only," Fabio replied, looking at the bag of mini cookies next to my sun lounger, which I'd been grazing on all afternoon.

I gave him two biscuits and he took them quickly, ate them and looked at Ed.

Ed looked away, then back to Fabio. "Are we eating, or are you just going to sit here teasing Kieran all night?"

Fabio stood, his hands on his hips, and his groin pointing towards me. "Maybe see you later, we're going to Melaka's bar after we eat."

Fabio left with Ed. He looked backwards and waved before he disappeared from view.

"Did you see that Jo, he waved at me? He likes me, you saw that didn't you?"

"He's straight. You know, that thing where men sleep with women, and not men. That's what he is."

"Did you hear what he taught me to say in Italian?"

"The whole youth hostel heard that."

"Whatever, he likes me. Why else would he be like that?"

"What was it you told me your worst nightmare is?"

"Falling in love with a straight man. I know, but this is different Jo, I know it."

One of the first things I'd told Jo all those months ago, was my fear of falling in love with a straight man. I'd already had a taste of what this felt like: I came out and quickly realised that my taste in men was quite wide ranging, including blonde, dark, posh, less posh, but all pretty much straight men, because for the most part this was all I saw in my life. I learnt this was an unfortunate combination if you're new to the gay experience. Time after time I would fall for these straight men, fluttering around them like a love-sick teenager, and every time my heart broke when I saw them with their girlfriend/wife. I could then no longer fool myself into thinking I'd "convert" them. Now, I had no excuse to repeat this since I actually went to places to meet other gay men. However Fabio just reminded me that I still couldn't be too careful.

"Let's get dressed and meet them in Melaka's. He told me where they're going. He must want me to come, or he wouldn't have told me." I did my best puppy dog eyes at Jo.

"Politeness? OK, but I warn you, this can only end in tears. I know what you're like. You'll be picking out curtains before tomorrow."

We met them at the bar and I asked about Fabio's life in Italy. He was a twenty two year old waiter from Venice; so far so good.

"I have many girlfriends waiting for me back home." He looked at the nails on his right hand, buffing them on his trousers.

My heart sank. Bollocks. Jo was right, why else would he remind me that he was straight?

"Let's dance," I said, taking Fabio and Ed's hands, keen to push this knowledge to the back of my mind.

Fabio stood up, re-arranged his Dolce and Gabanna T shirt and walked to the dance floor with Ed and me. We danced to a few songs while Jo observed from his table, sipping Malibu and Cokes slowly.

We all left the club together and walked back to the youth hostel.

"He danced with me," I whispered to Jo.

"So did Ed, it doesn't mean he wants to be your husband too. I detect a distinct whiff of *Obsession by Disco Kieran*. Remember, he is still straight," Jo whispered back.

"Yes, yes, they're going back to Ed's room to play cards for a bit. They've got a twin room, better than us in a dorm eh? Are you coming?"

Jo shook his head. "I think I'll leave this one to you. Good luck sweetheart, and remember, you're fabulous. Just don't get hurt. No black eyes, alright?" He kissed me on both cheeks.

I went to Ed and Fabio's room. We played a game where we had to describe what our type was. Ed described a blond surfer who also owned a yacht. Fabio described a women roughly akin to Jessica Rabbit from *Who Framed Roger Rabbit*.

"Dark haired, defined chest, a little bit of hair, good dress sense, Mediterranean maybe?" I said when it was my turn.

Fabio suddenly became very interested in the floor and started to yawn in an exaggerated way. I looked at my watch and realised I'd probably over-stayed my welcome.

"Thanks Ed, Fabio, it's been fun. Night." I left.

Fabio followed me and blocked my path with his arm. "Have you ever been with a woman?" When I shook my head, he continued, "How can you be sure without being with a woman?"

"How can you know you're straight without being with a man first?"

"It feels right with a women for me."

"Same for me. With a man."

"Have you met anyone since you were in Australia?"

"I've been with my parents up until yesterday, so there wasn't much chance."

"What about your friend?"

"He's not met anyone either, same reason."

"No, do you like him? You are very close, no?"

"Yes, but not like *that*."

"I thought you were together when I first saw you, the way you talk, the way you are with each other. You help him with things. Like a couple I think, yes?"

"I watched you dry in the sun after your game in the pool. I made myself and Jo a drink and we both sat staring at you through our sunglasses."

"Sunglasses straight ahead, eyes to the left."

I nodded.

"We're going to Ayers Rock tomorrow, what about you two?"

"That's where we came from, we're going to Adelaide now."

I shook Fabio's hand and walked back to kiss Ed's cheek. I left their room and crept to my dorm, trying not to disturb anyone. I climbed into my bunk bed.

Jo whispered down from his top level bunk, "No curtains then?"

"How did you know?"

"The rest of the hostel could probably hear you talking."

"Shit."

"I'll look after you."

What would everyone else say tomorrow, now they knew? If Fabio could cope with me actually saying to him that I fancied him, then why would anyone else really care that much when they knew I was gay?

I mourned the life we would never have together, but I wasn't really hurt about that. I had told him how I felt, and Fabio explained his viewpoint and I had to accept that. I could not force myself upon him anymore than a woman could force herself upon me.

I fell asleep, quickly drifting into a dream. Which contained gondolas, red Speedos and ice-creams.

Three

Alice Springs

e left Canberra behind and moved onto Alice Springs, right in the dry heart of Australia. Jo and I had talked about this day for as long as we'd planned to go to Oz together. Today was the day we would climb Ayers Rock.

We started the day as we intended to continue. We put on walking boots, sun cream and feathery costumes. I had second thoughts about the costumes, explaining to Jo that I felt embarrassed at climbing the rock dressed like an extra from a piece of musical theatre.

Jo stopped putting his costume on to count off his objections on his fingers. "One, you're never going to see any of these people ever again. Two, we've planned this for months, years almost, and you're not backing out on me now. Three, and most importantly, we're not extras, it's more like lead parts. Mum spent ages on these costumes, and I'm not wasting them,

I want a photo of us at the top of the rock in these dresses, anything else will be a failure of the holiday as far as I'm concerned."

We continued dressing in our twin room.

We'd treated ourselves to a twin room instead of a dorm room. We reasoned that if ever there was a time when a twin room would be money well spent, then it would be the time we would be dressing up in drag to climb Ayers Rock.

I sat on my bed unable to cope with all the change.

"I don't want to be here anymore. I want my home. Nothing is like at home. I can't even wash my clothes here, what sort of a stupid place is that? And you expect me to dress up like a pink flamingo and climb a bloody great rock. Are you mad?"

Jo sat next to me on the bed, put his arms around me and looked me in the eyes. "Why couldn't you wash your clothes? What happened?"

"They said that water is too expensive to use for hand washing in Alice Springs, and I had to use the washing machines. I told them I only wanted to rinse out my pants and some T shirts, and they said I'd still have to use the machines as it used less water. What a load of crap. I just wanted to do something simple, to take my mind off everything else."

"What, everything else?"

"Us, here, thousands of miles from home, all alone. No-one to help us. No real possessions. You know, just that sort of thing." I looked at the two spindly beds, bare white walls and our backpacks leaning against the far wall.

"Oh, that."

"I just wanted to do something normal, you know, something which doesn't involve sightseeing, travelling or making a difficult decision. Something normal. I'd mop a floor in the

YHA if they let me."

"I'm sure that can be arranged Kieran, if that would help."

I nodded.

During family holidays in Dorset when my parents' arguments or Paul's taunts became unbearable I would leave the static caravan, resting my copy of *Adrian Mole's Diary* on the table, and collect a bag full of washing and some washing powder. Paul would sometimes follow me on his skateboard, but as soon as he realised I was going to the washing block, he left me to it. *Perfect.*

I enjoyed swirling the clothes around in the warm water, watching the dirt disappear, then another swirl around to rinse them a few times. I liked the comforting sound the spin dryer made when I put the clothes in, and enjoyed seeing the water as it sloshed down the drain. I listened to the women as they washed their families' clothes, chatting about the latest episode of *Dallas* or *EastEnders.* By the time our washing was clean I was intimately acquainted with Dirty Den's latest exploits.

The whole time I was doing the washing, I didn't think about anything else. All those things which seemed too large to worry about. All I had to think about was getting the clothes dry. My family's arguments—about the next day trip, what to watch on TV, who was doing dinner or the washing up—these weren't happening anymore. My brother's taunts about me reading quietly rather than playing with him on the adventure playground didn't matter. The bullies at school hitting me. All gone.

And now, in this bloody hot country, where they were so proud of everything, they couldn't even sort out the water supply so I could wash some clothes.

"Do you want me to ask if you can mop the floor, or

something? I don't mind, if you really think that'll help." Jo held my hand.

"Thanks. I think I'll be fine. I just needed to, to have some time to think, before we do this, is that ok?"

"Course it is. Take all the time you need. We don't have to do it today. We're booked in this YHA for a while, we can do it whenever you're ready. I'm going to make a cup of tea, do you want one?"

I looked up through teary eyes and nodded. "Are you going like that?"

"I'm not getting changed, it took me over an hour to get this lot on. If we don't go today, you can take a photo of me and I'll send it to my Mum when it's developed. I'm sure they've seen worse things in their little kitchen."

Jo left in a flurry of bright pink ostrich feathers. I felt sick to my stomach. *I don't do unusual things—that's not what Kieran does. That's not what I do. Jo does that sort of thing.* I had come out to my parents, and Uncle. I had actually made my own plans during my gap year, despite what the official organisation had told me. I'd done all of these things since I met Jo. Things which could never have been imaginable. I realised I hadn't thought about *The Creek* since we'd left the UK, not once, not at all. Normally I took refuge with the characters at least a few times a week, but I'd not had chance for ages. Even before leaving I'd hardly watched it, as I'd been so busy getting ready to leave. Parties, goodbyes, visas. All of these things made me feel sick, but I'd got on with it and still done them. Jo didn't ever seem to pause for thought about these things, he just jumped straight in head first. Must be his acting—you can't stand on the edge of the stage, and not go on when your character is due. The whole play would stop.

I realised I didn't want my own play to stop; I wanted to continue living my life, to continue feeling sick to my stomach and playing on.

Jo returned to our small twin room, it had only a table between the beds and our backpacks leant on the wall. He was holding two mugs of tea. "Do you want me to leave?"

"No, who's going to do up the back of this gay ostrich your mum's made me?" I replied, holding my sparkly blue costume in one hand.

***

We had been climbing for an hour or so and had stopped at a convenient ledge for water and a rest. Jo took off one of his walking shoes and examined a blister the size of a pound coin while I reapplied sun cream. I took in our surroundings and noticed how our costumes contrasted so vividly against the dark redness of the desert. Jo sat down in his neon pink dress jutting out like a ballerina's tutu, matching tights, head dress and tail plumage made from dyed ostrich feathers. My costume was deliberately quite different, streams of blue sequinned fabric joining my hands to legs, like very loose bats wings with a blue sequinned leotard to cover my body. I'd opted for matching blue tights to cover my too thin legs. I too had a matching feather head dress, but had declined the offer of tail feathers when Mrs Davis offered me them.

To assuage Mrs Davis's worry we'd asked her to design and make our outfits for this part of the trip. It worked perfectly: she felt involved in the trip and obsessed about every detail of our outfits right up until we flew. All her worries about us being on the other side of the world and her precious son having to battle with spiders and snakes had faded into insignificance once she got the sewing machine out. She'd insisted we took a picture of us both in her outfits at the top of Ayers Rock so she could put it on her mantelpiece with her other proudly displayed photos of Jo.

"Look at that view, you can see for miles." Jo shaded his eyes from the sun and turned slowly, looking at the view.

"What's that over there?" I pointed.

"Those huge rocks are The Olgas. They look pretty small from here don't they? They're as high as a mountain and are about ten miles away, that's why they look so small."

I looked at him. "I'm glad you made me come in the end. I've got used to everyone looking now, well, I don't care about it."

"Like I said, you're never going to see them ever again. Who cares what they think?"

"It's about us, here, now, up this rock."

"Exactly!" He put his arm around me.

I stared into the distance and we sat in silence for a short while. Jo's pink tail feathers fluttered in the wind. I leant my head on his shoulder as he put his arm around me. I closed my eyes to really savour the moment. When I opened my eyes I noticed some of my sequins had fallen from my wings and commented how it sad it was.

Jo picked a load of blue feathers from my head dress out of his mouth. "Never mind that, I feel like I've just swallowed a whole bloody ostrich. At least you've not got a mouthful of your sequins. These costumes are a fucking liability."

I closed my eyes with a smile and we listened to the fluttering feathers and my costume's wings flapping like a kite.

Jo interrupted the silence. "What are you thinking about? And if it involved little red Speedos and Italian straight men, I don't want to know."

"Oh, it's nothing. I was just wondering what he's doing today. Do you think he's still thinking about me? I should have left him my email address. What do you think?"

"Who—Fabio?"

"Of course Fabio, who else?"

"What I think is that we're here and he's not. There are some things in life, which are just perfect for that time, and then they're over. I think that Fabio was one of those things. What was it you told me your worst nightmare would be?"

"Falling in love with a straight man. I know. But he was gorgeous, he was perfect in every way."

"Except for a small detail that he doesn't fancy you—that he doesn't fancy men at all in fact."

"What am I doing wrong? You seem to manage it ok. What do you do differently from me? What about Brighton Pride—you were going out with one, and you picked another up at the parade. Me, I didn't even have someone to come home to when I got home that night."

"You had me. You've still got me." He looked into my eyes.

"But it's not the same is it? We're not boyfriends."

"Come on, we've got a rock to climb. If we sit here any longer, we're not two queers climbing Ayers Rock in drag, we're just two poofs sat chatting while everyone else passes us looking and thinking what the hell are they doing here."

He was right, we *weren't* boyfriends. And because of that I didn't have him, not in the way I would have a boyfriend, not in the way he had a boyfriend. I didn't want Jo in that way, but I did want someone in that way, and him ignoring

48

what I'd said, made me think he didn't really want me to have a boyfriend as much as I wanted one.

We continued to walk slowly up the rock over the next hour and then I saw a flag which other walkers were gathering around for pictures. This was the top of Ayers Rock. We had done it, Jo and I had climbed to the top of the rock, in our costumes together.

"I'm the king of the world!" Jo screamed, as he stood behind me.

"Never mind doing a *Titanic*, there's no water for miles here, it should be *Priscilla*." I turned to Jo, posed with my hands on my hips and with a wiggle on each phrase said, "A *cock* in a *frock* on a *rock* you *twat*."

Jo looked at me. "I know, but I just wanted everyone to look, for a laugh. It's worked, they're all staring at us now" Jo said, and then he kissed me, a big sloppy lingering on the lips kiss with his eyes closed.

What the actual fuck? We're not boyfriends, and he does that? He ignores me pointing out we're not boyfriends, and then he kisses me like that?

A group of Japanese tourists looked at us and began to take pictures. Some families looked over and shortly after returned to taking their own pictures. Some scruffy backpackers looked up from taking pictures of each other stood next to the flag marking the top of Ayers Rock.

We took pictures of each other standing either side of the flag. We asked a passing Japanese tourist to take a picture of us together. He obliged easily, enjoying the opportunity to stare at these two unusual creatures in front of him.

I had done it, I'd climbed Ayers Rock, just like in the film. I remembered the moment when I had decided to travel to

Australia, and I thought about doing this as a joke. It was only when I spoke to Jo, he'd persuaded me it was something we really could do. And once his Mum got involved with the costumes, keen to have some input into our little adventure, there was no going back. Anything else while we were in Oz was a bonus as far as I was concerned. I couldn't think of much to top this.

We agreed to postpone the trip to The Olgas—some large circular rocks—for a few days and allow our feet to recover. Even though we had proper walking boots—despite my best efforts to avoid buying a pair—we weren't used to this sort of exercise. We hobbled down the rock and made our way to the YHA in Alice Springs.

I noticed other walkers as they stretched and checked their walking boots. I didn't know what they were checking about their boots—the souls, or laces? But since reaching the top I suddenly felt able to join their conversations about climbing rates, blisters and isotonic drinks—whatever they were.

"You have to start at sunrise or it's too hot to climb," I added to a group of walkers discussing plans for the next day. I continued with a lengthy description of the route we'd taken, and the contents of our backpacks.

Their faces reminded me I was still dressed like a Mardi Gras float. I smiled, remembered I had to be somewhere else, and quickly left.

We stayed at the Alice Springs YHA for another few nights. One day we visited the Olgas and walked among the huge boulders. Somehow they weren't as impressive as when we'd seen them from the top of the rock. They just seemed like big rocks when we were up close. The view of Ayers Rock and knowing we'd climbed it, was impressive however. Even so, I still had to pinch myself to realise I was in Australia.

I looked back at the line of other walkers who had joined us on the day trip and noticed Jo was chatting to a couple of girls. He'd mentioned them to me the night before, while we ate dinner in the kitchen. I had been too tired to pay much attention and didn't have the energy to make new friends, when I missed my friends from home so much. I hadn't really thought about how I'd cope without Hannah, Grace and Kev. I hadn't had time to write any letters or check my new hotmail account. Grace wouldn't have let *that* one by without reference to the hot males—which I'd yet to encounter. I didn't expect Kev to write—I knew letters and emails weren't really his thing, but Hannah would never let me forget it if I left it any longer. Jo said he'd get in touch with his friends and parents when we had some time away from sightseeing.

Marie and Jane were from Ireland—a couple of students about the same age as Jo and me—in a gap year before going to uni to study subjects which didn't exist in the 60s.

I walked quietly among the beautiful scenery and heard Jo's laugh among the girls' voices. I looked forward to getting back to our small twin room to read the Boy George autobiography I'd picked up amid the dross in the "bring a book, take a book" pile in the YHA. My feet killed me after I'd done more walking in the past three days than in the previous six months. Super noodles, shower, Boy George—the perfect night.

I felt a hard slap on my shoulder.

It was Jo, grinning slightly maniacally. "He'll come out, don't worry girls, won't you Kieran?"

"I'm a bit tired, why don't you go without me. I'm going to have a quiet night in. My feet are killing me. I just want a shower and some food before bed."

She pushed her short dark fringe from her eyes. "You're joking aren't you? You're on holiday and you're after going to bed like it's a school night. What's wrong with you?"

The other girl took her long blonde hair out of a scrunchie, leant her head forward and shook it all about. She looked up, hair in her eyes. "Come on Kieran, you've got to come out. Your man Jo was telling us about things you've got up to back home. I want to see if it's true or if he's just full of shite."

"Oh sorry, this is Marie." He pointed to the girl who spoke first, with short brown hair, a fringe covering one eye. "And this is Jane" He pointed to the girl with long blonde hair all over the place—in need of its roots doing I noticed. Jo said, "They're from, where was it again?"

"Ballamena" they both trilled.

"No, I'm going to bed, you go and have fun" I made a big show of yawning, stretching my arms above my head.

"What's his problem? Man problems?" Jane looked at Jo who shrugged. "Any men problems and I've been there, done that. Nothing I've not had before, went out got mindless pissed and forgot about it."

"Come on Kieran, I'll buy your drinks." Jo's arm was round my shoulder, he tickled my stomach.

I squirmed out of his way embarrassed at how ticklish I was, and also berating myself for the vicarious thrill his touch had given me. I grabbed both his hands and held them away from my stomach.

Jo smiled mischievously."You won't have to put your hand in your pocket all night. I promise. It'll make you feel better. Forget about Fabio and all the others."

"Fabio—I want to hear all about this Fabio" Marie replied. "Feck's sake, for that I'll buy your drinks too, come on Kieran, you know you want to."

***

We walked into the cabaret bar in Alice Springs—it seemed a safe bet—it had a neon sign in the shape of a pink platform shoe under its name.

Marie bought the first round of drinks. As the Archers and lemonade flowed, soon I had told them about Fabio and the bastard Ben. Both perfect; until they weren't, until they were both bastards.

"He deserves someone better doesn't he, Jo?" Jane kissed my cheek, twirling her long blonde hair around her finger.

Jo turned back to us, after he'd stared into the distance for the whole last section of our conversation. "Who—yes he does."

"Pay attention, we're trying to sort out this poor baby's love life, we need your help." Jane pinched Jo's cheek.

Jo took a sip of his drink. "I know what we need. Who wants to hear the story about the worst play I ever put on? And who wants a drink?"

We nodded and he bought a round of drinks.

"So my Dad made me watch this film, he'd gone on about it for ages, how it was a big sweeping drama (which I must admit did interest me), so I thought, I'd give it a go. Slow? Slow isn't the word, I thought it had stopped at some points. The first scene was this wedding and everyone goes to the main character asking him to do stuff for them, I mean I got that he was important after two people's visits. But did they stop there, no, there were about another five visits, I'm thinking, is this wedding ever going to end? I've actually been to real life weddings shorter than this bloody wedding scene."

Jane asked, "What film was it?"

"*The Godfather*. Seen it?"

Jane and Marie shook their heads.

Jo looked around the table, composing himself. "I thought, how can I make this more interesting? And somehow I ended up writing it into a musical. College had given us a chance to put anything on we wanted, as long as it wasn't offensive. Part of their "express yourself" module or something" he said, adding air quotation marks. "Up to then I didn't know what to do, and suddenly it was so obvious. I thought, we'll make it so bad, it's actually good. You know like that film, "*The Producers*." Anyway, the score on the film was pretty good actually, so that helped. I went all out, I had dancing horses heads in the chorus, people danced on stage with rifles like they were canes, I made the wedding scene like a musical within a musical.

He paused as Marie and Jane caught their breath from imagining the hilariously vile situation.

"Well, who knew, but it turned out it was just awful. Absolutely awful. We closed on the first night. Hardly got through the interval. People just left and didn't come back. In the end I think there were more people in the play than the audience. It cost the college thousands of pounds. We were never allowed to do our own plays after that, they had to be scripts from well known plays. I think we hadn't gone far enough to make it awful, but there you go. Drinks?"

We all nodded and Jo motioned to the barman for another round.

"Did you see it Kieran?" Marie asked.

"Before I knew him. Wish I had though."

"Get this will you sweetheart? I've run out of cash. My Dad's ex-Navy. Worked on boats all his life. He's one of those, just get on with it, don't sit about talking about it, types. You know. He wanted me to go into the Navy too. Turns out he's got me as a son." Jo laughed very loudly, his mouth open so far I saw his fillings. "Funny how things turn out isn't it?"

I told them about where I lived and why we had decided to travel to Australia together. They were interested when I told them how Jo and I had met. Jo sipped his drink during my account of us meeting.

I looked round and noticed that Jo had disappeared.

"Where's he gone?" I asked. Both girls shrugged and I continued with my life story.

"Look at this, look at who I've found!" Jo proclaimed as he sat down about half an hour later, followed by a muscular looking guy with a white shirt unbuttoned half way down his hairy chest. Jo started to stroke it when they sat at our table. Jo kissed the new man, everyone in our group, then the new man again.

"Isn't he gorgeous—my baby bear. What was it?" Jo frowned and looked at the man.

"Victor," came the reply.

"Polish—isn't he lovely. He's a student, lives in the UK, but is over here on holiday."

"I'm not really Polish, and my name's not Victor. I just say it is cos it gets me more attention."

"Worked with me, isn't he clever?" Jo stroked the boy's chest hair.

Marie and Jane smiled at me. I smiled back. We didn't really know what else to do, but smile.

Victor mouthed "sorry" to us as Jo continued to manhandle

him and started to whisper into his ear.

"We'll be back in a bit, we're going for a drink." Jo stood and led his prize downstairs to the dance floor by the hand.

The girls took a sip of their drinks slowly and watched Jo and "Victor" disappear.

Marie went first. "Is he always like that…when he's out?"

I nodded. "He's harmless, doesn't mean anything by it really."

We talked about our plans for travelling around Australia. I forgot about Fabio, Ben and all the other crap men. It was a relief to just enjoy the moment.

The barman walked up to our table, knelt down next to my chair. "If you don't control your mate, I'm going to throw him out. He's been insulting our customers all night and I've had enough of it."

"What's he said?"

"Someone offered him a cigarette and he shouted that he wouldn't take it because he didn't want to get AIDS. Look at him, he's a mess, he's all over the place."

I looked over at Jo, who was staggering across the dance floor, grabbing onto someone who wasn't "Victor" for support. "Are you sure he said that? He's not like that."

"I heard it, he said it at the bar. Your friend is a cunt of the highest order. You should do yourself a favour and get yourself a new friend." The barman left.

I watched Jo staggering from the outdoor area across the bar and to the stairs, which led to the dance floor. This time he held onto another man, dragging him along by the waistband of his jeans. I walked over to him, taking his hand out from the man's underpants.

"You've had enough, I think we should go. Come on, Jo."

"Who left you in charge? I was just getting to know my new

friend. We're going out the back for a bit."

The bouncer walked over to us, accompanied by a very angry looking man. He pointed at Jo and the bouncer picked Jo up and carried him out of the bar. Jo screamed and shouted and landed in a pile on the pavement.

The angry man looked at me. "Your mate is a fucking mentalist. He stood next to my boyfriend, flirted with him, right in front of me. He asked me if he could go outside with my boyfriend, and when I told him to fuck off he knocked my drink over and walked away."

"I'm sorry, he's had a lot to drink. He's normally very nice."

"You want to get yourself some new friends." The angry man walked away.

All this, and I wasn't even supposed to be here. I wanted to close my eyes and find myself in my room back at the YHA with my *Boy Ailsa* book. I closed my eyes, held them shut and counted to five. I opened them again and looked around the club at Marie and Jane sat shaking their heads, eyes wide open at our table. Others walked about trying to find their friends. I heard shouting from outside and noticed a crowd was gathering on the pavement in a circle. I heard Jo's voice from within the crowd telling someone to fuck off.

No, that's it, I'm stuck with it. I'm still here. This is my reality and I have to deal with it. Fuck it. He's not normally like this. I can't just get myself some new friends, it's not as simple as that is it?

I walked towards the crowd on the pavement.

Four

Adelaide

*A*fter the excitement of the wilds of Alice Springs, we moved onto Adelaide. It was a comforting city, large enough to be interesting, yet not too large to be overwhelming. Keen to distance himself from the incident at the bar with "Victor" Jo rediscovered his artistic side and insisted we split our time between museums and art galleries.

After three days of nothing but museums and art galleries, I became a bit sick of Jo's mantra: "You can never have too much culture." We stood outside a grand municipal building Jo had led us to early that morning.

What about if it all just seems the same, after a while?

Was it wrong that I wanted to lash the third Aboriginal Art gallery in as many weeks, and instead answer the call of the golden arches, after some shopping at the newly discovered Rundle Mall?

Taking a deep breath, preparing myself for a tirade of disapproving tuts and a side order of lecture, I looked Jo in the eyes and began: "I don't want to see any more of this for a while. Can't we just go shopping instead?"

Jo looked at me, stepping back from the shiny brass plaque outside the municipal building.

I was pleased I'd not met much resistance so far. "It's just, you know, after a few days of art and culture, all I want to do is watch some TV, do some shopping and sit on the beach. We are on holiday after all aren't we? Yesterday was the Museum of South Australia, today it's this art gallery, tomorrow it's…" I waved my hands in front of Jo's eyes.

"The Botanic Gardens, you'll like them, I promise."

I shrugged and avoided his eyes."I'm sure I will, but just not at the moment, not in the middle of all the other sightseeing. Can't we do something a bit more normal?"

"But you're not ready to go to a bar yet?" Jo tried, eager to establish the ETA for his next conquest.

"I'm going to say no, but that doesn't mean never." I'd tried to have a proper conversation with Jo about his behaviour on numerous occasions, but to no avail. Each time he pleaded complete ignorance of the evening, which made a discussion about his behaviour quite difficult. *Later. I'll definitely speak to him about it later.*

"I swear I don't remember anything about that night, nothing, which based on your description of the Polish guy, is quite a shame…" He drifted off, clearly trying to remember Victor's hairy chest. Right on cue, there it was, the serious memory loss he'd claimed every time I'd started a conversation about it. "But no, I completely understand. Mind you, I am a bit disappointed with you, and here was me, thinking you'd want to broaden your artistic and cultural horizons as far as possible. I mean, you hardly get Aboriginal art in Southampton do you?"

"A good point well made, but I do feel my horizons have been well broadened, in other ways, and artistically, especially since we arrived here. You're just trying to show me how sorry you are about the bar, and so we've made an extra effort of doing other things since then, but there are other ways to enjoy yourself than jumping on the next passing man with a nice body you find in a bar."

Jo smirked at me.

"And I should know, it's been a lifetime since I got *any*, as Grace would say."

"Better be careful, or it'll heal over, you'll be like a Ken doll, no genitals at all, just some welded on plastic underwear."

"Let's check out the main drag."

He looped his arm through mine and we started walking to Rundle Mall. I instantly missed Kev, an empty ache in my chest as I realised how much he would love to be here now. I told Jo, who smiled weakly as we continued walking.

I enjoyed the ordered nature of Adelaide, its grid squares made navigating, even as a new-comer, really simple.

Jo looked up at the now familiar logo. "Let's get something at Hungry Jacks before we get started, what do you want?" He returned with our drinks and we sat watching the shoppers passing by, formulating a plan of attack, which reached all our favourite shops.

"Shall we get any presents?"

"Who for?"

"Whoever, why, have you bought some already?"

Jo shook his head, and finished his drink. "I'm ready, shall we go?"

"Almost finished, so what about the presents?"

"If I see some I'll get some, who do you want to buy for?"

"Well, obviously, Mum and Dad, Paul, Hannah, Grace told me if I didn't bring her back something hideously tacky and stereotypically Australian she would consider it a failure of epic proportions, oh and Kev."

"If you want."

"Do you think there will be costume shop like in Sydney? We could get him a costume or something?"

"Doubt there will be, it's a lot smaller than Sydney, not as open minded you see."

"Ok." My eyes followed a very muscular man wearing only the tiniest denim shorts and a sun hat, walking a miniature dog. "Ok."

We spent a productive four hours of focused, using a list, arm wearying shopping. I'd found Grace a boomerang covered with Aboriginal Art, hence killing two touristy birds with one slightly tacky stone. She would love it. For Mum I'd bought some semi precious stones and Dad and Paul got a kangaroo leather wallet each, practical and manly, perfect.

Jo had concentrated on purchases for himself at this stage, explaining that there was plenty of time for gifts later in our trip.

I reflected on a morning well spent: the piece de resistance was my gift for Kev. After leaving a tourist shop full of didgeridoos and boomerangs, and while looking for some T shirts for Jo, we stumbled across a costume shop hidden down a side street off Rundle Mall.

"Why are we going here, they're not going to sell any GAP T shirts down there?" Jo had stopped walking and looked at the shop.

Jo stood outside, arms folded, looking through his purchases thus far. I forged on, and entered a treasure trove of camp and kitsch, which Kev would have loved. Being completely honest with myself, I loved it too, and soon was behaving like a child in a sweet shop, shiny belts, operatic masks and bright neckerchiefs all went in my basket. I explained to the shop assistant about my friend Kev, painting a quick picture by recounting his Brighton Pride outfit.

The shop assistant took my hand and led me through a metallic pink curtain into another room: two walls were covered in massive shoes of every conceivable type, metal heels, glass heels, red, leopard print, zebra print, and the other two walls had racks of clothes/costumes, depending on your persuasion.

I settled on two pairs of glass soled high heels, one red stilettos, "a timeless classic" and the other platform zebra print, "very of the moment, and great fun". I paid and wrote Kev's address on a piece of paper.

I left the shop and Jo was smoking slowly, looking at the ground. "Took your time didn't you? What did you get?"

I showed him.

"Nothing for Kev?"

"They're sending it straight home, save me carrying it around."

"Oh, I wanted to have a look at it, what did you get him?"

I told Jo and he looked even more disappointed. "Did you get me anything?"

"No, should I? I thought you weren't interested in all that stuff."

"Yes, well, not like *he* wears, all the time. Special occasions only. Some of it sounds alright."

"You wanted some GAP T shirts didn't you? I think that's up this way." I walked back to the main drag of Rundle Mall.

Jo had soon run ahead into one of his shops.

***

In McDonalds, surrounded by our purchases, Joe finished his burger and tapped my arm as a man walked past in a pair of red trunks, red swimming cap and goggles resting on the cap.

"What's he doing in here? Does he think it's an episode of *Bay Watch*? How can he look like that and eat this?" I stared at my half eaten burger and chips and reflected on my less than Adonis-like body.

"If he's swimming all day I suppose he can afford to have the odd burger, cos he's going to burn it off by tomorrow. Anyway, I didn't point him out so you'd get all sad about not looking like that, I pointed him out cos I knew you'd enjoy the view. You never know, he might want to take us for a drink. Go on, find out."

"He's not even a friend of Dorothy, look, there's his girlfriend, he's got his arm around her." I pointed to the queue.

"How much do you want to bet, he's as gay as me and you, and he'll want to have a drink with us?"

"It's his bloody girlfriend, I tell you, they're together, there's no way he's gay."

"Go on then, how much?"

"Ten dollars."

Jo shook my hand and walked over to Baywatch Man. After talking to them briefly he kissed both the girl and Baywatch Man on the cheeks and walked back to our table, holding a piece of paper.

"What's this?" I asked, mouth open.

"A prescription for back pain, what do you think? It's his number. He's meeting us in a few hours at Glenelg beach for a drink."

"And what about the girlfriend?"

"Sister. She's leaving us to it tonight."

"How did you know?"

"Number one, his arm's around her shoulder, not her waist, completely non-sexual. Number two look at his bag, Manhattan Portage, you can't buy those in Australia, so he's seriously into his bags to have one of those. Number three his chest hair—not one to be seen."

"What about the Polish guy?"

"He was in a gay bar, fair game, besides, he was a bear. How many straight men do you know who trim/shave/Immac their chests?"

I shrugged. "They've never mentioned it to me."

"I rest my case. Brad will meet us later, he's bringing his friend too."

"What's he called, Chip?" I sighed.

"Now now, don't be bitter, it's very unattractive in you. Ten dollars wasn't it?"

I handed over the money and finished my burger in shocked silence.

I couldn't concentrate on shopping for the rest of the afternoon, instead I followed Jo into his shops and held his bags as he continued his afternoon, sponsored by Mastercard.

Back at the YHA I started to panic about what to wear: "Did he say he liked me, what should I wear, is it too hot to wear jeans, or is shorts in the evening a bit naff? Jo, what on earth am I going to do?"

"Put my shopping under my bunk, I'll sort it out later. I might send it home actually like you did. But I'm going to wear something new tonight."

"Hello, panicking here, what to do?" I flapped my hands in front of my face.

"As long as you don't wear any of that stuff you bought from the drag shop you'll be fine. Jeans and a shirt are fine, no trainers, no hoodies. Think summer waiting job."

Controlling my breathing, I replied, "I'll show you before I decide. I'm off to have a shower, oh and thanks."

During the whole journey on the tram to Glenelg beach, when I would normally have been enjoying the ride, I shook my foot as my legs crossed in front of me. Jo stared out of the window looking for any passing talent.

He held my foot and told me to stop.

"I didn't know I was doing it, what's wrong with me?"

Jo leant in and whispered in my ear "Because for the first time in ages you might, just might get *some*—a bit of action, and you're worried you've forgotten how everything works. Which bits fit with which other bits." He leant back and folded his arms across his chest.

Disgusted, I looked him in the face. "No, that's not it at all." My face flushed red.

Jo turned to look out the window.

I felt my face heat and tried to stop my foot tapping.

***

We arrived at the bar, a modern white building with a glass

front separated from the beach by a pavement. Brad stood up, while holding out his hand enthusiastically. Kiss or shake, which was it to be? Both as it turned out. Both cheeks too, with an alcoholic tinge.

He introduced his friend Chuck who was exactly as I'd predicted: broad, blond and very tanned, bright shorts and a Hawaiian print shirt. They lead us to tables and chairs stood on wooden decking above the sand. Jo immediately sat next to Chuck, resting his hand on his leg and playing with his blond leg hair.

I sat next to Brad, maintaining a respectable distance, allowing me to survey what sat before me: light brown linen trousers and white linen shirt half-unbuttoned, showing a completely hairless chest and pecs you could cut yourself on. I felt myself shift in my trousers, pleased I'd not opted for shorts and instead my smart jeans and a T shirt, no option of being unbuttoned, and bloody right too, with that in front of me.

"I got you one of these." Brad pushed a camp cocktail towards me. "Few of them and you'll be right." He smiled.

Nervously I took a sip and realised it wasn't as camp as it looked. After small talk about the weather and how much better it was than the UK, I asked where Brad came from. He'd lived in Adelaide all his life, never left South Australia. This made the conversation about where I lived quite hard work, so after trying to describe the New Forest in relation to London for a tortured ten minutes, I stood up and asked who wanted a drink.

Jo looked up from exploring Chuck's back teeth, leaving his hands in Chuck's groin and shouted, "Same again" before returning to his previous position. Standard Jo really.

"I'll come and help you." Brad offered, standing and putting his large hands on my bum, which sent a jolt straight to my groin.

Despite being bored by the conversation my groin couldn't deny what it felt, and this, it liked, so putting up no fight whatsoever, we walked to the bar together. Towering above me Brad stood behind me at the bar, pushing himself into my back while playing with my belly button underneath my T shirt. I spent an enjoyable five minutes or so, waiting at the bar for our drinks, as Brad pulled back the waistband of my trousers, and explored the front with his large fingers.

I walked back to the seats with our drinks, leaning forward to disguise my obvious lust for Brad. This only spurred him on, and by the end of the next drinks I was sat on his lap, persevering with a conversation about music tastes. He hadn't heard of any of my music, including Abba, which at first made me question his gay credentials, but a quick glance at the bulge in his trousers soon put paid to that.

Jo stood up, disentangled himself from Chuck and while rearranging himself in *his* trousers proclaimed, "We're going to a club, change of scene. Coming?"

"Na, we're gonna talk a stroll along the beach, maybe catch you later." Brad tweaked one of my nipples under my T shirt.

Were we? Is that what I wanted to do? Beach, sounds harmless enough, what could go wrong? My thoughts were slowed by the cocktails and not all of them were coming from my brain.

I shrugged and smiled at Brad.

And then there were two.

"Come on cutey." He took my hand and led me to the soft sandy beach where we walked hand in hand like on a brochure for a honeymoon holiday company, in Mikanos.

I tried to restart the conversation, commenting on the

moonlight, sound of the sea, asking where his parents lived. All were met with a smile and "Yeah" accompanied by a squeeze of the hand and more.

"So this is it." He stopped outside a white art deco beachfront block of flats, all clean lines it looked like the front of a cruise liner.

"What do you mean?" I focused on the curved glass in some of the windows.

"This is where I live."

"It's nice."

"It's nicer inside."

"Is it?"

"Come on, I'll show you." He took my hand and led me through the door, and up a few flights of stairs. I noticed the decor was well refurbed art deco, tasteful, classy, nothing tasteless could happen here.

He opened his door and took his shirt off straight away. "Shower?"

"If you want, I'm fine."

"Get all the salty air off, refreshing. I do it every time I'm back from the gym, swear by it, come on."

I looked around the flat, well refurbed art deco continued. It's all fine. "How long have you lived here?"

"Couple of years." He untied his trousers and they dropped to the floor. "Look, do you want to, or not?"

I looked at the crumpled trousers on the floor as he stepped out of them, they'd take ages to iron now, maybe I should hang them on a chair. I looked up his muscular legs and noticed a pair of light blue trunk pants with a well known label across them. *He* could be an underwear model for Calvin Klein too.

I didn't even know his surname. Or what his parents did.

Or where he went to school, although, judging by his UK geography knowledge, that was doubtful.

"I know you want to." He looked at my crotch and walked over to me. "Let's get you out of these clothes, they're filthy, clean you up, and get something fresh on." He slipped off my T shirt, unbuttoned my jeans and suddenly I was stood in front of my very own Rocky, just wearing my underpants, and conscious of my pigeon chest and weedy legs.

He took me by the hand and led me to the bathroom where with one swift movement he removed his, and my underwear. We were soon soaping each other's bodies all over in the shower.

He led me to the bedroom, still dripping, and clutching a towel each, although we could have hung the towels up on ourselves at that point.

It was like having sex with a slippery bouncy castle, muscles everywhere, we slipped and slid across each other, adding lube to our already wet bodies, laughing and kissing each other all over.

He told me he loved my little legs and flat muscle free chest, then in one movement reached in his bedside cabinet for a condom and rolled one on with a smile and a glint in his eyes. "I've got a whole drawer of them. Flavoured, different sizes and some glow in the dark."

He loved me, my body!

I hadn't forgotten which bits went where, and neither had he it seemed. Brad knew very well which bits went where, and he mixed it up a bit too, which I enjoyed. The glow in the dark condoms were great fun, we strode around the bedroom like Star Wars Lightsabers until we fell on the floor and made proper use of them.

And then it was over. We lay in a salty heap together.

I fell asleep, the room spinning slightly and my head buried deep in his plush pillows.

I woke and worked out where I was, a pile of damp towels on the floor next to the bed. I looked at Brad next to me noticing the curvature of his pecs and perfect square jaw, just starting to show a little stubble. I moved over next to him and put my arms across his chest, keen to absorb his body heat.

He moved away.

Undeterred I repeated my manoeuvre so we lay spooning.

He looked at me, got out of bed, put his dressing gown on and left the bedroom.

"Tea? Coffee? Orange juice?" he shouted.

"Tea."

"I've got to go in a bit, so you'd better have a quick shower. You remember where it is?"

Remember where it is? I could draw you a diagram of it, we spent so long in it last night. Last night he couldn't get enough of the smut, all over my body like he'd lost a contact lens, and now it's like we've just met.

I climbed out of bed, covering myself with the damp towel and walked to the shower.

Part of me expected him to join me in the shower again, but he stayed in the kitchen making our drinks.

I put my clothes on which smelt of last night's sex and sea and met him in the kitchen.

"Tea's on the side, you've got ten minutes and I'm going."

"What you doing today?"

"Gym, dunno really, I'll give Chuck a call, see how he got on."

I can tell you exactly how he got on. But I smiled instead over my mug.

"I'm going as soon as I'm washed, so…" He looked at the door. "See you around." He disappeared into the bathroom.

I left my tea, put on my shoes and left, closing the door quietly behind me.

Walking along the beach back to where I knew I could get a tram back to the city centre, I felt a strange mix of elation and depression. For that night, that one night it felt as if I imagined it always would, when you found that person, the proper one, Boyfriend, Prince Charming. Ok, so he wasn't exactly Einstein in the conversation department, and I still didn't know what his surname was, but I could have drawn you a picture of his perfectly manicured man bush.

I realised then, I'd never see him again, and yet that was ok. That was exactly as the universe had meant it to be. Just one night of fun, uncomplicated, basic fun, and nothing more. No one had died, I hadn't done anything I didn't want to do—I'd done a few things I hadn't done before, but there's nothing wrong with broadening one's horizons is there? He didn't want to meet my mother, I didn't want to hear about how his day at work had gone, I couldn't ever have really imagined picking out curtains with him. How could I take someone seriously who didn't know who Abba was?

I arrived at the tram stop, the sun shining and a smile which became a smirk spreading across my face, as I remembered the details of last night.

Jo's never going to believe this one.

I made time to tell Hannah and Grace about this, feeling slightly guilty, and a bit turned on as I typed the emails.

Grace replied the next day…

From: myrealnamewastaken@hotmail.co.uk

To: discokieran@hotmail.co.uk

Hiya! :throws arms into the air with excitement:
   A quick one, (what was that about a quick one Shaz?!) while I'm in the library, taking advantage of the internet before I officially start my shift. I can't believe it, you've gone and got yourself a seriously big portion of some, well done that man. Don't worry about feeling guilty, I doubt this is the start of a new Kieran, sleeping his way around Australia—you can leave that to Jo. There's nothing wrong with a bit of harmless fun like that. I'm trembling with envy. As for me, not a sniff of it, unless you count the middle aged brown cardiganed man who keeps requesting unusual books at the library every time I'm there. No, I didn't count him either!
   Will reply properly after I've finished keeping the elderly of Gosport in interesting reading materials.
   Lots of love Disco Grace xx

Hannah took a bit longer…

From: hannahgreeneloves-steps@hotmail.co.uk

To: discokieran@hotmail.co.uk

Alright m'darlin'
   Just getting the hang of this email lark—at college in the computer lab when I should be in the library researching something or other…
   YOU'RE SUCH A SLAG! (Someone said there was an abbreviation for a winking face, but I'm buggered if I know what it is, so "winking face")

72

Adelaide

Love you
XHX

Five

April—May 1999, Melbourne

We were going to a house party, a night out, how exciting. What to wear? Mark from the Bar had invited us. We had been in Melbourne for a month since we got bar jobs from the notice board in the YHA. Jo had started to run out of money, and needed to earn some more. I was slightly smug as I was still solvent, but I was happy to work anyway. It did somewhat restrict our sightseeing ability, as we always had to be back within a few days for our next shift, but it was nice to have regular money. Jo didn't seem to have much left at the end of every week, but he did seem to be having a great time mixing with our new friends from the Bar.

The Bar did have an actual name, but it was so awful, a play on words like so many hairdressers called "Fringe Benefits" but worse, we couldn't bear to actually say it, so we both referred to it as just the Bar.

We shared a room in a house not far from the Bar, and

soon settled into a regular routine: work, beach, nights out. The Bar was, almost exclusively, staffed by back packers like us, in their early twenties, and so there was no shortage of excuses for a night out. Happy Tuesday, Happy Birthday, Happy Leaving—you get the picture.

Tonight was happy birthday for Mark who had worked at the Bar for the grand total of six months, this would have earned him five stars on his name badge, if we did that sort of thing. He was, in comparison to the rest of us, an old timer. Mark was celebrating his twenty-fourth birthday in Australia by having a fancy dress party—themed as superheroes (which I later noted some had stretched slightly)—in his house share in a studenty suburb of Melbourne.

I had noticed Mark during my time at the Bar, and gradually got the courage to speak to him. He was that particular sort of handsome which is quite intimidating when viewed from a distance. When I saw him closer the impression just became stronger. The first time I'd worked with him I returned home and described him to Jo to see if he'd clocked him too.

"Longish brown wavy hair, a square jaw, permanent five o'clock shadow, piercing blue eyes, and a nose which would normally look too big, but on his face was like a cherry on the top of a fairy cake, finishing his face off to perfection."

Jo nodded. "What's he sound like?"

"I think he's from Yorkshire, and he's got a soft lilting accent, which sort of wraps itself around you like a fierce wind."

"That's a very butch way to describe a man, Kieran." He pursed his lips.

"Not the point. Do you know who I'm talking about?"

"Course I do you fucker! I was winding you up!"

So when Jo had told me Mark—this Mark—had invited us

75

to his house party I could hardly contain my excitement. We'd spent half an hour guessing which superhero he would come as. My favourite was He-Man, Jo went for Spiderman.

We arrived at the party and were both proved wrong. Mark answered the door dressed as Robin, I could see his smile, revealing perfect white teeth, five o'clock shadow, and as he removed his mask, I saw his piercing blue eyes and bits of his wavy dark hair emerging from the mask. I couldn't keep my eyes off his body, easily visible through the tight costume: red T-shirt and yellow tights, perfectly accessorised by the campest shoes this side of the Atlantic: yellow and red boots with wings on each side sprouting from the ankles.

I looked at Jo as Mark took the wine from us and hugged us in turn.

The evening progressed and after the third circuit of the party mix, even Tiffany's "I Think We're Alone Now" sounded a bit tired. No-one really cared if she was *still* alone. There was a revolution, Robin strode over to the hi-fi and inserted another CD.

I walked over to him as he chose the track to start the music with. He looked up at me as I said that it'd better be a good song he put on. Stood next to him as he looked through the track listing, I could feel his breath on my face. I looked at his dark features as he studied the CD case intently. He put on *Just Like Jesse James* by Cher: She sang about how he drove the women folk wild and he'd shoot them down with one flash of his pearly smile.

I started dancing again and Mark joined the circle of twitching and swaying bodies. He smiled and moved in time to the music opposite me, laughing at the trashy lyrics. After a while the tights and cape proved too much for him so he took a rest. As he sat on the arm of the sofa I saw him looking at me as I danced. I danced with my back to him so I had to look over my shoulder to see him.

"I feel a right tit in this costume, I wish I'd not bothered with fancy dress."

"At least you've not got to get home wearing your costume, me and Jo have to traipse across town looking like this." I looked down at my Wonder Woman outfit, feeling annoyed that I'd not kicked up more of a fuss at the fancy dress shop when they said they'd run out of Superman outfits as Jo had the last one. Jo had persuaded me that as Superman and Wonder Woman we'd make a perfect pair.

Mark laughed.

"You could always go to the red light district to make yourself a bit of money."

I laughed.

Jo walked up to me. "What are you two talking about?"

"Just talking about our costumes, what did you come as?" Mark looked him up and down in an exaggerated way.

"Isn't it obvious, I'm Superman, isn't the big S on my chest a giveaway? I spent ages looking around for the costume, it was the last one in the shop, and you don't even know who it is."

Mark smiled at me and I smiled back.

"Oh, I get it, right, well if that's all, leave you to your little conversation shall I? Kieran, don't leave without me, I don't want to get home on my own." And Jo left.

The thought of catching trams and buses home on my own as Wonder Woman filled me with dread, so it was unlikely I'd leave without him. At least together, people would realise the joke we'd attempted, and we'd both feel like complete tits, *together*.

The party continued and a parade of random guests arrived and left. This included a contingency of music students who were so painfully *very* that I had to stop myself laughing at them. They stood in little cliques, dressed in jeans and T-shirts, having obviously taken a long time to choose their costumes, discussing the various benefits of modulations and why *technically speaking* all modern pop music was rubbish.

What would Grace do? I walked into their little circle of musical snobbery and said, "Did you know, "Dancing Queen" has got a two octave range? And "The Winner Takes it All" is widely regarded as the best pop song ever written. So if you think that technically all pop music is rubbish, I think you'll find you're wrong." I stood with my hands on my hips, grateful now for the Wonderwoman outfit.

They tried to argue back at my points, but I was really fired up now, not quite three sheets to the wind, but getting on for one and a half, with a good wind behind me.

"And don't even get me started on your "technically speaking."" I made the air quotation marks with my fingers."I watched a documentary about a music student who studied Abba's music. He said it had all the hallmarks of classical music in its complexity."

The *very* music students sat open-mouthed.

I walked to the kitchen for a drink, pleased with myself.

"How's it going with Robin?" Jo handed me a drink.

"It's going very well with, Mark actually. I've just pissed off a load of smug music students, so all in all it's going pretty well—you?"

"Yeah, good. I got stuck with one of those music students in here earlier when I got myself a drink. Talk about boring, I didn't know someone could be that dull. He started talking about his journey to college in minute detail, this bus that train. I wanted to jump out the window. Thank God someone came in so I could leave."

"Let me know when you want to go. I'm going back to see if Mark's dancing." I kissed Jo's face and walked out the kitchen.

"Kieran?"

I turned to face Jo again.

"Yes?"

"You do know he's straight don't you? Remember your worst nightmare."

"Who said anything about love" I replied and continued to walk out the kitchen.

I sat down and faced the people on the sofa: *Batman*, *Robin*, one of the *Baycity Rollers* and an assortment of girls. Without realising, I had invited them to a one off showing of "An Audience With Kieran Donovan." They asked me questions about my college, which university I was going to, where I lived, and my friends. Eventually Batman got up the courage to ask me about being gay. Then questions came thick and fast: How did you know? When did you know? Have you ever slept with a woman?

After a while I paused and stood. "I'm going to get myself a drink. I'd like a break from this impromptu heterosexual outreach programme."

Jo was sat on the work surface chatting to a blonde girl. He stopped talking to her and looked at me. "You ok? Do you want to go home?"

"I'm just warming up. Why would I want to go home?"

"Don't let them take the piss. You're not a performing seal, if they ask anything you don't want to answer, just ask if they would answer that question. Always works. And if they ask you to tell them about coming out to your parents, just say—ok, but could you tell me about one of the most painful experiences of your life too, then we're even. That normally works." He winked at me and chinked his glass against mine which I'd just filled.

Re-invigorated by Jo's advice, I returned to centre stage on the chair opposite the audience.

"Who's seen the film *Threesome*? Alec Baldwin? A woman accidentally shares a room with a straight guy and a gay guy because she's called Alex and the computer thought she was a guy so it put her in the guy's dorm at university."

Some nods around the room.

"They're good friends, but this is complicated by the fact that the straight guy fancies the girl, the gay guy fancies the straight guy and the girl fancies the gay guy. Is everyone still with me?"

More nods.

I was really getting into my stride now. I rubbed my hands together. "Anyway, one of the film's theories is that sex with someone of your own gender is by definition better than sex with someone of the opposite gender." I paused for effect.

"How can you say that? Why?" Mark's cute face looked confused.

Batman added, "I don't think so, no way."

I looked at them both, then reminded myself of the stride I had been in. "The theory is that as a man you know what to do to a man's body to push his buttons, but a woman's body is a bit of a mystery—because a man doesn't have the same bits. Same with girls."

"I can see that, yeah, but what about the emotions with sex?" Mark still looked confused, that sweet little boy lost, confused, which I found really sexy.

"That's another discussion, but I'm just talking about the physical side. Not a bad place to start I thought, seeing as you were all asking quite detailed questions to me."

Mark continued with this line of questioning, "Who do you like on TV at the moment?"

"Paul Nicholls is cute, especially in his pants, like in that drama on BBC."

"So what would you do, would you try it on with him?"

"Like *I've* ever got a chance with Paul Nicholls."

"What about me, I'm in pants, with this costume, and you "haven't tried it on with me." He put his hands on his hips and stood with his legs wide apart like a cowboy.

"Well, I didn't think you wanted me to." I looked into his eyes and blinked exaggeratedly.

"Well, I do, and I feel hurt that you "haven't."" He stuck his bottom lip out.

I just sat there and smiled at him. Everyone else sat quietly, looking at the floor, unable to know where to look as a man with a girlfriend was doing some A grade flirting with me. *In public. In pants.*

The blonde girl asked, "Why don't you just ask Kieran what you've been dying to ask all night? If he fancies you?"

Mark shrugged.

"Well if that's your translation as asking that, then yes I do fancy you, like she said. Didn't you pick up on me flirting with you earlier tonight?"

"No. I guess I didn't know how men flirted."

"Same as women do." I flashed him a fake smile.

"I guess I wasn't really looking for flirting from a man." He paused, then continued, "what about uniforms, do you like a man in uniform?"

"Nurses' uniforms are cute, the little white tunics with the black trousers are cute. I'm used to that, when I worked in the hospital."

"So what about *me* in a nurse's uniform, what would you do if *I* was wearing a nurse's uniform?" Mark tilted his head to one side and pursed his lips.

The blonde girl coughed, and I realised where I was again.

Mark looked around the room, then back at me. "I feel like a right poof in the Robin outfit."

"Didn't you realise, *all of us poofs* wear tights, underpants on the outside' and capes." More exaggerated blinking.

Mark shook his head and looked at the floor.

By half-six-of-the-bleary-eyed-morning-after-o'clock, even Mark and I had run out of conversation, I dozed lightly in the chair. However, by half eight, the light streamed in through the flimsy living room curtains to wake everyone up. I glanced at the sofa: Robin lay with Madonna's head across his chest. Batman's ears were looking decidedly limp as the Baycity Roller lay on his chest.

After much coercion Mark made tea for everyone, excluding himself.

"That's very *new man* of you Mark," I said as he passed my tea.

"Yes I suppose it is." He stood up from the sofa and pulled the tights and pants into a more comfortable position. More complaints about how stupid he felt in the outfit. "I really need someone to rip these off me…how about you?" He stared straight at me.

"Now, that's not fair, flirting back with me, it's like taunting a child with sweets he can't have."

"Ok right." He looked away.

Jo burst into the living room. He looked like he'd just run through a branch of Claire's Accessories covered in glue. He scanned the room, found me and ran over.

Holding onto my top and staring straight into my eyes he quickly said: "I've got to go, I think I've done *a bad thing*. Can we go now please?"

I whispered to him, "What have you done this time?" Aware of the drill by this stage in our friendship.

"I'll tell you when we've gone" he whispered back.

I mentally rolled my eyes.

***

We sat on the tram among the other passengers. All around us people sat quietly, dressed and washed for a new day. Jo and I stood out like a pair of dishevelled sore thumbs covered in costumes. We stank of cigarettes and alcohol, our eyes showed we'd not slept, and our clothes were more than a bit incongruous with eight-of-the-fresh-new-day-o'clock in the morning, as Grace would have described it. I watched as our appearance amused some of the bored commuters around us, as they slowly got the significance of Superman and Wonder Woman being together.

"What happened?" I steeled myself for the response. We'd been here before.

"You know you were chatting to that Mark for most of the night, the guy dressed as Robin?"

I nodded.

83

"You know his friend, dressed as Batman? Well, turns out he's called Chris." Jo paused as I nodded and shrugged, unclear what was so bad about that. "And that blonde girl, who sat on the sofa with you and Robin, that's his girlfriend—Ailsa she's called. Anyway we got chatting in the kitchen when he got himself some drinks in a break from your "Audience with Kieran Donovan" show."

I remembered Batman disappearing for a while from the sofa, but hadn't thought anything of it at the time. At the time I'd rather enjoyed bathing myself in the adoration and attention from Robin and the others.

"He told me how interested he was in what you were saying about sexuality, and your theory about sex with someone of your own gender being by definition better."

"Yes, so. Can you get to the point, this tram journey's going to be over in twenty minutes, I want my bed when I get back. Can you please just get to the point, I'm starting to wilt here."

"Ok, ok, so anyway, of course I pointed out to him that he had a girlfriend, the lovely Ailsa. He nodded and walked closer to me. He asked me if I wanted a cigarette outside with him. So I followed him outside. So, we're outside smoking, and he walks up to me and said he'd like to see what it's like to kiss another man. So I kissed him. He said it was more stubbly than he'd expected, which is funny because I'd shaved that morning. One thing led to another and soon we're in the bath having sex. When we'd finished he offered me another cigarette and we left the bathroom separately. Someone had banged on the door asking how long we thought we'd be. I ignored them, but Chris told them he'd not be long, which was a lie as it goes." Jo folded his arms and looked at me. I looked around the tram and noticed all the bored commuters were enjoying the floor show we'd unintentionally put on for them.

I whispered back to Jo, "But you knew he had a girlfriend, and you'd been chatting and dancing with Ailsa at the party. And let's not forget that Ailsa and Chris both work at the Bar, so you've got to see them afterwards."

"I hadn't thought about that. What if Chris doesn't want to talk to me at work anymore? I don't think I could cope with that."

"Never mind *that*, isn't it more awkward with Ailsa? Working with her when you've shagged her boyfriend in a party, while she was upstairs talking to me? Isn't that a bit more difficult?"

"I hadn't thought of it like that before. She'll be fine. I'm not going to tell her, are you? And you can bet Chris won't say anything. Maybe things will all be fine, now you've put it like that. I just need to make sure I'm extra friendly and fun to Chris. Don't want him snubbing me; we have a good laugh at work, sometimes he's the only thing which makes a shift bearable."

I looked at him, speechless, unable to comprehend his logic. I saw a row of white high-rise buildings next to palm trees lining the road. We were near home.

"Oh Kieran, I'm so pleased you listened. It's really helped. I feel so much better, turns out there's nothing to worry about really is there? Isn't this our stop, quick, press the button." He stood up and we walked off the tram. "Have you got anything for stubble rash? My face is covered."

Six

Chapter 6

S hortly after the party, Jo decided it was time to move on. We'd spent just over two months in Melbourne, seen the sights, been to more parties than I'd thought humanly possible, earned a bit of money to help us on our way, and sat on the beach checking out talented lifeguards on too many afternoons off to mention.

Add the fact that, exactly as I'd predicted, Chris didn't want to speak to Jo after the bathroom incident, and it was definitely time to move on from Melbourne. Jo insisted it was because we'd worked at the bar for too long, and used it as an excuse for us to leave. I saw the way Chris looked at Jo now—he had a sadness in his eyes when he saw Ailsa and Jo both working behind the bar. Chris told me he hadn't meant to go as far with Jo as he had, "Only a kiss. I just wanted a kiss." But once in the bathroom Jo, while kissing his face, had taken Chris's trousers down, sat him on the bath and moved down his chest and started using his mouth elsewhere. "He said he was still only kissing me, just down there." Chris looked away. "But then he was. And it was too late." What man is going to say no to that when he's being kissed *there*? Chris didn't stand a chance.

Ailsa asked me what was wrong with her boyfriend, and I lied that I didn't know. I wasn't going to tell her, I couldn't tell her. Jo told me it didn't matter because we'd not see Chris and Ailsa after we left the bar. I couldn't help thinking about the damage he'd done, which would remain long after we left, like a bruise on their relationship. Jo didn't seem to understand this and just waved my comments away with his hand and a "Don't worry, it'll be fine, I'm sure it's not the first time."

We had a huge leaving party. It was meant to be a surprise, but Jo got wind of it and insisted on taking control. I confronted him about the big party, he explained, "I want everyone to remember us after we've left. I want them to all say "wasn't Jo and Kieran's leaving party brilliant?" I want them wearing black arm bands when I, I mean we, leave. Don't you Kieran?"

So I went along with his plans, it was easier for everyone that way.

I wasn't *really* bothered, I'd been to so many other leaving parties since working there I knew we'd be forgotten as soon as the lights went off in the bar for that night. Except for one member of staff, who'd remember one of us for much longer.

We had an Australia themed party. Not the most original idea, but Jo had learned from the leaving party at The Duke and bought more little koalas, kangaroos and flags than I'd ever seen. The bar looked like it was Anzac day.

Jo wanted to hire a silver bus for our arrival, but the bar

manager told him only if he paid for it. We stuck with the koalas, kangaroos and flags.

Jo made a speech and thanked everyone for the laughs we'd had since working there. "So if you ever need some help turning this place into a cabaret bar, just let me know. People came from all over the UK to see my production of "Cabaret." Kieran and I are off to continue our travels around Australia, I asked for a silver bus, but was reminded we didn't have enough money. Next stop Surfers Paradise. Working here has been more than enough for a holiday, so we'll be taking it easy when we get to Surfers. If you see us on the beach, say hi."

I stood next to the bar sipping my drink. I noticed Chris and Ailsa talking in one corner: Ailsa staring at the ground, shrugging off his attempted hugs. I had just wanted to hand in our notice, have a few drinks with the staff and leave the next week. I didn't want this big fanfare, I wanted to get on with our holiday, keep the memories I had of the bar and move on.

We caught the Greyhound bus early the next morning. Jo wore Jackie O style sunglasses, which were the size of a couple of tellies and slept for the whole journey. I read our *Rough Guide's* section on Surfers Paradise. I looked out the window at the familiar sights of the city and had my own "Muriel's Wedding" moment: "Bye the Bar, bye trams, bye house parties, bye house share, bye Melbourne!" I murmured quietly to myself as our old life disappeared into the distance.

June—Surfers Paradise

We arrived in Surfers Paradise, mile after mile of sandy beaches next to concrete towers and rows of shops selling surfing equipment, beach towels and snorkel masks. It wasn't quite the tropical paradise I'd expected, but it felt good to leave Melbourne behind. Away from the repetition of work, away from the politics of the Bar, away from the mess which Jo had created with Chris and Ailsa. A fresh start, sightseeing, surfing (well, watching people surfing, I had no intention of actually surfing), and feeling like we were on holiday again.

We checked into the YHA, treated ourselves to a twin room—the thought of going back to a dorm after having our own room for so long in Melbourne hadn't appealed, so we'd agreed to stick to twins from now on. I bought some food from a nearby shop while Jo checked out the YHA's facilities. I returned, dropped our food off in the kitchen and went to our room for a lie down. I felt exhausted after the party and the coach journey. Although I hadn't done anything wrong, I still felt somehow guilty for what Jo had done to Ailsa and Chris. I read a while and fell asleep.

Jo shook me gently and I woke, I looked at my watch and realised I'd been asleep for just over an hour. "You're going to want to wake up for this."

"I was well gone, I must have needed that." I rubbed my eyes and yawned, gently coming awake.

"I'm sure you did, but you're going to need this even more. I've been checking out what there is in this YHA and I think you're in for a surprise. There's a pool room, laundry room, and a bar, which is where this gets interesting. I sat in the bar killing time while you slept and before long I was talking to Duncan, the barman. He was telling me all about the places to go out here, where to avoid, the best places to go surfing."

"What does he look like?"

"Well, his voice is certainly like a powerful wind blowing over you. He definitely is *gay best friend* gorgeous."

Since coming out, Jo and I had noticed that whenever we met a new girl they inevitably had a gay best friend who was described as being gorgeous. "He's absolutely gorgeous, he's my gay best friend, you'll love him." The problem with such a build up was that invariably the person didn't live up to the expectations which their friend had built up with us. If only they really were as gorgeous as described, they would indeed be an Adonis of Greek stature. From this Jo and I used it as shorthand for someone who was genuinely as gorgeous as we imagined. This was not faint praise indeed.

Hence, Jo's description of Duncan as being "gay best friend gorgeous" was enough to get me out of bed.

We walked to the bar where Jo ordered us drinks and introduced me to Duncan, who was drying glasses behind the bar. He shook my hand and I got an eyeful of his arms, well displayed by the white vest top he wore with bright red surfing shorts and flip-flops (or thongs as the Australians called them. Rest assured that had caused much confusion and hilarity the first time I'd discovered that.)

We ordered drinks and Jo introduced me, and between serving drinks, Duncan from Reading, told us about himself:

He was travelling around Australia for a year, and had stopped here for some work, as he needed some money. He wanted to work in the police force when he got back to the UK, but needed some time out first, as he'd gone between jobs and university since leaving school without a break. He had just split up from his girlfriend of five years, so thought now was a good time to leave everything and come to Oz. He explained that he used to work in pubs, which is why getting the bar job was easy.

"That's enough about me, what about you two, what brings you two here?" Duncan asked with a slight West Country twang.

"We're starring in our own version of *"Priscilla Queen of the Desert."* Jo replied immediately.

"I remember that film. Lots of music and costumes. That guy from Neighbours was in it wasn't he?"

"Guy Pearce. He played Adam." I rested my head on my hands on the bar and stared at Duncan.

Duncan smiled and asked, "Do you two play cards, cos we've got a bit of a game going on tonight. Nothing serious, the game's called golf, and we play for matchsticks. It's just a laugh. You can watch for a bit first if you want. So what do you reckon? Tempted?"

If only you knew. Very tempted.

"Yes, where do you want us?" Jo looked around the bar.

"I finish at ten, we're meeting in the lounge area through there." Duncan pointed to a seating room off the bar.

"See you then" Jo replied as we walked from the bar to sit outside with our drinks.

As we sat, I checked we were out of Duncan's earshot. "You said gay best friend gorgeous, you didn't say he was straight. That changes everything. I can't believe this."

"I said he was gay best friend gorgeous, I didn't say anything about him being gay. Anyway, he's friendly, he's invited us to play cards, he's lovely to look at. What's your problem, let's just go with it. If something happens, then so much the better. God knows you could do with some action, it must be like Pavlov's dogs for you. When was the last time?"

"Mind your own business."

"That's what I'm worried about."

"Brad, in Adelaide."

"That was two months ago."

I looked away.

We played this golf, card game—at first I found it hard to understand but after a few hands I realised I was really competitive.

Between hands, Duncan walked outside for a cigarette. I didn't smoke, but wanted some fresh air, and taking a leaf out of Jo's book took this opportunity to spend time with Duncan alone. It had worked for him, so why not give it a go? We sat on the chairs in the small yard area out the back of the YHA, we could hear the sea crashing on the beach in the distance. Tower blocks stretched along the seafront far into the distance. *They'd never allow this in the UK,* I thought, putting off making conversation with Duncan.

"How's your year of freedom going?"

Duncan inhaled his cigarette, paused and then breathed the smoke out as he replied, "Better than I'd thought actually. I was with Iz for so long I forgot what it's like to be with anyone else. I can do what I like, don't have to ask anyone. She did me a favour actually."

I nodded, indicating I wanted him to continue.

"It's not just doing stuff, I mean, other things. I've not been with anyone else for the last five years. Well, now I can. I was a bit of a goer in my early twenties, but then I met Iz and I settled down. I suppose I'm doing what I should have done five years earlier. Wild oats and that! What about you? What's it like travelling with your boyfriend?"

"Jo's not my boyfriend, we're just friends."

"It's just how you are together. He takes charge, and looks

after you. I suppose it's like I did with Iz. Just thought that's how it worked with you lot too. One of you looking after the other one."

"*You lot?* What's that supposed to mean?" I asked, wanting him to spell it out for me. I enjoyed making straight men squirm like this. Kev did a good line in squirming straight men, and I'd learned from the master.

"You know, gays. I mean, gay men." He paused, waiting for me to confirm he was right. "You are, aren't you, and Jo?"

I nodded.

Duncan took another deep drag of his cigarette and nodded too. "Thought so. I'm not as stupid as I look. I might not have grown up in London, but I know a thing or two."

"You don't look stupid at all." I smiled and turned to look at him, taking his bait.

"Must make it easier for you lot." He paused, thinking of how to express what he was thinking. "Sometimes I don't understand how men and women can be in a relationship together, cos they're so different. You know, Men are from Mars, Women are from Venus, or some shit. Iz was always reading books like that. Women always want to talk about stuff, their feelings, and men, well, we just want to get on with things. Why bother talking, when you can have sex? She always wanted to make it romantic, and I just wanted to do it."

"Are you still talking about sex, or other things?"

"Yes, no, everything. Anyway, we're so different. But cos men are similar, it must make it easier when you're together. None of that "how does it make you feel, and why have you hurt my feelings" crap. Simpler."

"I suppose, I hadn't thought of it like that. I've only ever had relationships with men, so I don't know what it's like to have

93

one with a woman. There isn't only one sort of man, and one sort of woman, so things still get difficult for two men. It's not as simple as that, but I get your point." I felt it was important to concede his point partially.

"Iz always needed to have a reason for sex. What do they say, women need a reason, men just need a place? That's got to be simpler for you lot hasn't it?"

"Suppose it does. Can I have a drag of your fag?"

"Didn't know you smoked."

"Strictly speaking, I don't, it's just everyone goes on about how nice it is and I wanted to see what it's like."

Duncan handed me his cigarette. "Here you are. Take it easy, or you'll be sick."

I ignored Duncan's advice and took a huge drag on the cigarette. I felt sick and light headed. *Why did people enjoy this? How can this be fun?* I wobbled on my feet and Duncan held my arm to stop me as I almost fell over. *It's worked.*

"Alright, maybe I should take that off you. Do you want some water?" Duncan asked as he led me back inside the YHA, holding my arm to steady my progress. In between the sickness I smiled to myself as this was the most intimate I'd been with Duncan. I enjoyed being looked after by him, feeling his strong arms and hands guiding me to a seat inside the YHA.

We played cards until two o'clock in the morning. We came to the end of a thirteen "hole" game, and I announced I'd had enough.

"Are you ok walking to your room Kieran?" Duncan looked up from his cards. "You don't still feel sick do you?"

I caught Jo's eye as he looked at me after Duncan said this. I quickly looked away from Jo and returned to Duncan's gaze. The other players sat around Duncan on low chairs set against the wall in a bright lurid green. I was relieved not to have their itchy material next to my legs anymore.

"I'm fine now, I just need to lie down. What are you doing later in the week? Do you fancy doing something together, you know, later this week. If you're busy, or don't want to, that's ok, we can play cards again."

"Not tomorrow, but the day after, I'm working from six, so we could do something during the day. Look see you in here at twelvish, once I've got up. We can see what we fancy doing then—depending on how late I stay up. Alright, night Kieran." A couple of other players looked up, their backs straightened after leaning over the low table covered in cards. They nodded a good night to me then returned to their cards.

I walked slowly to bed, making more of my sickness than was strictly true. When I got to our room, as soon as my head hit the pillow I fell into a deep sleep. My dreams were never very subtle; in this one, I dreamt I had sailed to Mars with Duncan in a large silver bus.

***

The next day as he finished work, Duncan suggested playing pool. I'd spent lunchtime in the bar, ostensibly reading my paperback, but really just brewing my own particular brand of eau de toilette—Obsession, by Disco Kieran. Jo knew I did a good range of such scents—at least it was better than his scent—Easy.

I explained to Duncan I'd never played before and so it would probably be more fun to play on his own.

"Now, when's playing on your own more fun than playing with someone else? I can't think of any times. Come on, I'm going to teach you how to play pool."

He explained the rules of which I remembered less than a third. I missed a few shots as I held the "cue" (who knew it was called a cue?) nervously. Duncan stood behind me, put his hands on top of mine as I held the cue, and showed me how to line it up with the ball and the pocket you're aiming for. I "potted" (again, who knew?) the ball, the first time during that game. I turned round to see him smiling at me. I felt his body against my back and bum. *What was this about—was this about him teaching me to play pool, or something else?*

That evening Jo had a very clear idea what this was about. "He fancies you, but he doesn't know how to do anything about it, so he's doing what he'd do if you were a woman—flirting. I bet you could feel him, stiff as a board, when he stood behind you. He won't actually make a move on you, but if you do, then he's all yours. It's textbook. Loads of the straight boys at drama college were exactly the same."

"There were straight boys at your drama college?"

"You're missing the point Kieran."

Time progressed, with us spending more time together like this. We spent a day on the beach. Jo made some excuse about having to work—although I'd not heard anything about him getting a job, and rest assured, if he really had a job, I'd have heard about it. So it was just me and Duncan on the beach.

I wanted to pack a picnic, but Duncan wanted to just get a hotdog from a stand nearby. We settled on a small picnic, with the option of hotdogs. He swam in the sea, while I read my paperback of *The Llama Parlour*, by Kathy Lette. He asked me what it was about, listening intently as I described it. He only read books with black covers, spy stories, thrillers, that sort of thing. We talked about our plans when we returned to the UK. He had to move back in with his parents, just outside Reading. He was worried about how he'd cope with this after living with Iz for the last five years. We reflected on the co-incidence that my parents lived quite near to his, and we discussed meeting up when we were both back. A part of me knew this would probably never happen, but I enjoyed imagining it, and revelled in making plans together.

There was a nicely awkward moment when he asked me to rub sun cream into his back. I obliged Duncan's request, thinking about Margaret Thatcher in the nude throughout. "Do you want me to do your back?" he asked.

I nodded and quickly lay on my front before succumbing to his hands as they massaged my back.

"Your neck's very tight. You're on holiday, you shouldn't be stressed," he commented as he felt my neck.

"I just worry about things. Jo has a habit of needing to be looked after."

"I thought it was him who looked after you. Well he's not here now, so there's nothing to worry about. Apart from whether to trust that van for hot dogs or not."

"It's not quite that simple with Jo."

He made comments about women as they passed in bikinis, expecting me to agree with him. I responded by commenting about the men as they walked past.

We ate the picnic I'd prepared, chatting easily. He commented how much nicer it had tasted than the hot dogs.

"I'll have to think of a way to thank you for this," he said.

"I'll let you know."

We walked back to the YHA in time for him to start his shift.

He squeezed my shoulder as he ran ahead and left me walking slowly back.

He turned round and said, "Fancy a game of golf tonight when I finish? Get some others together eh?"

"Sounds good, see you later." I waved.

And he was gone.

Jo was laying on his bed when I returned. I told him about the afternoon I'd just spent with Duncan. Jo asked for more details as I told the story, had he lingered on my back when he'd massaged in the sun cream? How had he asked me to put sun cream on his back? What did he say when I mentioned a cute guy I saw on the beach?

I couldn't answer most of these questions, but was pleased for Jo's interest. I felt a bit lost during the day without Jo. Somehow, I felt as if I'd cheated on Jo with my friendship with Duncan. I didn't tell Jo this, as he'd probably laugh, but it felt right to be sharing this story with Jo, as usual. Poring over the details of an encounter together. It felt right, normal, usual, comfortable.

Ten o'clock, I'd assembled a group of other hostellers, all interested in playing the card game. I walked into the bar to tell Duncan who was just finishing his shift. He'd told me this earlier and I'd made a mental note of the exact time, stored for use later.

He smiled as I walked into the bar, finished serving a customer, waved to the other bar staff and followed me. He walked past the living room area into the kitchen.

"We're all sat in there." I pointed to the living room.

"I've got to eat something, I've not eaten anything since our picnic. I could eat a scabby horse between two bits of bread. Won't take long, I'll just make a quick snack. Come with me if you want."

I told Jo to start explaining the rules of the game, and play a few dummy rounds and that I'd be back with Duncan in a few minutes.

I walked to the kitchen where Duncan was in the middle of making a cheese sandwich.

"Do you want me to do you Welsh Rarebit? Or Welsh Rabbit as Mum calls it?" I stood next to the work surface, poised to grab the cheese.

"What's that?"

"You worked in pubs and you don't know?"

"Never heard of it. You said you did A level Geography and thought Lisbon was in Australia, so Jo told me."

I made a mental note to kill Jo later. "It's sort of posh cheese on toast. Do you have some mustard powder, and Worcestershire sauce?"

I cobbled together my version of Welsh Rarebit while Duncan made us both a drink. He ate it quickly and licked his fingers afterwards, smiling at me.

"Very nice, better than what I was going to make definitely. I'd better do the washing up and then we can play cards." Duncan looked around the kitchen to where I'd prepared the food.

"Done it."

"When?"

"As I went along. It seems there's a lot I can teach you about catering."

"You'll have to think of some way I can thank you." He smiled lasciviously.

I was eating a banana.

"Yes, something like that." Duncan added. "Are we playing

cards or what?" He walked into the living room area and I followed.

We played until four-of-the-early-hours-in-the-Antipodes-o'clock, which meant it was only now not too hot to feel as if you were melting when you moved too quickly.

"I'm going to bed. I can hardly see straight anymore," Duncan announced, standing.

I felt my eyes very heavy and agreed. There were only three or four old campaigners who had lasted this long, so I felt I wasn't bowing out too early. I stood next to Duncan.

"You going too?"

I nodded. I followed him as he went to the bathroom. Duncan went into a cubicle next to the sinks, I noticed he hadn't locked the door. I stood by the row of sinks and slowly washed my face. Duncan continued to talk to me even though he was in the cubicle.

"I don't think I could ever get used to this heat, even if I lived here? What do you think Kieran?"

I stumbled for some filler to say, as my brain noticed that not only had he not locked the cubicle door, but he had also left the door slightly ajar as he continued to speak to me.

I dried my face. "No, I prefer the seasons you get in the UK, they're proper seasons."

"Good night wasn't it? Good game we had, didn't we? I could have played longer, but I just need to relax now."

"Yes."

There was a pause while he moved inside the large enough to fit two people cubicle and I stood by the sinks, like a spare something at a something or other.

His voice continued to come from within the cubicle, "You going to bed?"

Chapter 6

He's straight, he hasn't stopped telling me how much he likes women, how he fancies them, how he's looking forward to sleeping with women who aren't Iz. My brain hurt.

The silence spread out in front of us like a large expanse of water—absorbing all sounds and reflecting our thoughts clearly. I folded my arms, unfolded them, and then folded them again.

Silence.

"Yes, night Duncan, see you in the morning." I left the bathroom. The pull towards the cubicle and the pull towards the fact of him being straight were so strong I felt as if I would tear apart.

Seven

Chapter 7

I woke at eleven-of-the-bleary-morning-o'clock and dragged myself out of bed. I was grateful for booking another twin room and not being woken by ten backpackers getting up from seven onwards. I noticed Jo sleeping soundly in the other bed.

I made two cups of tea and brought them back to our room. I shook Jo gently and put his tea on the stool next to his bed. He brushed the hair out of his face, rubbed his eyes and slowly sat up in bed.

"Good night? What time did you go to bed?" I handed his tea to him.

"Five, six, I didn't look. You?"

"Four, I couldn't keep my eyes open. Did my teeth and went straight to sleep." I paused, thinking about the bathroom with Duncan. "I think Duncan was flirting with me last night."

"How so?"

I told him about the bathroom incident. Jo listened and sipped his tea throughout.

"Doubtful," he proclaimed. "You're not his type."

"What, I'm male?"

"You need to seize the moment with him. Straight men are always the same. If you miss your opportunity that's it, they're back to being all "grr, look at the tits on that". You've got to pick your moment carefully or it's gone."

"Speaking as an expert from sleeping with so many straight men?"

"Kieran, there's a lot you don't know about me. I did have a life before I met you."

His comment hung there between us, like a little wasp which had just stung my arm.

"Beach? My tan's fading. I want everyone to think I'm South American when I get home," Jo said, getting up and grabbing some clothes from his backpack.

"Ok, meet you in here in fifteen minutes."

"Fifteen minutes, how do you think I can get ready for the beach in fifteen minutes? I'll see you in an hour in the living room area. You can sit and read one of your little books while you wait. You're always going on about how you don't get enough time to read, see, everyone's happy." He left.

I was dressed and ready, towel, sun cream and paperback within fifteen minutes. I sat in the living room area reading my book. I suppose it was kind of Jo to suggest me reading while I waited for him, I had mentioned to him that I didn't get as much time to read as I'd thought. Sometimes I just wanted to sit and read, so this was the perfect opportunity for that. The *perfect* opportunity.

I couldn't really settle into the book, I kept returning to the wasp sting comment. *What things had he done before, which he'd not told me about? And why would he suddenly confess to being an expert on straight men?*

Jo came to see me in the living room area three times, each time wearing a different T shirt and needing me to advise whether it suited him or not. I pointed out that it would soon be scrunched up under his head to be used as a pillow once we were on the beach, but he was insistent on picking the right one.

T shirt agreed, we made our way to the beach. After some deliberation, we found a suitable spot, placed our towels on the sand, and resumed our usual beach positions: me reading my book with my T shirt on, and Jo alternating laying on his back and front to ensure even coverage, between all over sun cream top ups.

I read the same paragraph four times so took a deep breath and tackled the wasp sting.

"What experience have you got of straight men? You never said anything before."

"I didn't think it was relevant." His eyes stayed closed as he lay on his back in the sun.

"Even though I was clearly falling for a straight man, who you pointed out to me? You still didn't think it was relevant?"

"It's not your sort of thing."

"What does that mean?" I asked, getting angry now, wishing I'd ignored the scratchy wasp sting.

"I took some risks, and they paid off, that's all." His eyes were open now.

"What like?"

"Do you really want to know? Is this what's happening now?" I nodded.

Jo remained laying down with his hands behind his head and sunglasses on. "I was friends with this guy at college, let's say he's called A."

I put my hand up in protest. "Why don't you want to tell me his name?"

Jo smiled and adjusted his position in the sun. "It's easier if I don't. We had been working late on a play for a few weeks. He had been driving me home afterwards—I said I'd give him my bus fair. This was before I could drive. We talked about a girl he wanted to go out with and I gave him ideas for things to say to her when he saw her around college. We talked about plans for the play.

"One afternoon he drove me home, we'd finished earlier than usual and it was a bright sunny day. As we drove through the forest I said that I was looking forward to topping up my tan, that summer and asked whether he like to sunbathe. Soon we had talked ourselves into stopping in the forest to start our suntans early. It had been a pretty miserable summer up to that point, so we wanted to make the most of the weather. We walked into the forest, took our T shirts off, sat on our jackets and lay in the sun.

"I couldn't help notice A's body, he must have gone to the gym or something, but he was pretty nice looking. He wouldn't have looked out of place on a float at a Pride festival wearing tiny Speedos. I made an effort not to stare at him too much, but he must have noticed me through my sunglasses.

"What are you looking at?" he asked. I shook my head and closed my eyes again.

"I don't mind. It's a compliment, I spend enough time at the gym, so it's nice when people notice. Do you want to feel my arms? Hundreds of press ups I do every week for these."

"Although I felt embarrassed, I thought, well, he's asked me to do this, and I'm not forcing myself on him, so why not. I leant over him and felt his arms and he smiled up at me. Fuck it, I thought, in for a penny, in for a pound. I leant down and kissed him. When he didn't punch me I couldn't believe my luck.

"You can work out the rest." Jo paused, waiting for me to ask a question. I said nothing. "I had to catch the bus after that. I passed my driving test soon afterwards so it wasn't that bad."

"That's what I should have done with Duncan last night?"

"Sounds to me as if he gave you the perfect opportunity and you wasted it. It doesn't take much, and they're all yours. Timing and grabbing the opportunity, that's all it took." Jo turned over to bronze his back.

"Took, what do you mean took. Are we talking hypothetically or in reality?"

"Why do you always have to make things so complicated Kieran, by over-thinking things?"

"Because that's who I am. That's what I do. Don't change the subject, what happened to you last night. Why did you come to bed after me, what did you do?"

"I told you, it's not your sort of thing."

"If you don't tell me, I'll, I don't know what I'll do, but you won't like it. Tell me, we're meant to be best friends, best friends don't have secrets."

"It's nothing much. I went to the bathroom after you'd gone to bed. Noticed Duncan in the cubicle. I started to chat about the card game, how hot it was, you know nothing much. I saw the cubicle door was ajar. He was leaning against the wall opposite the door. We talked, and I joined him in the cubicle, and—look Kieran do I need to draw you a picture? It's nothing,

106

it's not like he was your boyfriend, just some straight bloke you fancied. Nothing, we'll be gone soon and you'll never see him again. Can you get me an ice cream from one of the shops? I've got a few dollars in my shorts."

"*Can I get you an ice cream?* That's what you ask me to do, after you've just told me that! What the hell did you say to him, what magical words did you whisper in his ears to enchant him into hanging up his straight boots for the night and putting on a big pink fluffy pair of gay ones? Eh? What did you say?"

"I can't remember, nothing much, I don't know. Does it matter now? It's not like I forced him is it?" He was still laying on his back, resting his head on his arm.

"Who knows, I'm not sure what you did. Seems you can do anything if you put your mind to it."

He sat up and faced me, his eyes still covered by his sunglasses. "Look, I'm sorry. I didn't know you'd be this upset. I didn't mean to hurt you. It just sort of happened. You hadn't done anything with him. You're not together. It was just all talking."

I leant back, resting on my arms, wishing I'd not scratched the waspy sting. This was much worse. "Give me your money and I'll get us an ice cream. I need some space away from you for a bit."

"Get yourself something from this too," he said, handing me a ten dollar note.

Like that's going to make it alright? A couple of dollars worth of ice cream and it's all fine. Give Kieran a present, pat him on the head and he's fine. Good little boy Kieran. I walked away from Jo, not looking back, or saying anything.

I took a long route to get the ice cream, sat on the wall watching the hordes of tourists walking past. They smiled, holding hands in couples, laughing at each other's jokes, taking pictures of the beach and tacky shops. I watched a woman hand her ice cream to her boyfriend as she adjusted her shoulder bag, before he handed it back to her. He pointed out she had ice cream on her face and handed her a tissue to wipe it off.

That's what I want. Someone to hold my ice cream. Someone to look after me, to help with the small things. Small but important things.

I don't want to walk around my whole life with ice cream on my face and no one to tell me it's there. I don't want to put my bag on and drop my ice cream. I want someone to help. And I thought that person was Jo.

I stood up and began walking back to the beach, via a row of shops selling all you could ever want in the way of tacky touristy beach tat.

Perhaps he did it to show me how it's done. Maybe he wasn't thinking, maybe it just happened. I mean, it's not as if Duncan was actually my boyfriend. We were just friends, I didn't *really* realise anything else was on the cards. I missed the signs, and Jo picked up on them. It wasn't really his fault I didn't do anything was it? I was paralysed with fear, so I did nothing. Story of my life that is.

I arrived back at our spot on the beach.

"What happened to the ice creams?"

"It's ok, I forgive you. You didn't plan it. Like you said, it just happened. And it's not as if you slept with my boyfriend is it? He's just a friend, we'll probably never see him again when we leave Surfers. No harm done."

"That's good news, I'm glad we've got that sorted. Now onto the really important things—what happened to my ice cream and my money?"

"What?"

"You've got some ice cream on your mouth, so don't tell me you didn't buy any." Jo handed me a tissue. "Let's go out for dinner, my treat. Show you there's no hard feelings. It's all water under the bridge. What do you say to that? Free lunch—dinner actually, but you get the point."

"They say there's no such thing as a free lunch." An image of Jo and Duncan in the cubicle together suddenly popped into my head. I immediately blanked it out. I wiped my mouth with the tissue, took a deep breath to compose myself: "I want expensive and Chinese, nothing else will do."

"Expensive and Chinese it is. Although I think they call it Asian here, but the love is there." Jo replied as he kissed my cheek gently while holding me.

All I could think of was what his mouth had done the night before.

***

Over the next few weeks I realised I needed some space and time away from Jo to think about what he'd done, so began to take walks alone, listening to the mix tapes Grace made me and the CDs everyone from the hospital had bought me. It was like having Grace in my head, talking—well singing—to me. I read so much into the lyrics of the songs, sometimes I found myself walking along the beach wiping tears from my face. With the CDs I felt as if I was in my own version of *Muriel's Wedding*, working out how to escape. But I couldn't quite work out *what* or *who* I needed to escape *from*. Was Jo like Muriel's best friend, or more like those cliquey girls who'd told her she was nothing? He'd not told me I was nothing, and yet it had been far from plain friendship sailing since coming to Oz together. I would visit the local internet cafe, keeping my music playing all the time, blocking out the real world. I emailed Hannah about the last few months. She replied within a few days:

From: hannahgreeneloves-steps@hotmail.co.uk

To: discokieran@hotmail.co.uk

Hiya!

It's lush to hear from you. I was worried you'd dropped off the face of the earth. It's been months, since your last email, and all I've got is a post card here and there. It's nice to see you've mastered this email thing then eh? This is much more like it, a proper Disco Kieran newsletter. I've made myself a cup of tea and settled down to write my reply, so I hope you've got enough credit in the internet cafe.

I bet you're really tanned by now aren't you. Are you actually wearing shorts? This I have to see. In the whole time I've known you, I've never seen you in shorts—other than swimming shorts, and that doesn't count. What's happening with your hair by now? Has all the blond grown out? I'm all about the fact that your roots will need doing by now. Send some pictures ASAP so I can add them to my wall of friends pictures in my bedroom. At least it distracts me from Himself, but I don't want to go there at the moment.

Just to say, last week, he burst into my bedroom, while I was watching TV (without knocking by the way) and accused me of eating all the food in the fridge. He said I use the house like a hotel, coming and going all the time, and don't contribute anything to it.

This is ridiculous because I've not eaten downstairs with him for at least the last six months, I always buy my own food, and keep it in my fridge in my room, so why would I eat the horrible Asda shite he buys? Mum wants me to get on with him better, and I said that I'll get on with him better when he stops being such a homophobic small minded arsehole. Mum didn't have much to say to that one. I'm doing stuff with Mum, away from Himself, otherwise I don't see Mum either, and this seems to be working. We went to town (yes it was Southampton, where else?) a few weeks ago and had a nice mincey day together. Coffees, shopping, bit of lunch. She took me to the new Bench shop in town and I was like, "I might be a lesbian Mum, but I'm trying not to live up to ALL the stereotypes" which made her laugh. She'd read something in Woman's Own about a woman's lesbian daughter liking Bench stuff, and thought, "I'll have some of that for Hannah."

Well, that's a whole paragraph about Himself, and I said to myself I'd not bore you about him, so that's it. Any comments welcomed, also feel free to ignore Himself and the issues if you'd prefer—it's done me well for the last five years.

Right onto the important things. So you're back to falling in love with straight men again are you? Fabio, Mark from the party in Melbourne, and now Duncan. Kieran, you really do have to change your taste in men. You're gay, you need to find a man who's also gay, that's kind of the basis on which it works you see? How many times have we talked about this, how it will always end in tears, and this time it seems no different. You remember your exploration of the concept of slag with Brad ages ago? We want more of that and less of the others, understand?

Sounds like you had a great time at the bar job in Melbourne, I can't imagine you pulling pints, or whatever measure they use there. You'll always be my care assistant. Did you pick it up easily once you'd been there a bit? That leaving party, superheroes sounds a good laugh. I'm impressed (and slightly disappointed you didn't get further) with your flirting skills with Mark and his Robin costume. I read your email and imagined you holding court in the living room at the party, telling the music students where to fuck off, and also flirting with Mark too. Very impressive. Well, it would have been if you'd actually shagged him. Sounds like you'd have had a pretty good chance at that if Jo hadn't rushed in and made you leave. He's a very dramatic person isn't he? I don't just mean his plays, but he seems to always have some sort of drama around him don't you think? It's not a criticism, because I know how much you love him, and how much fun you have together, it's just something I noticed when reading your email.

Did he really shag Chris in the bathroom at the party? I didn't think Jo was like that. You'd not mentioned he was so...how can I put it politely...free and easy with his affections. Poor Ailsa, do you think she knew what had happened when you saw her upset at the leaving party? Jo just wanted to leave it all behind and move on. Were you planning on keeping in touch with the friends from the bar? I suppose that'll be a bit harder now won't it?

Is Surfers Paradise like a scene from Muriel's Wedding? All high rises and surfer shops, with miles and miles of beaches. Sounds nice to me. Well, nicer than the New Forest, it's been a miserable winter here and as I sit now, it's raining hard and it's freezing out. I've got some Abbacadabra to keep me going in the computer's CD player as I type. Aren't computers amazing, multitasking, like the best women do!

How long have you been at the YHA in Surfers? Sounds like you've made good friends with this Duncan—again another straight man to fall in love with. Seems to me that Jo just encouraged it by pointing him out to you when you checked in. Or does Jo always live in hope that any straight man can be persuaded? What is it they say? The difference between straight and bi is about three pints of lager!

Sounds to me like you might have had a good chance of having your way with this Duncan, had you just made it happen. You know what I say, if you want something you've got to make it happen. Things don't just happen, you have to make it happen. If I'd waited for you to talk to me when we first met at the hospital, I'd still be waiting now, but I made it happen, and look at us now? I can't imagine my life without you in it, our friendship is so precious to me, and I miss you so much all those thousands of miles away. Whenever I hear that song by Annie Lennox I think of us singing it in the corridor. Carolyn was livid wasn't she? Makes me smile every time I hear it on the radio.

So how are things with you and Jo at the moment? Are you still speaking to him after what he's done? I'm not sure I would be. I understand your point about it not being planned, or malicious, but still, it did happen. It's not like this Duncan mauled Jo like a big dog—they both wanted to do what they did. Fair enough Duncan wasn't your boyfriend, but Jo did know you liked him—in fact he pointed him out to you in the first place, and it's not as if Jo's not had much action since you went to Oz. Maybe he should spread the love around a bit! If it goes on for much longer you can officially apply for your virginity back again! It's been months and months for me, my application's in the post I tell you.

Look, just make sure you look after yourself. You know I'm here if you need to call me, and I'm always only an email away. Still, make sure you take care of you—not everyone else—you. I know what you're like. And say hi to Jo from me, tell him he's such a drama queen, he could appear in the West End, all the drama he has! Tell him if he messes you about he'll have to answer to me, and

I'm a big butch lesbian—I can put up flat pack furniture in five minutes, and can take him in an arm wrestle any day!

Well, that's 1300 words and I've reached the end of Abbacadabra's first album (flight one). I must get on with my dinner, something to avoid the boiled cabbage nightmare being served downstairs. Email soon with news and dramas.

Lots of love
Hannah xx

Eight

July 1999 — Queensland Rainforest

*W*e travelled north to the rainforest. It couldn't have been more different from Surfers if we'd flown to another continent.

As we got off the Greyhound coach in Cape Tribulation the sky opened and it didn't rain cats and dogs, as it was the first time it had rained for more than a few spots since arriving in Oz, it really put its back into it. It was like the weather was showing us what a proper tropical storm could do to knock our parochial little UK raining cats and dogs into a cocked hat. There were big round sploshes of water coming down with no air between them. Within seconds there was a few inches of water on the ground causing brown splashes of puddles to reply to the big round sploshes from the sky. It was like a symphony of rain in both directions. It was raining cats, dogs, kangaroos and koalas. This was rain Oz style. I squinted at the sky to see if there was enough blue to make a sailor a pair of trousers: thoughts of Mum filled my head. I want to be home. I miss Mum and her sayings. I want a shepherd's pie. I want to relax, I want to not be moving from place to place. I want to leave my bag and not worry that it's going to be stolen. I want to wake up in the middle of the night and know how to get to the toilet without having to work out where I am first.

There wasn't enough blue in the sky to make a sailor a pair of underpants, never mind a pair of trousers. There would be a lot of sailors walking about with no trousers today. I spat out the water and rubbed my eyes.

"Where's this YHA then?" I looked at Jo.

"I'm not sure, but we'll find it soon."

I looked at my backpack as it stood on the ground. It was soaking wet. My clothes had soaked through and I felt my underpants were now wet. I put my hands in my pockets and noted my wallet had also got wet. *Probably ruined my money too.*

Jo was looking at a map which allegedly showed us where the YHA was.

I sat on my backpack, held my head in my hands and shut my eyes. If this is supposed to be fun, give me not fun any day. I don't want to be here, I'd rather be at work. This was the apogee of crapness from the last few weeks. I thought of Duncan and Jo again and my stomach tied itself into a familiar knot. It wasn't supposed to be like this. It was meant to be like *Priscilla Queen of the Desert* not like a scene from *Trainspotting* (I'd exaggerated the last part, but at that moment I'd have done anything to be home in my bedroom, watching *The Creek*.)

Jo walked over to me, produced an umbrella from somewhere, and held me tight. We sheltered under the umbrella. Although it was too late as we were already soaked to the skin, it somehow made me feel better. I buried my head against Jo's shoulder. We got into a taxi, which had appeared from nowhere, and were soon at the YHA.

The YHA was a series of wooden huts on stilts in the rainforest. I felt as if I'd stepped into a fantasy novel, I kept expecting goblins and fairies to spring from behind a tree.

Jo led me into our hut. It had a bedroom with two single beds covered with mosquito nets, bedside cabinets and a writing desk. A door led to our own private en suite bathroom. This was pure luxury when compared to sharing a bathroom with all the male residents of a YHA—although as I'd noticed, that in itself could have its own advantages.

I was so soaked, and my get up and go had completely got up and went, that despite Jo telling me to take my clothes off, I couldn't even kick off my wet jeans. Jo took over and gently helped me out of my clothes, wrapped me in a warm fluffy towel and led me to the bathroom. He'd run a bubble bath. This really was untold luxury, I'd not had a bath in months, the other places only had showers so I'd got used to showering quickly each morning. A bath before bedtime was part of my home ritual, which I must have told Jo about when we first met. I couldn't remember telling him this, but how else would he know? This habit was much to my Dad's irritation as he would shout upstairs and implore me not to use all the hot water each time.

"Take your time, I'll make dinner for when you're out," Jo said as he closed the bathroom door.

I lay in the bubbles for what seemed like hours. I closed my eyes and thought of our trip so far. People's faces flashed into my mind: Fabio; Mark in his Robin costume making tea at the party; Duncan helping me play pool; Marie and Jane's faces when the bouncer told us what Jo had done in the club; Chris and Ailsa's upset at the party. When you put it like that I suppose it was quite dramatic. I'd not thought of it like that before, all together it seemed worse than each thing on its own. Drama seemed to follow us around during the trip. We'd had good times too, it's just that I'd not expected to spend so much time clearing up after Jo's mess.

I left the bathroom and found Jo had laid out a clean set of clothes on my bed. I dressed, dried and styled my hair, put my shoes on and checked myself in the mirror. I walked to the YHA's kitchen and found Jo putting the final touches to our dinner.

He turned from the hob, "You look lovely. Feeling better now?"

"Much better thanks. I feel like a human again, not like some wet sack of clothes. What's for dinner? Do you want me to help with anything?"

"Just sit over there, I've laid that table." He pointed to an area on the wooden bench seats where he'd laid out cutlery and glasses.

I sat and he brought over two bowls of noodles with sweet and sour chicken.

"Where did you get it, it's the middle of nowhere?"

"Never mind that, is it ok?"

"Ok? It's my favourite, I can't believe it. Thank you so much."

"I wanted to say sorry."

"What for?"

"I know it's been a bit hard lately, what with Chris and Ailsa, and then Duncan. I wanted to say sorry. I didn't mean any of it. It just sort of happens. Sometimes I find myself in these situations and I think to myself, "how did I get here?" And

I turn round and you're there to help." He smiled as he sat opposite me and we both tucked into the food.

"That's ok, that's what friends are for isn't it?"

"I suppose it is, but I wanted to say thank you."

"It's very kind of you. Exactly what I needed, especially Brad! Not long till we fly home you know."

Jo nodded. "Just Perth, then it's home. I thought this would be a good opportunity to toast our holiday, and congratulate ourselves on actually making it happen."

"That's what Hannah says—making it happen."

"Sensible girl is Hannah. Here's to us, going to Australia, best friends and our fabulous holiday together. Here's to many more like this."

"Many more like this." We raised our glasses of water and chinked them together.

We ate our meal remembering the high points of the holiday. Jo didn't mention the things I'd remembered when I lay in the bath. He seemed to have forgotten them, and only talked about the good times. I wished I could be more like this, focussing on the positive rather than the negative. I suppose overall the holiday was a success really. I remembered Brad's shower and his refurbed art deco flat and smiled to myself.

"It's not over yet" Jo said as we finished our noodles. He smiled and produced a huge chocolate bar from under the table next to him. "And there's more. Follow me."

"What about the washing up?"

"I'll do it later, come on." He stood and took my hand to lead me to the hostel"s living room area. It was fairly standard small square room with sofas around all four walls and a small TV in one corner. The room was empty of people, in contrast to the TV rooms of other YHAs we'd visited on our trip. Normally they were a rabble of people talking, eating, and some actually watched the TV. I don't know how Jo had done it, but he'd cleared the room. We sat on the sofa next to each other, exactly like when we watched TV at his house.

"Unfortunately they don't show The Creek here, but after extensive audience research, I spoke to some other backpackers who I thought would share your TV taste, I found out there's something which should be almost as good. And it's on tonight, in a few minutes."

Jo broke off a few squares of chocolate, and handed me the rest of the bar. He switched the TV on and we watched as the opening credits started on an American comedy by the same people who made Friends, starring Kirstey Alley. *Veronica's Closet* was about a woman who owned an underwear company, it had it all: a bitchy assistant; a philandering ex-husband; and a PA of indeterminate sexuality. It was perfect. We laughed at its witty yet obvious jokes, and I forgot the stresses and worries from earlier that day. For that half an hour, it was just me, Jo and Kirstey Alley in the room. We laughed easily at the characters' quips, and agreed that some of them reminded us of people from The Duke.

As the credits started to show, I looked at Jo and said, "Thank you. This is perfect. It's everything I wanted, it's just perfect."

"Well, I am your *best friend*, so what else should I do?"

I felt a slight rash of the wasp sting coming back. I pushed thoughts of the incident with Duncan to the back of my mind. I went back to my happy place, right here, right now. I remembered us watching *The Sound of Music* together after a night out. I leant in to kiss him and hugged him close to me. "I love you."

"I love you too." Jo stared into my eyes.

That was what it was *really about.* The other things were just things, which had just happened—Jo didn't mean for that to happen, he wouldn't do something like that deliberately. Things just got out of hand sometimes.

As the credits ended I noticed a knock on the door and the door opened slightly. There was a group of people waiting outside the room. Jo sat up and replied to this activity, "Yes, it's all yours now. We're done."

The others sat around the seats and someone switched the channel over to something to do with sport—a green pitch and people running around after a ball—I didn't pay much more attention than that. We collected what remained of the bar of chocolate and left.

We moved onto Cairns for a three night boat trip snorkelling around The Great Barrier Reef. The boat moved to different parts of the reef each day. It felt like another planet, swimming at the surface of the water, the sun on my back, flippers splashing gently in the sea, staring through the mask to the bottom of the clear warm water at the reds, oranges and greens of the coral moving gently in the currents. Below us were shoals of bright orange and white striped little clown fish or smaller shoals of yellow and black plate sized fish. Sometimes we saw a lone three feet wide turtle, gracefully propelling itself with its fins doing their version of breaststroke. We saw scuba divers swimming down among the fish and corals, trails of bubbles rising from them to the surface where I swam. Every time we swam to a different bit of the reef, we both returned to the boat full of stories of the new things we'd spotted.

Our final stop in Queensland was the small town of Port Douglas, a short coach trip from Cairns. Here every other person was a tourist, cameras round their neck and backpacks on their back. There we took a boat trip up the wide brown tropical Daintree river into Daintree Rainforest. The tourist guide—we went with a group, it felt safest—told us it was the largest continuous tropical rainforest on the Australian continent. The rainforest grew right up to the edge of the sea. It was full of birds, as many different types of birds as fish in the reef, from little sparrow like ones to huge ones that looked like a black turkey with a bright turquoise neck.

Nine

Perth

~⟋⟍⟋⟍~

*E*ven before we'd left the UK, everyone had talked about how amazing Perth was: the most remote city in the world; "Australia's sunniest capital city"; un-crowded beaches; amazing shopping; etcetera etcetera ad nauseam.

Even before arriving, it suffered from *gay best friend gorgeous* syndrome. No matter how amazing it was, poor old Perth could never have lived up to the fanfare it had received from pretty much every Australian I'd spoken to, and numerous Brits too.

What sort of magical hold did Perth have over people I wondered? Did they brainwash people, or replace visitors with robots, only programmed to rave about how unbelievably amazing it was, a sort of Stepford Wives tie up with the Australian Tourist Board?

Evidently Jo had been replaced with one of these *Stepford Wives* robots, because for the last few weeks it was all he'd talked about. I had wanted to change the return flights to leave from Darwin, in the rainforest, a much more interesting option, but Jo insisted on keeping Perth in the itinerary. "Otherwise we'll miss out WA completely, and I'm not having that."

WA is Western Australia for those who aren't familiar with the vernacular. As you can imagine, Jo was very familiar with the vernacular, by this point.

Working out there was no budging Jo on this, I decided to take more of an interest in Perth, the final part of Oz we'd see before going home. After consulting a map, I concluded that Perth was basically the only thing in WA, which seemed to make up about half of Australia. So is this country really half-full of nothing?

We arrived on the Greyhound Bus in the middle of Perth's CBD, (that's central business district to those who haven't done A level geography), in the middle of the night. All money for additional internal flights long since exhausted, we'd endured about a week on the bus from the rainforest to reach the oft hallowed city of Perth.

Relieved for Jo's organisational skills, and too tired to object to anything else, he swept us to a nearby YHA where we shuffled to our beds in a dorm of thirty other backpackers.

Five hours later people began to stir, making noise as they dressed for the day, and as the light seeped through the barely there at all blinds they became less quietly apologetic.

At six I gave up, made myself a tea and sat in the kitchen thinking about returning home.

Home, a word which carried so much weight and memories. Not just my parents' house, not just the village, but all the places I'd been to while growing up there. I remembered walking along the windswept sea front with Grace before I flew away, nights in Hannah's bedroom avoiding Himself, getting ready for work at the hospital. All meant *Home* to me.

Jo shook me awake holding a mug of tea in both hands. "You been here long?"

"What's the time?"

"Gone nine. And it's a beautiful sunny day, so it's living up to its name."

"What?"

"Perth, *the sunniest capital city.*"

"Right."

"I've got some tips for places to see, been talking to some of the people who work here."

And when he said people, he meant men.

"And?"

"There's this little island off the coast, Rottnest, and they've got these little mini kangaroos, quokkas they're called." His eyes glinted in that unmistakable way.

So the kangaroos aren't even as impressive as elsewhere?
"Right..."

He counted the points on his fingers. "The CBD's meant to be amazing for shopping, and there's this bit called Freemantle by the water so we've got to go there. Come on, get dressed, I'll meet you by reception."

I stood up slowly, my neck aching where I'd fallen asleep in the chair.

"Don't forget, sun cream, it might be the last sun we see for a while once we're home."

I met Jo by reception where I found him deep in conversation with a Swedish backpacker who'd meant to stay in Perth for a week, but was still here, working at the YHA three months later.

Another Stepford Wives robot.

Jo leant across the reception desk and kissed the Swede on his cheek, linked arms with me and we left the building.

"He's not gay is he?" I looked back at Sven or Bjorn or whatever he was called.

"He's got a girlfriend, but they're very open minded, these Nordic types. I thought shopping first, then lunch in Freemantle, more shopping, and we can check out some bars tonight."

Do you remember the start of *Neighbours*, where they zoom in to a suburban area of houses? That's what Perth is like, miles and miles of similar looking suburbs with a city centre that could be anywhere. Freemantle is an area Perthians are proud of, unfortunately after a day of shopping with Jo in the blazing sun, all I wanted was my bunk in the YHA, or more preferably my bed at home.

I could see the general attraction, it was very clean, well ordered, plenty of shops, and yes, sunshine, everything you'd want in your perfect city. But when it all came together, it somehow was less than the sum of its parts. It was missing the culture of Sydney, the country town atmosphere of Adelaide. It was all a bit too planned, a bit too perfect, like Milton Keynes in the sun.

In fairness to Perth and its legion of robots, it could have had wall to wall go go dancers in every restaurant and chocolate on tap and I'd have still just wanted my bedroom and some Ovaltine (which you can't get there anyway). By this point in the holiday, it no longer felt like a holiday, the end point was so near, I could almost feel it. It was like the end of a party, where you're waiting for your friend to finish talking to the interesting person you met in the kitchen, and you know you're almost about to go, but you've still got the journey home to negotiate, and you'd give anything to do an *I Dream of Genie*, blink your eyes and instantly be home.

As we sat in a bar at the end of a long hot day, surrounded by Jo's shopping bags, I reflected that at least I didn't have to put up with Uncle Colin in Perth. Ok, so he'd taken the shine off Sydney, but here it would have all been a bit too much. I blinked my eyes in an attempt to magic myself back home, but nothing.

"I'm getting another drink, you want one?" Jo stood, hovering next to our table.

I shook my head.

"Something to eat?"

I shrugged. Did they do Mum's shepherd's pie here? Doubtful.

"I'll get some chips."

He returned with a cocktail for himself and a cup of tea for me. "Chips are on their way. Have this." He passed me the tea.

I smiled as I took a sip.

"You looked tired. You ok?" He peered over the cocktail glass, behind a mini paper umbrella.

"Tired, bit homesick. Nothing, I'll be fine. You've got a good haul though, look at all this stuff." I gestured to the bags around our feet.

"I know, I certainly can shop when I put my mind to it. And you were a perfect companion. Didn't get much for yourself though."

"Money. I'm worrying about the stuff I've put on my credit card already, without getting more. I got quite a lot in Adelaide remember?"

He nodded.

"Is any of this presents, or is it all for you?"

"There are some presents yes. Mum and Dad, and some friends. And yes, a lot of it's for me, but I'm the one who's here, I need things to remember my trip, they don't."

Moving on from Jo's slightly strange logic, I asked him about his plans when he got home. I was looking forward to seeing Hannah, Grace and Kev, and studying again while feeling nervous about living in London. Would it all be too much for me, too much of a change from home? Had I chosen the right subject to study? What reading should I do in preparation for the first term? My mind raced and I was keen to return and start on the ever-growing list.

Sipping his cocktail, Jo leaned back in his chair: "There's loads of Prides in summer, so that'll keep me busy. Mum's sorted all the uni stuff out, so I'll just put some bits in her car and off to London in September. Bob's your Uncle and Fanny's your Aunt!"

No he isn't and no she's not either. I admired Jo's ability to just sail through things, oblivious to problems, not even thinking of issues which may come up, just taking things if and when they faced him.

"Feeling better after the tea?"

I nodded.

"Fancy something a bit stronger?"

"Like what?"

He opened his hand and showed me two small white tablets.

"Where did you get them?"

"The Swede on reception. Comes here all the time, said it's a good way to end the day."

"Right here, right now? What about the shopping, how are we getting home? Don't you think about anything?"

Waving his hand he said, "It'll be fine, trust me." He put his hand to his mouth and then took a gulp of his drink.

"Fucking idiot, I can't believe you, we could get caught, put in prison, deported, anything!"

"Only if you carry on like that, don't worry, kept one for you." He showed me one tablet in his hand.

I stood up, taking some shopping bags with me and started to walk out.

"Kieran, come on, stay, it'll be fine, don't go!" he shouted.

"What the fuck am I doing with your fucking shopping, you can stick it, you can stick it all, and you can look after yourself. You're on your own, I'm going." I dropped his bags and left the bar.

I ran quickly from the bar, my throat dry and my head pounding, needing to get as far away as I could from him, and those things. I ran until I didn't know where I was, bloody Perth, bloody Freemantle, where was I?

What if he died? What if I've left him and he dies in that bar, surrounded by his shopping? How's he going to get back?

It'll be fine.

I heard a siren, an ambulance? *Is that him, being rushed to hospital, choking on his tongue?*

A vision of his funeral flashed before my eyes, I saw his parents, bloodshot eyes, dressed in black standing by the graveside as I read the lyrics from his favourite song from a musical. Jo's Mum grabbing hold of my arm and asking me quietly: "I thought you were *best friends?*"

I turned round and ran back to the bar. His seat was surrounded by his bags, but where was Jo?

I ran to the bar and asked if anyone had seen him. The girl pointed to the corner, where a small dance floor was completely deserted except for Jo, dancing alone. I walked quickly to him and grabbed his shoulders.

His eyes lit up, his pupils were enormous. He immediately gave me a kiss on the lips and hugged me tighter than he'd ever done before. "I knew you wouldn't want to miss all the fun, come on, let's dance together."

"Are you ok?"

"Course I am, come on…" He grabbed my hands and led me onto the main dance floor.

At first I stood opposite him trying to notice any twitching or foaming from his mouth—I wasn't sure what the signs would be, but these seemed a pretty safe bet.

After a while he took both my hands. "Why aren't you dancing?" Everything's ok, I'm ok, you're ok, it's all ok." He looked deep into my eyes and continued: "I love you, you know that don't you?"

Slowly I started dancing and yet again I felt like we were the only two people in the bar. Jo's grin was infectious, once I realised he wasn't about to drop down dead in front of my eyes, I loosened up and was soon enjoying myself.

I'll talk to him tomorrow about this. Not now, but tomorrow. That's when to have a stern word with him.

We ended up in a club, both dancing on the podium next to the paid dancers, with our tops off. At that moment I felt indestructible, like I'd reached the perfection of friendship—if only I disregarded what had happened earlier that night.

***

130

Soon afterwards, I tried to talk to Jo about how irresponsible he'd been, how he'd left me with no option but to come back and look after him. He maintained he'd done nothing wrong. "People do it all the time, no problems."

"But you knew I wouldn't leave you."

"I knew you'd look after me, isn't that what friends are for? *Best friends.*" He looked innocently directly into my eyes. "If you'd got really drunk you would have trusted me to look after you, wouldn't you?"

"Well yeah, but that's a bit different."

He looked away nonchalantly. "How?"

"Illegal for a start."

"Details. I'm talking principles." He turned to look me in the eye.

Principles, now that's where it all got a bit confusing. Jo explained that the basic principle behind a friendship was looking after each other, and how that trumped everything else. And that's what made our friendship so perfect, addictive, yet at the same time confusing and painful.

We gave each other space over the next few days. I reflected on Jo's argument about the principles of friendship. Jo continued shopping.

One evening he walked over to where I was eating alone, carrying armfuls of shopping bags. "How much longer are you going to keep this up?"

"Don't know what you mean." I shrugged and still didn't make eye contact.

"Pull the other one, it's got bells on. I apologised didn't I? We had fun that night didn't we?"

"Once I realised you weren't going to die." Still no eye contact.

"Kiss and make up?" He held out his arms to hug me.

I put my cutlery down and leant in for a hug. *Did he apologise?* Did he *actually* say sorry? I didn't want to spoil the moment, so I filed that thought for later.

"I know what we should do before we leave. Everyone goes on about kangaroos in Australia, but what about these quokkas? No one back home will have heard of them, something to impress people with once we're home."

I shrugged, still thinking about when to open the apology file.

"Come on, it'll be fun. Mini kangaroos, a boat trip to an island, what's not to like?"

On the boat I looked at the sun, trying to memorise its heat and the gentle sea spray against my skin, leaving salt marks. Jo talked about what we should do once on the island, the best places to spot the quokkas, and where to eat. All gleaned from the friendly Swede at the YHA reception. He was evidently a very talented man.

Like the sea spray, I let his words wash over me.

I opened my eyes and walked over to a man I'd spotted before I'd drifted off. Pleased he was still there, and still staring at me, I held out my hand to introduce myself. Blond curly haired Clyde worked on the island's cafe and offered to show me the best bits of the island. He lived in Perth, but hadn't yet been replaced by the robots as he didn't once mention how amazing the city was, much to my surprise.

Jo held out his hand to introduce himself: "I'm Jo, we're together. Not together, *together.*" He smiled. "Travelling together. So can you tell us what's good to eat then?"

"What?" Clyde asked, bemused.

"The cafe, you work there."

"Yeah right. I was thinking more about your friend, what was it?" He looked at me.

"Kieran" I looked at him, taking in his five star Australian-ness: all over tan, uniform of tailored shorts and short sleeved shirt, smart sandals with no socks, showing tan lines on his feet.

"That's it, we were gonna catch some rays once I finish my shift. I know some great dunes where no one will come to disturb you." He winked unsubtly at me and licked his lips.

Why did I feel like I'd seen him before?

I agreed to meet Clyde at the cafe when he finished and we left the boat.

"You're definitely getting some there." As we walked away Jo winked just as unsubtly as Clyde.

"You think?"

"Definitely. Did you see the way he was looking at you?"

"Like a hungry dog looks at its dinner?"

"Exactly. Come on, let's check out these little kangaroos, I want lots of photos so I can prove to everyone we saw them, or they'll think I've made it up."

After a few hours of quokka spotting, the novelty of seeing the little creatures had somewhat worn off. Jo had a few films worth of photos, and I'd had more than enough. We ate in Clyde's cafe where he was no help whatsoever in recommending anything to eat, and he called me Kevin every time he visited our table.

At the allotted time, Clyde came to our table, where Jo was nursing a drink and playing with the remains of a distinctly mediocre sandwich.

"Ready?" Clyde asked, taking my hand.

I stared out the window at the sea, thinking if it was the same water I'd swam in back home, or whether I'd drunk some of it already. I remembered a statistic from geography, in London the water has gone through everyone at least eight times.

Jo shook me. "Hello, earth to Kieran, anyone there? Clyde asked you something."

I looked at my hand, dwarfed in comparison to Clyde's large tanned hand, noticing the hairs on his arm, bleached by the sun.

We walked to the beach together, arriving at a quiet sand dune, where he spread out a towel, which would have at one point been bright red and yellow. He lay on the towel, taking his shorts and shirt off in one quick movement. His blonde curly hair formed a V on his chest, which was completely tanned, no tanning lines whatsoever. Even in his tiny little bright blue sculpted underpants I couldn't see the tan lines on his legs. He patted the towel next to him. "I don't bite, unless you want me to" he laughed.

I sat next to him and he began stroking my chest and nuzzling my neck.

"What's wrong eh?" he asked, taking a break from my neck.

"Just thinking, about the water. I wonder if some of this has been around the other side of the world, and if I've swam in it."

"Eh?"

I tried to explain what I meant, mentioning the geography statistic.

"You gonna take off this T shirt?"

"I don't want to burn."

"You won't burn if I'm on top of you."

"I'll keep it on, I think. So what do you do when summer's over?"

"What do you mean?"

"Will you go to uni, or go travelling, or stay at your parents'?"

"What about these jeans, let's get these undone, and see what's happening." He felt my groin. "Not a bad start." He unzipped my jeans and started to investigate their contents.

My groin wanted more, but my head was still thinking about where I'd seen him before.

"Chook!" I exclaimed.

"What?"

"From *Muriel's Wedding*, that's who you look like."

"Who's wedding?" He continued to play with the contents of my underwear.

And with that, I pulled myself together and left the faded beach towel and Clyde behind.

Jo sat open mouthed when I told him what had happened. "He's offering it to you like that, and you stood up and left? Call yourself a gay man? He was properly gorgeous, not gay best friend, but proper gorgeous. What a waste."

"He'd never heard of *Muriel's Wedding*. A gay Australian, and he's never heard of it, now I'm sure *that's* illegal somewhere. I just didn't feel like it."

"Now that, I'll never understand."

"No, I don't suppose you will, but I do."

It was all so inevitable, so obvious, and I wasn't quite ready for that again after Brad. The way I felt then, I knew my heart couldn't have coped with the emotion of it all, so instead I opted for a long hot shower with my eyes closed.

Two more days until I was back in my own bed. My own bed with my own wardrobe and my own TV and all my other friends, once again. I closed my eyes and remembered my room, with piles of videos by the TV. I was itching to drive

Priscilla once again, having not driven at all for so long.

Ten

August 1999

We finally landed at Heathrow on the first Friday in August. The flight seemed to take twice as long on the way home as on the way there. Every hour as I approached home seemed like an entire day. A wet and windy Heathrow greeted us. Despite it being summer, the British weather hadn't differed from exactly what we'd expected.

Our parents met us at the airport. I later learned there had been quite a big debate about whether only one set of parents should pick us up to save on petrol costs. It seemed a bit silly since they were both taking us back to Hampshire all the way from London. Options included one parent from Jo and my side, but since they couldn't agree which of each side's parents should go, it was agreed, begrudgingly that they would both go in two complete sets.

Jo's mum stood by his dad who held a luggage trolley, primed and ready for use. Mum was beaming next to Paul who held our trolley. Dad stood quietly next to Mum.

Mum hugged me and held me too tightly. "Hang on a minute, when did you get your ears pierced? You never told me about this," she exclaimed as she let me go.

"Because if I had, you'd have told me not to do it. And anyway, it's only one ear, I'm not a bloody pirate."

"That's enough of that language, Kieran. We won't have any of that. Dad, what are we going to do about the ear-rings?"

"He looks like a right little queer. You know what they say, right ear, right queer," Paul added, with relish.

"Which is why it's my left ear if you'll take the time to notice" I said, flapping my left ear lobe theatrically. "Everyone has pierced ears now anyway. Anyway, can do what I like, I'm an adult now, so it's up to me. Where's the car?" I looked at the cars surrounding us.

Mum stared at my left ear and I saw on her face she realised there wasn't much she could do.

Dad looked at Paul sternly. "Leave him alone Paul. You got a hug for me too?" I hugged Dad. "Right follow me, we put it in a special car park. It's a bit further to walk, but I looked at the charges for the other car parks and thought, they're not taking *me* for a ride, so it's just over here."

He pointed into the distance and strode off ahead of us, seemingly pleased to have something to do again now the emotional hellos were over. It was nice to see things hadn't changed since I'd gone—same old Dad with his practical considerations.

I looked behind me and saw Jo and his parents hugging each other in formation around the luggage trolley. I waved to him, shouting, "I'll call you."

Jo's arm broke away from his parents' hug, waved at me and

I turned to look at Mum, smiling.

"Still you're back now. Safe and sound, I was so worried about you, and now you're here." She hugged me again, looking at my ear. "Earring doesn't really matter I suppose does it? Your hair could do with a bit of something, what do you reckon?" She felt my hair, noticing the dark roots then took my hand and we followed Dad.

"That sounds perfect."

As we walked to the car, the English summer welcomed us back with open, and wet, arms. I smelt the wetness of the pavement, I noticed the greenness of everything, even among the grey concrete and tarmac of the airport. I noticed the familiar typeface of signs, and number plates of cars. I saw a red post box, much classier than the yellow Australian ones I'd got used to for the last few months. All these things, I'd taken so much for granted, as the background to my life, were suddenly much more precious and special to me. Leaving had made me realise how much I enjoyed living where I did.

My bedroom was exactly as I'd left it. My videos stacked next to my TV and VCR, gathering dust. My cuddly toy collection in the corner, hiding my ever increasing collection of Attitude and Gay Times magazines.

That night Mum made shepherd's pie, topped with three types of Cheddar cheese.

"I bet they didn't do this in Australia did they?" Mum asked as she dished up.

I looked around the kitchen, Dad was reading a computer magazine while Mum rushed around. Paul waggled his right ear lobe and stuck his tongue out at me. "No, they didn't."

"Three types of cheese this has got. Bet they don't have three types of cheese in Australia do they?" Mum handed me a plate.

"Is this what I've got now, you're going to ask if they do things in Australia like we do here?"

"I just want to make sure you're happy here, before you go off again to uni. Right, it's ready. Dad, put your magazine down. Paul stop doing that, if the wind changes you'll stay like that." Mum sat and we started to eat. "I'll do your hair tomorrow if you like, I'm here all day—got the day off work when I told 'em you were back home. I got more of the bleach if you want me to do it blond again. I know that's how you like it."

"Thanks Mum, that's great. How about in the afternoon, first I've got to get my old job back. I'm going to see if Carolyn will give it back to me."

***

I drove to the hospital, Priscilla eventually started after a bit of encouragement. I'd left strict instructions for Mum to drive her a few miles every week while I was away, so she wasn't too shocked when I asked her to take me on the familiar journey back to work.

For the last two months in Australia my life had been sponsored by Barclaycard. I'd run out of money; once I had got used to spending it in Oz, I couldn't get enough of it. Every time I told myself the biggest cost of getting there was spent, so why skimp on not having a boat trip, or another meal by the sea. Jo helped me spend too, when he'd forgotten his card, or hadn't quite enough for that round of drinks. I hadn't wanted to complain about my lack of real not sponsored by Barclaycard money to Jo, as I knew he'd make us go home earlier. I was just getting used to the freedom of being away, and didn't want to suddenly rush back as soon as my money ran out. I'd brought a credit card, for emergencies only. Unfortunately, the definition of an emergency changed somewhat during the trip. By the final few weeks I put everything which accepted credit cards, on my credit card: YHAs, tickets for Greyhound coaches, meals out, food shopping, The Great Barrier Reef trip, and gifts for friends and family. All emergencies, within the new definition of the last few months.

Carolyn was in the nursing office talking to one of the domestics. I knocked on the open door and waited.

"Oh, look who we have here!" She rearranged her ample bosom in her dark blue dress. "Don't you look tanned? How time flies." She looked at the domestic, who I didn't recognise, and said, "I'll find you in a while. I think me and this young man have got some catching up to do, don't you young Kieran? This is Kieran, he used to work here as a healthcare assistant, and then he left us to travel around Australia. He's come back to tell me all about it haven't you? Either that or he's asking for his old job back."

I smiled at Carolyn as the domestic left the office.

"You can shut the door. Do you want a drink? Then we can sit down and you can tell Auntie Carolyn all about it?"

Auntie Carolyn? I don't remember her being this friendly before.

Carolyn held our drinks, having filled me in on changes since I'd left. She sat opposite me, her stockinged legs crossed, her dark blue nurse's uniform stretched over her thighs, the shiny decorative buckle stretched across her waist. She took a sip of her instant coffee and she pulled up one leg of her tights.

"So, young Kieran, what did you get up to? Actually, don't tell me everything, I'm sure I'll hear more than I need to through Hannah. Just tell me the best bits, and make sure they're clean."

We talked for a while, I gave her a PG version of events: I described the blue sea, sandy beaches, climbing Ayers Rock, Sydney Opera House, working in Melbourne. I felt like I was an episode of *Holiday*, I kept expecting Carolyn to change into Judith Charmers and cut to a video tape of my trip.

She looked at the inside of her mug, checking for one last bit of coffee. "Well, that's all very nice, but I'm sure that's not why you've come here is it? What can I do for you?"

I looked her in the eye, then to the window. "I've got this credit card, and you see, I'm not going to university until September, so I'm here for the next four months. So I was wondering, are there any shifts going? I'll do anything, nights, days weekends, anything. I just need some money you see." I bit my lip.

"It's nice to hear you value the job here so much, and how you're so interested in caring for people still."

"No, well, I do enjoy working here, it's just, well obviously the money would come in handy before I go to uni, and it's work I know, and a place I know. So I thought…"

"I'm sure we can find the odd shift here and there Kieran, for a certain care assistant who was so missed after he'd gone. I had patients asking me for the first few months you'd gone, where that nice young blond man had gone, and when he was coming back."

"Did you? What did they say, what words did they use?"

"That's enough of that, let's look at this off duty and see what gaps you could fill." She wrote down various shifts over the next four weeks, copied it and handed it to me. "So we'll see you the day after tomorrow for a late shift. Are you sure you're ok to start back that soon? You don't want a break to get used to being back?"

"It's fine, I've just sort of slipped back to it all quickly. See you tomorrow."

I returned home, told Mum my news and she celebrated by showing me her well stocked cheese shelf in the fridge, and making me cheese on toast—with three varieties of Cheddar. We spent the afternoon together while she cut and bleached my hair.

"Your ends are terrible. Did you get it trimmed out there?" Her state registered hairdresser skills were in full swing.

"Once maybe. I can't remember. I didn't have a lot of money to spend on haircuts, it was all about food and accommodation."

"You thought you'd wait until you got home for me to do it for free did you? It's like that is it? I see. You're paying something towards house-keeping while you're here now, until you go away in September. It's not a bloody hotel you know!"

"Fine by me. Bet you don't make Paul do it when he's my age."

"That's up to me and Dad. You and Paul are different, so we have to see how it goes when he gets to your age." She paused as she mixed the peroxide cream and bleach powder in a plastic bowl, adding two packets of artificial sweetener to lessen the sting—another of her state registered hairdresser tricks. "How did you get on with Jo? All that time with each other, you must have had a few arguments?" She fished unsubtly, checking for lumps in the peroxide mix.

I thought about telling her, but didn't want to change the way she thought about Jo. After all, he'd been so kind to me that night in the YHA when we watched *Veronica's Closet*. It seemed so unnecessary to tell her about the other things. Such small things when you looked at the whole trip together. Mum would only worry if I told her. Best to leave it and just talk about the good memories. Also who wanted to talk about men you fancy with your mum?—not me, or at least not yet. I had some friends who were really open about things like that with their parents, but I didn't feel ready yet. The fact that Mum had agreed to peroxide my hair again, after the first time debacle, was progress. I didn't want to spoil that.

"We had a great time. I've got loads of photos I'll show you later. Us at the top of Ayers Rock, walking through Kings Canyon, on the beach at Surfers Paradise, everything. I'll have these memories forever. I'm so pleased I went with him."

"That's nice, I'm glad you got on." She painted the white cream all over my hair, the gentle burning sensation grew as it touched my scalp. "I was a bit worried, thought he might steal the light from you. He's a very nice boy, don't get me wrong, but he can definitely be a bit you know, over the top sometimes I think. On the one hand, it's good because of his drama studies, but on the other hand, it might cause fights, which is difficult when you're with each other all the time. No, it's good you got on. I said to Dad, it would be fine. I knew you'd know what you were getting yourself into with him." She paused. "How long do we leave the bleach in so you don't go ginger?"

"An hour."

"That's right. Shall we have a look at some of these pictures, or do you want to show them to Dad as well?" She put a shower cap on my head, then wrapped a towel around it all, securing it with some special hairdressing clips she pulled from her hairdressers apron.

"Let's show them together, or I've got to do it three times."

She smiled. "Dad wants to see what you got up to after we left."

***

Grace opened the large Victorian door to her large Victorian house. She flung her arms around me. "Well, hello. How the devil are you? How devilish are you? How is the devil? Are you the devil? Questions, questions… come in. I've just been in the east wing, this morning, and I thought we could move onto the south wing later…"

I followed her to the kitchen where she handed me a card with a picture of a cartoon man with large yellow hair. Inside it read:

Kieran,

Hello!

This is my greetings-card equivalent of a "welcome" doormat. The Big Hair slogan is in anticipation of any exciting Antipodean hairstyles you may have picked up. Here's hoping it's not a Neighbours-era Jason Donovan mullet. Brr, what a horrible thought…

Lots of love

Grace xx

She hugged me, put the kettle on to make tea and, leaning against the work surface asked, "So? How's things? News, dramas, men? I see your hair's been sun-kissed as I predicted, or is that a touch of *salon de ma mere*? Very nice by the way, nothing like I'd feared. Tea? Sugar?" She searched through the pine cupboards for the required ingredients then opened the pine effect fridge for the milk.

I nodded. "It's so good to see you. It's been so long. I don't know how I'd have managed without your news keeping me going." I sat on the pine bench at the long pine table watching her mum hanging washing on the twirley round washing line at the bottom of the well manicured and very long garden.

"And yours certainly spiced up my life here. While I was mastering the alcoholic jiggery-pokery behind the bar, during my shifts as a 'host' at the pub, you were falling in love with a legion of muscled straight men, climbing Ayers Rock and let's not forget the portion of *some* you had too! It was *me* who couldn't have managed without *you*."

"Host"? You didn't say that?" We both did the air quotation marks with our hands.

"Basically, 'host' is a way of saying barmaid/waitress/whatever, and shouldn't be thought of in the parasitic sense of the word. Nor should it be thought of in the 'Soho nightclub hostess' sense of the word—chance'd be a fine thing!"

"So the bar job's going well?"

"One bloke wasn't too happy that I'd left a three inch head—fnar fnar—on his pint of Heineken so I had to start that one again, but other than that I'm doing as well as can be expected for someone who goes to the pub about once a year. Actually, I'd not thought of it like that before, with this job I can claim to be all interesting and cosmopolitan, like I go out all the time. When people ask where I am, I'll say 'I'm in the pub' when I'm actually working. Mind you, they might start thinking I'm an alcoholic, and I don't want that. So yes, it's going well. Not long now till I go to uni, I can't wait. What are you doing from now until then?"

"Back at the hospital. Yes I know, but it's easy—because I know the work, and because I got my job back easily. I could have spent a month looking for something, and I just walked in and they gave me my old job back."

"I can see what you did there." Grace paused, handed me my tea which had been stood for a while on the, you guessed it, pine work surface. "How's Jo?"

"Fine."

"When did you last see him?"

"At the airport, I waved as he was being hugged by his family."

"So have you fallen out, since 'Duncangate'? I was pretty surprised when I received your email. I didn't have a chance to reply before you came home. It seemed a bit silly to reply once you were back here. Do you actually have internet at your parents"?"

"Dad has, but we have to ask to use it, and explain why we want to use it. He comes in to the study after fifteen minutes and points out how long it's been by tapping his watch and looking disapprovingly at me. Better to just call me, or write a letter."

"I thought about that, but what with the high flying life of a 'hostess' and the library, I didn't have time. I thought it would be better to just talk to you when we met."

"Some things are better said than written I suppose."

There was a pause between us as I sipped my tea and Grace thought about what to say next.

"Which would you prefer—a few episodes of *The High Life*—" She displayed a home video like a gameshow host. "—finding out what the camp trolley dollies have been up to

147

and shamelessly stealing some of their put downs, or a mince around Fareham or Gosport to scour the shops for bargains? The choices are endless—well strictly speaking they're not, but all the same, the choice is yours."

I thought about the two options put before me, and then thought about 'Duncangate', as it had been christened, including air quotation marks of course. I hadn't seen Hannah yet, and I started to think about what she'd have to say about that little incident too. She'd been pretty clear in her last email. How could I avoid more questions from Hannah, who was never one to let an issue drop if she thought she'd get some mileage out of it. Grace on the other hand, was more gentle with her line of questioning.

"Do you really want to go shopping?" I looked at the video.

"My feet are pretty sore. Because the combined hours of both jobs, I spend a lot of time on my feet and I am beginning to worry that they're going to swell up like barrage balloons and leave me no choice but to wear slippers whenever I go out. I did ten hours in the pub the day before yesterday, and did another six at the library yesterday. The pub shift was really busy as I was 'on the floor'—ooer as I said the first time they told me, but the joke did wear a bit thin—instead of serving behind the bar. Essentially I don't like the waitressing side of things because of the injurious nature of the work involved," Grace gabbled, obviously excited to be able to talk to me face to face after so long.

"How so?"

"Scalding fingers from picking up meals that have been sitting on heated shelving. Sore arms from carrying huge trays, and I mean *huge*, full of food and very heavy empty plates. An extremely sore arse from bumping the kitchen swing doors open while carrying a tray. Hideously deformed feet thanks to running around in shoes more suited to working in an office than a pub. I just can't find a pair of flat, comfortable, black, slip-on shoes. Actually come to mention it, perhaps I could do with going shopping..." She put the video down then leant against the work surface.

"Shall we make another cup of tea, take some biscuits to the living room and just carry on like this?"

"Only if you lead on the mincing, and we can watch some of *The High Life* as a break from it all."

"Done."

Safely ensconced in Grace's living room on her sofa, we both sipped our tea.

"Now it's time for me to don my Claire Rayner hat and deal with 'Newly back from Australia, of the New Forest.' What a fair old pickle you've got yourself into, eh, luvvy?"

"I don't know what you're talking about." I looked out the bay window to the gravel drive and her mum's VW sparkling green, just like the ivy climbing up the wall.

"Pull the other one, it's got bells on it. I've got the email. Don't force me to get it from my folder and read it to you."

"Folder? Did you print it out or something?"

"I take my correspondence very seriously, as you should know. Different folders for different senders, all stored by date order. Once I started to colour code it all, but ran out of steam for that one."

"Ok, alright. What do you think? Everything, hold nothing back. Tell me what you really think of Jo and 'Duncangate' as it's now evidently been named."

"Remember, you asked for this ok?" She took a deep breath and put her tea down. "It sounds to me that Jo is a bit of a big old tarty tart, who does things before he thinks, and then apologises afterwards, thinking that everything will be better because of the little word beginning in s."

"S?"

"Sorry you nit! Ok, so he's your best friend, and ok, so you went to Australia together. And I'm not denying you have good times together—I heard about a lot of them before you went away. And I'm sure you had some great times when you were down under—fnar, fnar—but the thing I have a problem with is the way he treats you."

"Like what?"

"That bloke from the bar in Melbourne…"

"Chris."

"That's the one."

"We made up about that. I told you about the *Veronica's Closet* night he did for me afterwards didn't I?"

"Yes." She stared into my eyes, then looked out the window. "Jo's good at apologising isn't he?"

"What's that supposed to mean?"

"He does things, and then apologises and it's all fine."

"What's wrong with that? Some people don't even apologise, at least he does that."

"Yes, but if you apologise for the same things time after time, it sort of shows you don't really mean it. Does he understand what he does to you?"

"I don't know what you mean."

"Does he know how upset you were when he shagged Duncan, after you'd told him how much you liked Duncan?"

"Look, he said he was sorry, I don't know what more to say. Anyway, if that's all he's done wrong, as far as Auntie Claire Rayner's concerned, that's not too bad is it?"

"But that's just it Kieran. That's *not* the only thing he's done. What about all the times he gets drunk so you have to drive him home?"

She stood, and began pacing the carpet, sometimes counting off points on her fingers. This was serious. As she counted the various Jo related events in Australia I felt my stomach churning. Every one of them was true—exactly as I'd told her they'd happened, only when they were all laid out together in a list, counted on Grace's fingers I felt a cold hand grab my heart. *But he was my friend, these things happen. Don't they?*

"He doesn't mean to. He just loses track of time, and gets carried away. And anyway, I don't mind, I wouldn't want him to drive home like that. I don't mind looking after him. It's fine."

"Exactly!" She stopped pacing and crouched in front of me on the sofa.

"Exactly what?"

"He knows that, which is why he knows he can get away with it. And if you ever threaten not to help him he plays the 'best friend' card which he knows you'll take, because you're such a good friend. I should know that, I've been through enough with you. And how he behaves in night clubs, when he's got a boyfriend, leaving you to sort things out with the latest man he's picked up for the evening, while his boyfriend's downstairs? He treats you like you're some sort of relationship counsellor crossed with a mediator."

"So what's different about me helping you? And since when did it become wrong to ask for friends' help with relationships?"

"When was the last time I did something really stupid, made a complete mess of something which you had to clean up?"

She was stood now, arms folded.

"What about that time you'd bleached your moustache and left it on too long and you called me to help you cover it up? And how about that guy, who worked with you while you did work experience at The News—you obsessed with him for the whole summer. That's where we got Obsession, the eau de toilette idea from. And you accidentally sent him an email which was about him, but meant for me. I was there, in the pub after you finished, working out a plan for how to sort it out. So it's not all plain sailing with you is it?"

"His name was Alastair.", Grace sipped her tea and looked up from her mug at me slowly. She continued, now adopting a Scottish accent, "Ooh, Shona, who shat in your handbag?"

We both started to laugh.

Dropping the accent, Grace sat next to me on the sofa, putting her arm around me. "Ok, so you're good at clearing up other people's mess. Maybe that's why you're such a good care assistant!"

"Ha bloody ha. So Jo's not so bad after all is he?"

"Do you want to watch some of "The High Life"?"

I'd won. She understood. She finally understood how it worked with Jo and me. That he wasn't being any different from my other friends. That's how it works with best friends. If anyone would understand it would be Grace.

We spent the afternoon watching the campy escapades of "The High Life" and said "oh, dearie me" in a Scottish accent so often that Grace's mother walked in and asked us what was wrong. By the time we'd explained that it was just a quote from the TV series about two Scottish trolley dollies, she was completely lost. She asked what was wrong with them to say that all the time. Eventually she offered her help if anything else went wrong, with us, and we thanked her for the offer.

I laughed so much my sides hurt and my eyes watered. There wasn't anything wrong as I sat with another of my best friends, Grace, on the living room carpet, watching TV and talking. How could there be anything wrong? I was sure that Grace would continue on her voyage of understanding when she met Jo, which, if it was up to me, would be quite soon.

***

The next day I visited Hannah at her house for lunch before we both started a late shift. She met me at the back door, and we walked through the kitchen upstairs to Hannah's room. I waved at her parents, just to be polite on the way up. Her mum looked up from a pair of trousers she was sewing and asked me if I was alright. Himself tapped the ash from his cigarette into the ash tray, our presence barely registering.

Once upstairs in her room, the door closed, Hannah put the kettle on and started to prepare our lunch—a Chinese ready meal from Tesco. I use 'prepare' in the loosest sense of the word: she pricked the wrapping with a fork and put the containers into her microwave. Hannah was the sort of girl who would order Chinese takeaway for Christmas dinner if she had guests; she would do it in such a way that no one would mind.

"What's *he* doing here during the day?" I sat on her sofa and noticed she'd redecorated again—the walls were deep red with gold Chinese writing scattered about.

"Lost his job again. Told his boss to fuck off and got sacked.

Mum went doo lally tat when he told her. They can't manage on her wages for long, all the debt he's got them into. He's driving her up the wall, being here all the time." She busied herself making our tea at the mini kitchen bar against the wall. "She's used to having the house to herself during the day between night shift. Normally she gets home, hoovers, dusts, cleans the bathroom, makes a cuppa tea, has a fag, then goes to sleep for a couple of hours, and by two, she's up again, batting about in the house—sewing, that sort of thing. Soon it's seven and she's got her uniform on and she's off to Tesco to stack the shelves again."

"So you're glad to get away when you're at work?"

"Bloody right I am. Can't stand it here at the moment." She handed a mug of tea to me. "It feels like a bomb is about to go off, and it's usually Himself. Sweet and sour, or oyster?"

"Oyster."

"There you are. Tuck in." She handed my food over then sat next to me on her sofa. "Never mind all that, what about you? Have you got used to being back yet? Back to the hospital straight away I noticed?"

"I needed the money. I'm ribboned for money, and I don't want to start uni like that."

She forked a mouthful of food in. "Jo? You heard from him?"

"Yesterday. He called to ask how I was settling in."

"That's nice. Sounds like you had a great time out there. You told me about who Jo shagged, was it just Brad with you?"

"In Adelaide."

"So you're still talking to him?" She asked casually, a mouth half-full of food.

"Brad?"

"Jo you nit!"

154

"Yes—why wouldn't I?" I shrugged.

She mentioned 'Duncangate', but conceded that she'd already said it all before in her email, and there was no point in going over it again.

Relieved for this small mercy, I replied, "It's all fine now."

Hannah forked a mouthful of food into her mouth, avoiding my eyes. "Listen to me Mister, *we'll find you your Prince Charming*, just you wait. I'm not much better though. I went to that gay club in town a few times, met some people, but there are so many freaks out there. I don't know how else to describe them."

"Tell me about it."

"Did you get home-sick when you were away? Bet there were things you missed."

"It wasn't like being on holiday. Being away that long is so not like a holiday. Getting a job changed that. Living out of a backpack gets a bit boring too."

"But it was nice to travel with a friend?"

I nodded emphatically. Between mouthfuls of Chinese, I told Hannah about the *Veronica's Closet* night, explaining that Jo had noticed how home-sick I was, and knew how to cheer me up. I didn't think it was worth bringing up 'Duncangate' again, and the fact that Jo had actually done the '*Veronica's Closet* night more as an apology for his behaviour than to alleviate my home-sickness. I knew that Hannah would let that colour Jo's well-meaning and kind behaviour that night at the YHA. So what if it was as an apology, rather than just to be nice, he'd still been kind to me, and that was what mattered.

"Aren't you the lucky one? Sounds like you two are more like Boyfriends, capital B, what you did on that *Veronica's Closet* night. Snuggling up on the sofa, very cosy."

I nodded.

"Finished? I've got fruit and nut, or some bananas that have been sat in the bowl for over a week. I thought I'd better get some fruit to balance the other stuff, but every time I think about what to have for pudding I just end up having something else and they slowly sit there going black."

"Tempting as the bananas sound, can I have the fruit and nut?"

She handed me a chocolate bar. "Done. Shit, it's gone one, we'd better go or we'll be late. Sure you're ok to give me a lift to work?"

"What's the point in us both taking a car to the same place? It's greener, better for the environment."

"Never mind the bloody environment, I couldn't give a shite about that. If we can carry on chatting, that's all I'm arsed about m'darling."

We grabbed our bags, took another chocolate bar each and left, shouting "bye" as we walked past Ange and Himself in the living room.

"Hannah, what time are you back tonight?" her step dad asked.

"Don't know what we're doing yet. Might go into town with Kieran. Bye."

I looked at her and whispered, "Are we? I'm ribboned, I don't want to go into town."

"I know, but I don't have to tell him what I'm doing do I? Besides, we might decide to go to town after work, who knows, anything could happen."

Yes it could, I thought as we drove to work. Anything definitely could happen.

Eleven

Chapter 11

~⚬⚬⚬~

G race had been talking about going to London Pride for weeks. She said she was missing out on all this, and how on earth did I expect her to be a helpful and sympathetic friend if I didn't show her some of 'my new culture'—her quotation marks. I pointed out to her that we'd been comparing camp stories and noticing camp things years before I'd come out to her, so she hardly needed any extra tutoring on 'my new culture' (of queerness). I reminded her of the time she'd written to me with a sticker from a particularly camp type of apples she'd spotted while out shopping with her mother, I enjoyed the *Pink Lady* sticker attached to the letter and had mounted it next to my TV in my bedroom. I also reminded her of the flyer for some shows at Portsmouth Guildhall including one entitled *All the Queen's Men* which she'd boldly 'highlit' (or highlighted depending on your persuasion) for handy reference. Grace acknowledged these 'forays into the arena of campness' as she'd described them, but remained resolute that it was essential for her to attend London Pride.

"Besides" she'd said, "I've not met this Jo of yours, despite hearing so much about him that I feel as if I should know his inside leg measurement and shoe size, so I think it's only proper for me to actually see him face to face."

I had conceded this was a good point, and so the scene was set. Grace and Jo would finally meet.

After a number of phone calls we agreed to meet in Salisbury at Out! where the minibus started its journey to London. Jo made his own way there, and I picked Grace up from her house, as she was still yet to either learn to drive, or buy a car. Both activities had been on her to do list since I'd met her, and unfortunately due to lack of funds, and lack of confidence, neither had moved any further up the list. After the first car/wall incident in her Mum's car, I'd tried giving her a lesson in the same car park near the seafront in a small town near Gosport, which had resulted in Grace driving very slowly into a traffic cone, and since then she had never asked to 'have a go' at Priscilla's controls again. Much to my and Priscilla's relief it has to be said. In the meantime, Grace relied on the kindness of friends to transport her around Hampshire and in this instance, Wiltshire. I was on this occasion one of those friends, and I was happy to give Grace some of said kindness to facilitate her learning more about 'my new culture'.

I bought the tickets through Out! I asked Bruce if we could bring an honorary fag hag, and he said it was actually compulsory.

"If you hadn't asked me that, I'd have been disappointed Kieran. The minibus is going to be half full of queers and half full of their friends, and more power to us for it. It all makes for the rich tapestry of life as my mum used to tell me."

"Does that mean I can have a ticket for her?" I stared at one of my recent additions to my bedroom wall: A1 the boyband, stood in a swimming pool, all chest and smiles, allegedly with no trunks underneath. It was from my Naked edition of Attitude Magazine. Word of its publication had gone round Out! like wildfire and my copy had been well thumbed on that particular evening.

"As long as you think she's *sympathetic* to gay people." He paused, "Yes, it does. How many extra tickets do you want?"

I looked at my list of names on my bedside cabinet."It's just my friend Grace as well, so that's me, Jo and Grace. Three please. Kev's coming, he mentioned something about some others coming too. Has he spoken to you?"

"Kev's got his order in, don't you worry. I'll put you down for three places in the minibus. If any others come out of the woodwork, just give me a week's notice and I'll see what I can do to squeeze you in. Alright?"

Grace and I pulled up outside the Portakabin where Out! took place, the soundtrack to *Queer as Folk* blaring out of Priscilla's windows and roof. We stopped and in a move, deliberately designed to copy a scene from this TV show, both shouted: "Where's the do?" as I opened the door.

Grace got out of the car and looked around the car park where groups of teenagers milled around chatting and smoking next to cars while Bruce and other youth workers attempted to take some semblance of control over proceedings, with the careful use of a clipboard, roll of tickets and a mobile phone. I noted, Bruce wasn't succeeding.

I looked around and couldn't see Jo's car—unless he'd

changed it again. He had a habit of buying cars which were on their last legs, just one MOT short of the scrap yard. He insisted it was cheaper to do this, rather than constantly pay for MOTs, servicing and other silly luxuries like that. I wasn't remotely convinced of this, particularly when you took into account the amount of time it took Jo—and me for the last three cars—to buy each of the replacement cars from various auctions around Hampshire.

I had sighed to myself when he'd called me after his last purchase had failed its MOT with a list of advisories as long as your arm, just two months after we'd spent a day buying it from an open air car auction in some far flung part of north Hampshire (it may have even been Surrey, such was the distance we'd travelled to reach it). I reflected to myself that there were other places I'd rather have been on that long day than in the rain, bidding on a fifteen year old Nissan with Jo. But I did like to help Jo, and it was always fun to spend time together—Thelma and Louise—in jokes, making jokes about other people to get us through the day. Of course, a day shopping in Southampton would have been nicer, but I didn't like to point this out to him, especially as he was at that point, without transport to get him to Southampton. Instead I had smiled and agreed to meet him in a few days to buy the next car.

Now, Grace tapped my shoulder. "So which one's Jo?"

"Can't see him yet, he'll probably be a bit late. He's not great with sticking to times. He's always rushing from one thing to the next, so he's usually late, but it's fine, that's just Jo for you."

I had once tried to broach the subject of his tardiness, to which Jo had replied: "Hang on a minute, let me check my diary, oh I don't have one" and shrugged his shoulders innocently.

Not worth a huge row, so I'd not mentioned it again, I just knew that wherever and whenever I met him, he would always be at least twenty minutes late. This was in spite of being the proud owner of a special time-the-laps, waterproof, scientific watch. Again, this wasn't something I'd broached with him either.

Now, I saw Jo's current car—a 1985 Ford Fiesta in a fetching shade of red and rust—pulling into the close where we were gathered. He parked a few hundred yards from the minibus, where we were now stood. He got out of his car, surrounded by a cloud of blue smoke, a clunk and a bang as the engine stopped, he held a black backpack covered in rubbery red spikes and ran towards us. As he approached I heard him shouting at us. "Quick quick, they've got guns, they've got knives, they're after me, they're going to kill me, help me help me!"

The groups of teenagers stopped smoking and milling and looked at Jo as he ran towards us.

He dropped his backpack to the floor, hugged me and looked at Grace.

"You must be Grace? I've heard so much about you, Kieran's always talking about you, it's 'Grace says this, Grace says that' nice to meet you finally. I'm Jo."

"Hiya, yes I'm Grace. They shook hands."Nice to meet you. Can I ask you something?"

"Always." He bowed as he handed her hand back.

"The guns and knives. That's *Queer as Folk* isn't it?"

"Yes. You've seen it?"

"Only bits" she lied, having seen and pored over every single episode shown to date. "You see, I'm new to all this. I suppose you could say Kieran's showing me the ropes." She smiled at me, then turned back to Jo, full eye contact. "But I do have a good memory for bits of dialogue from films and TV. Always on the hunt for a good quote. I want to go into journalism."

"You stick with us and we'll show you plenty of the ropes. You've got to make an entrance." He held his hands either side of his body and did a twirl. "And you've got to be able to hold a conversation at a party haven't you? He told me about your work experience at The News. I'm doing drama studies at uni, I'm going to be a professional actor."

"Hence, the big dramatic entrance, yes that makes sense. Nice, I can see what you did there." Grace paused, looked at me, then Jo."You can stay. I think I'm going to like you."

They linked arms and walked towards the minibus, leaving me behind, suddenly feeling a little bit like a spare part in my own life.

We sat in the minibus together not quite at the back, yet not right behind Bruce who was driving. I didn't feel enough of a swot to chat to Bruce all the way to London, but I definitely didn't feel like a *sit at the back of the bus and smoke and swear* type person either. In the middle felt right for me and two of my best friends.

It was a shame I couldn't have had Hannah with us too. Hannah and Himself had recently had an argument, the result of which had taken the appeal off her going to Pride with me. Himself had found her 'lifestyle' magazines in her bedroom. There followed an argument about morals and doing things under his roof which he was unhappy with. Hannah pointed out it was hardly news that she was gay since she'd come out months ago. She'd asked whether these so called morals included snooping in her room and hitting her mum and her whenever he liked, and Himself had hit her. First thing I knew was a messy heap of red-eyed-Hannah sat in her car outside my house half an hour later. She had been living with me

162

since then, occasionally seeing her mum when she begged her to come home and promised that Himself was sorry. I told Hannah that as soon as she left home and went to university, this uncomfortable chapter of her life would be over, and she would be free to live her life as she wanted. Unsurprisingly Hannah, complete with a large black eye, didn't feel there was much pride in being gay, so had declined my invite to London Pride.

As we arrived in Richmond, a south west suburb of London, where we were to catch the Tube to central London, I surveyed the other members of the minibus party for a familiar face. I hadn't had a chance to work out who I knew from the group as I'd been talking to Grace and Jo for the whole journey. Now that everyone was leaving the minibus I started to search for familiar faces as everyone stood in Richmond station's car park.

Nicola was a friendly girl with long dark brown hair—she'd been on a poster used across Hampshire advertising gay youth services for young people. Mags, her girlfriend, had bright red hair, thick rimmed glasses and a T shirt with something about fucking up the system written across it. The irony of this hadn't been lost on me as I'd noticed her getting out of a very very large, very very new BMW as she was dropped off at the meeting point in Salisbury. The system can't be all that bad if it's given your parents that sort of wealth, but then again, who was I to question?

Or course, there was also Nick who was constantly on the lookout for even the slightest smallest chance of a shag off pretty much anyone male. This attention had quickly become very tedious, and was made much worse by his bad breath, awful hair (bleached blond with terrible root growth, which was unforgivable in my book) and constant boasting about things he'd blatantly never done. These boasts ranged from sleeping with a member of *Take That*, to having a father who had invented microwaves. Whenever asked for evidence of these claims he suddenly developed an interest in someone over the other side of the room. His incredulity of how I could work in a hospital looking after people never failed to annoy me.

Nick hung around with the 'it couple' of the group, Steve and Neil: one half straight looking garage mechanic and the other half-campy high maintenance and a bit theatrical. (Steve's words to describe Neil, not mine.) They'd been together as long as I'd been coming to the group. They were the Posh & Becks of the group, if you will.

I watched someone climbing carefully down the minibus steps dressed as a mid eighties *Madonna*: black lace gloves up to his elbows, layered ra ra skirt with polka dots, fish net stockings, high heels and makeup which left you in no doubt who he was meant to be.

I walked over to the minibus with Jo and Grace following me, and held *Madonna's* hand to steady him as he reached the ground.

"I see you've dressed down for today Kev," I observed as he teetered on his six inch heels I'd bought him in Oz.

"At least I made an effort, what have you come as?" Kev pointed to my clothes and tutted loudly.

"I'm a normal gay man, they wear things like this."

"If you say so" he paused, balancing on his high heels, kissed both my cheeks, and gave me a hug. "Come here you, I've missed you so much. Thought you were never coming back, that you would leave me all alone in a little village outside

Salisbury. Lost in Wiltshire." He squeezed me tight and said into my ear that he loved me.

"You soft old queen. What are you like?" I said I loved him too into his ear then pulled back to take in my fabulous quirky cross dressing friend. I wiped my eye. "Have I told you about our outfits?"

"Sorry I couldn't get the hang of email. I was waiting for a proper letter, full of all the fabulous things you'd got up to. But none came." He pursed his lips.

"Too busy doing them to write about them, sorry. Don't forget the presents."

"How could I? I've got some of them on now! How much do I owe you?"

"Nothing, they're presents, that's the point. I've got loads of pictures to show you—Mardi Gras and Ayers Rock. I thought I was going to pass out in the heat. And *the spots* after all that slap. How do you manage?"

"I'll tell you another time, over those pictures." He paused. "Have you met Tony?" He pointed to his friend.

Tony was a camp Goth, all black lace and leather, with long black nails, a black wig of straight hair which came down to his elbows and vampire makeup. Tony and Kev, evidently shared a love of all things dark and dragish. Tony did a camp wave, the silver rings on his fingers glinting in the sun as he smiled.

Kev walked past Tony. "Don't overdo it, love." He stood next to a woman. "This is Donna, Tony's friend."

She wore a white wedding dress and Minnie Mouse ears. Donna extended her hand for me to shake firmly. "Alright, me boyfriend wasn't really up for this London Gay Pride, so I thought I'll give Tony a bell and see if he wanted to go. Turns out he's going anyway, and wanted someone to go with him, so 'ere I am, with me gay husband!"

Jo and Grace introduced themselves to Tony and Donna. We stood around chatting about our plans for the day—some claimed to have been to hundreds of Prides before, and others were Pride Virgins. I looked at the group stood around me as we waited for Bruce, his clipboard and mobile phone to work out our next move. *Fabulous darling, absolutely fabulous.*

Jo caught my eye across our little group, winked and smiled.

If anyone had described this situation to me a year ago, I'd have told them it was about as likely as me giving birth to a child, personally myself. Yet here I was, about to lose my London Pride virginity on the same day I'd introduced Jo to one of my other best friends.

Bruce, pumped up in a tight black T shirt and blue jeans, blew his whistle, then enviably confident with his sexuality so I'm going to be really camp gesture waved his arms and clipboard about. "Quiet everyone, I'm going to explain the plan for today." He paused as someone near the back of the crowd shouted something about getting twatted. "Yes, thank you for that. Well actually, we're getting the Tube to Green Park, where we can walk to The Mall, where the march begins. It'll last about an hour and a half. It finishes at Victoria, where there is a gay pub, where we can have a drink, for those of you who are eighteen. The festival's at Finsbury Park, which is a Tube journey away from Victoria. We'll get the Tube with you for those who aren't used to travelling in London. The festival finishes at ten and so you need to be back here, the car park of Richmond Tube station by eleven. I've got my mobile phone on me, you've all got the number because my glamorous assistant Doug." He pointed to Doug in his rainbow T shirt and trousers who bowed and held his hands out in a hey presto gesture. "Who's handing out cards now. *Do not be late.* That's eleven o'clock, Richmond Tube Station car park—as in where we are stood now. That's also on the cards too. Right, now follow me to the station and we're off to central London."

We took up almost an entire car of the Tube train. It was fortunate that the train started at Richmond so we could make ourselves comfortable in our carriage. The couples sat next to each other enjoying the freedom of London to hold one another's hands. Nick put his CD player on and sang along to *Steps* songs loudly and out of tune.

I watched as the train filled with non-Pride passengers, each one noticing us in our carriage travelling in our own pink bubble. Tony and Kev were comparing nail varnish and adjusting their wigs. Donna had struck up a conversation with a builder wearing paint stained overalls carrying a toolbox. I caught snippets of her conversation, including "Gay hubbie" and "He helped me pick the dress—charity shop. Imagine donating your wedding dress to a charity shop. Poor cow, she must've been." The builder nodded and smiled, not able, or trying, to get a word in edgeways.

We arrived at The Mall and followed Bruce as he held his clipboard high in the air like a beacon, his bicep bulging impressively from his T shirt. Some other member unfurled the banner they'd made for the youth group. It proudly proclaimed 'Out! A friendly space for young people to be themselves in Wiltshire and parts of Hampshire.' It could have done with a bit of editing I thought, but at least it got the message across. Nicola and Mags held it and the rest of the group stood underneath.

After a few false starts, the march began and we walked through the streets of central London. I waved at members of the public who stood on the pavement on the route of the march, feeling bolstered in confidence by everyone around me doing the same. I briefly noticed, and then decided to ignore, a group of men standing on a bank of grass on the edge of the march wearing placards proclaiming "It's going to get worse" or "Leviticus says it is against God" Tony and Kev waved camply at these men, who ignored them.

"You've got to look them in the face and smile at their silly messages." Tony adjusted his black leather and lace fingerless gloves.

"If you're abusive to them it gives them more reason to say how vile we are, this way they just think we're a bit queeny, and there are worse things than that." Kev puffed up his skirt and flicked his hair, a huge grin on his face.

Soon we fell into a comfortable rhythm on the march, taking turns to hold the Out! banner and each worrying slightly about whether we'd end up on TV if a news camera filmed us on the march.

I felt pleased I was finally out to my parents, so whether or not I was broadcast on national TV didn't really matter in that sense. Tony and Kev were out to their parents, with varying degrees of success. "Mum's alright—I didn't have much option but to tell her, I mean look at me" Tony said, gesturing to his clothes. "But Dad just doesn't really talk about it, which is fine cos he's hardly ever there so…"

"Last week, my old dear helped me pick this lot out from Oxfam." Kev gestured to his clothes.

The march ended at Victoria, as Bruce had predicted. The banners from other groups gradually flopped and were packed away as the crowd dissipated around Victoria. Some made a beeline for the Tube to make their way to Finsbury Park, others went straight to The Stag—an octagonal gay pub made of 1960s concrete and devoid of any windows. I could hardly contain my excitement at the prospect of going inside. *Me, going into a real London gay pub—would you Adam and Eve it? I looked about for some jellied eels, pie and mash and a pearly king and queen. There were plenty of queens about but not of the pearly variety.*

Bruce waved his clipboard above his head and started to shout to get everyone's attention. "Right, that's the march finished. This is the gay pub I talked about. We're going in for a drink—for those of you who are eighteen mind—before we get the Tube to the festival. If you want to make your own way to the festival, that's fine, but remember when you need to be back at the car park. Those who are…" Bruce's voice faded as I felt myself being pulled away from the grey concrete entrance of The Stag.

I looked down and noticed Jo's hand in mine as he led me away. Jo was holding Grace by his other hand and we were joined by a tired looking Donna—her dress looking quite dirty and worse for wear by now and Tony who was holding Kev's hand, helping him walk on his heels. We continued until we reached a park not far from Victoria and Jo stopped.

Jo stood in front of the group. "I'm not going to that pub, it looks vile. Let's go to Soho, it's only just over there." He pointed to the far side of the park. "I won't have it said that we went to London and didn't go to Soho. If anyone back home found out, I'd never live it down. The fact you're here, means you agree with this. If you don't then you'd better get back to Victoria and catch the Tube with the others." He paused to wait for an answer, none came.

We continued to walk across the park and soon found

ourselves on a main road. Jo strode confidently ahead of our group, periodically asking strangers for directions, while we followed him. Soon we were in what I assumed was Soho—the rainbow flags and men holding hands gave it away somewhat.

Jo stopped outside a large pub on the left of us. "We're here, Compton's of Soho. Shall we?" He gestured towards the door.

"What if we get ID'd, I've not got anything with me?" Kev rummaged in his black lacy handbag.

"I don't think they're bothered about that sort of thing, don't you think we qualify to get in, I mean look at us?" He gestured at our smorgasbord of a group. "We look like a load of extras from *The Rocky Horror Picture Show.* I think they'll get the message. It'll be fine."

It'll be fine. Jo's catch all, get through all phrase. He walked to the door, smiled at the plainly dressed bouncer who opened it for him. The bouncer nodded and smiled at us all and let us in without a word.

As the door opened I felt a wall of smoke, sweat and testosterone which knocked me back slightly. There was a large wooden bar to the left, as we walked in. Various tables and chairs stood between the door and the bar, each full of groups of men, mostly wearing leather, with short hair and beards.

I looked up and noticed a mezzanine floor with some empty tables. "Shall I get a table, I've seen one up there?"

Jo nodded, and walked straight to the bar. Tony followed him and Kev followed me to the mezzanine. I looked at Donna and pointed upstairs. She put her thumbs up and made a drinking motion so I left her at the bar with Jo and Tony. Grace shrugged and followed us.

Shortly after I'd settled down on our table with Kev, I took in the sight before me. A pub, about three times the size of The Duke, completely full of gay men, and a few women, containing only a few people I knew, miles from home. If I smoked, I'd have lit a cigarette and laid back to enjoy it, or whatever it was people who smoked normally did in situations like this. Kev had already lit one, his eyes closed as he inhaled, and I was slightly tempted to ask him for one. Before I had chance the others joined us, Jo put my Malibu and coke in front of me, Tony put a coke, and I assumed vodka in front of Kev, and Donna sat down next to her pint of lager, adding a bottle of something for Grace.

Donna was chatting to anyone who'd listen, "Can't stand all them girly drinks, Malibu, Archers, crap like that. I'm a pint girl, always have bin, always will be. Fits in well with this place don't it? If my Gary could see me here, he'd have a fucking shit freak. All these men around me. And ain't they just *gorgeous*?" I noticed an implied *gay best friend gorgeous* in her tone. "I'm moist just sat here."

"Donna, thanks for that beautiful picture you've just painted for us all. But if you don't mind we don't need that much detail." Tony pretended to be sick and turned away from Donna.

"Sorry, got carried away."

"You do realise they're all gay, the men?"

"I know, but it's the way they look, it's like we're in a bikers' bar or something."

Kev looked around the table at us all. "It's what is called, a bear bar." Silence. "A bar for bears, gay men who are, like this—beards, leather, short hair, butch."

"I wondered what it was all about. How'd you know?" Donna rolled her eyes in a *now it all becomes clear* gesture.

Kev showed us the cover of a free gay magazine he'd been

reading as we waited for our drinks to arrive.

Donna nodded and took a sip of her pint.

"Bit different from The Duke isn't it? Imagine if that was a bear's pub." Kev looked up from the magazine, his eyes wide.

"Imagine me with a beard and clothes like that. Oh, the horror!" Tony replied, laughing.

We stayed in the pub for a few hours, gradually getting used to our surroundings. Kev stood up and began lip syncing to a Madonna song as it started, while Jo and Tony stood either side of him, miming backing vocals and making exaggerated hand motions. I looked around, expecting someone to tell us to stop, or leave, but no-one gave us a second glance. After the initial looks we'd gathered as we walked in, probably more to do with the fact that we were clearly not a group of bears, we'd been left completely alone in our little provincial non-bear bubble. I couldn't remember feeling this happy in a very long time—the only thing which would have made it perfect was having Hannah sat next to me, but I knew why that wasn't possible and didn't want to dwell on it.

"What about the festival? Are we going or are we staying here and getting more drinks?" Donna asked no one and everyone as she finished her pint and banged the glass on the table before burping loudly.

Once we got over the burping, this question was met with a few shrugged shoulders, and some nodded heads. I was keen to see whether the fuss everyone had made about the festival was worthwhile, and was satisfied with the current Soho pub experience to move on. "We have come all this way, it seems a bit silly if we don't actually go to the festival doesn't it? I mean we've gone to Soho, so if anyone asks we can say that."

Jo patted me on the back then looked around the table. "I

agree with Kieran, we'd look like a right bunch of twats if we didn't actually go to the festival, especially when we've got here so cheaply with Bruce and the group. Anyone else want to come with us?"

Donna wiped her mouth, suppressed another burp then said, "I want to do tequila shooters off the bar, and then go to another bar. Someone told me there's one where they have almost naked men dancing on the bar."

Jo smiled, it didn't reach his eyes. "How about we don't, but we say that we did?"

Donna looked at Tony who was sipping his drink in a more civilised manner than Donna had managed so far. Tony smiled at Donna, looked at me and Jo, nodded, finished his drink then stood up. He took Donna's hand. "I've had enough, let's go. I'm sure there will be loads of semi naked men at the festival, if not, well we can always come back here later."

I looked at Grace who was quietly sipping her drink with a huge grin across her face.

A walk and a Tube ride later we arrived at Finsbury Park. I was disappointed to discover that far from being a green and relaxing suburb as its name suggested, it was in fact a slightly down at the heel north London area, which happened to have a park nearby. We walked past hair weave shops, fried chicken emporiums and corner shops, which all promised to send money abroad for less than the previous one. I noted a distinct lack of any high street names in Finsbury Park, no familiar names or logos here.

"It's this way, follow me," Jo proclaimed as we left the Tube station.

We all dutifully followed him.

Once in the park, it became clear that the group would have

to divide into smaller units if we were all to get what we wanted out of the remaining few hours of the festival. Kev, Tony and Donna headed for the cabaret tent, which left me, Grace and Jo debating which part of 'my new culture' to experience first.

"*Steps* are on stage in an hour, and I'd really like to see them 'sing'," Grace said, inserting her own air quotation marks, to indicate that she knew there would probably be as much singing as Kev and his backing singers had done in the pub earlier. "And like to see what camp old pish is for sale, so I can take it to uni with me and be all 'aren't I so down with the kids and cool about all this,'when I meet my new uni friends. Those are my two requests."

I looked up from the free festival guide Grace was holding. "I'd like to see Steps too, and I want to see if they've got any signed photos I'm interested in. Other than that, not bothered."

Jo looked at both of us and smiled broadly then clapped his hands. "Sounds like we can accommodate your requests. Sounds good to me. I want to go to the dance tents and 'throw some shapes', as they say. So where first?"

Grace unfolded her free festival guide and map and angled it so we could see the layout. "The biggest dance tent's just over there, so shall we start there? Just as long as we're in sight of the stage for Steps in, ooh, fifty minutes now." She looked at her watch. "I think I could be persuaded to 'throw some shapes' too!"

The dance tent was very full of a variety of men and women, dancing in circles around piles of their bags. Some had clearly had more than a few cans of beer, judging by their bin-lid sized pupils and chewing mouths. Jo disappeared briefly, which made me anxious in case he returned with some little white pills. He returned with a bottle of water for each of us. He handed them around and said, "Make sure you don't get dehydrated, dancing in this heat. You've got to look after yourself, even if you've not done more drugs than, ooh possibly life itself, as some of this lot seem to have done." He looked around and nodded in confirmation of his statement.

"Yes, I did wonder what the chewing was about," Grace replied, laughing.

We cheersed our water bottles, did a group kiss which Jo taught us involved leaning into the middle of a group hug while dancing and kissing each other, and danced to versions of our favourite pop songs we'd not previously heard before. I felt as if I were on a completely different planet from my normal life—the hospital, my house, my brother. I closed my eyes and listened to Sophie Ellis Bexter's voice over a thick bass beat, as the strobe lights flashed along to the music. I felt two of my best friends' hands in mine as we danced together. I wasn't going to allow anything to spoil this perfect day for me—it would be forever remembered in this way.

We saw *Steps* 'sing' and it was every bit as good as I'd imagined. We all inserted our own air quotation marks to ensure the irony of the situation wasn't lost. We all sang along to their latest single, *Love's Got a Hold On My Heart* and even did the prescribed dance. The group performed five songs, much to the crowd's delight, and I felt as if I was at a *Steps* concert with Jo and Grace. For someone who claimed to need to learn more about 'my new culture' she seemed pretty knowledgeable of the dance moves and lyrics of the *Steps* songs. Jo really put his back into the performance, and even sang along to some of the songs, rather than our rather feeble lip syncing.

We went to the 'market village', all agreeing it was more than a bit *very,* since it was basically a collection of stands selling various rainbow themes and coloured pish. We were in heaven. I bought a signed photo of Craig Kelly, or Vince from Queer as Folk, as he was better known. Grace bought a rainbow friendship bracelet, sailor model with a T shirt which read 'yes I am', rainbow fridge magnet and rainbow note book. "For all my camp notes for use in future letters and emails," she explained.

Jo looked at her hefty bounty of camp paraphernalia and asked, "Is there something you want to tell us Grace? We're all friends here, you can tell us. Come on, there's no shame if you've realised you want to drink from the furry cup of love."

Grace looked at her bags of rainbow coloured pish, bit her lip. "I am not gay. I can see why you'd leap to that conclusion and I do mean leap. However, just to clarify for everyone's benefit, I'm immersing myself in this new culture. That and I've always been a bit of a collector of this sort of camp old pish, and now I'm officially a fag hag, it's given me an excuse to ramp up my collection of said pish."

I looked at them both. "Well, I think our work here is done. Shall we find somewhere to sit and people watch?"

Jo said, "Maybe in a bit, I'd like to walk about a bit more. We can see what the other dance tent's like, and I want to get to the front of the stage to see *Cher*."

"*Cher's* here?" Grace's ears pricked up. "You're shitting me. Well in that case, I'm there."

"It's not actually *Cher*, it's a tribute *Cher*, I'm sure it'll be good all the same. Follow me." Jo took our hands.

Via a bar, Jo led us to the second, larger dance tent and walked to the middle of the dancing, sweating throng of people. We stayed there for a while, both Grace and I looking for somewhere to sit, while Jo danced frantically.

176

Chapter 11

He then, enthusiastically and a bit drunkenly took us by the hands to the other dance tent, again taking us right to the middle of it. He jumped onto the stage, and began cavorting to the music, while we stood next to a speaker beneath the stage. I looked to Grace, who was clutching her camp bounty in various bags, close to her chest.

"I can't just leave him on his own. We've got to stick together," I shouted into Grace's ear.

She shrugged her shoulders at me and clutched onto her bags harder.

We waited another few minutes, which seemed like an hour, and I pulled Jo's trousers as he danced on stage. I motioned to explain that we wanted to leave, he smiled back at me and danced more emphatically. I looked at Grace and shrugged.

She leant towards me and shouted into my ear. "If *you* won't tell him, *I* will. My ears hurt, my feet feel like my shoes are full of blood and I want to be somewhere, anywhere which doesn't have music so loud it hurts my brain." Grace pulled Jo's trousers hard, he leant down near her face.

Jo climbed off the stage and Grace lead us out of the dance tent. We found some trees far away from the music and sat. Jo immediately stood up and danced next to the trees, sipping his drink from a plastic cup.

"What did you tell him?" I asked Grace.

"I told him I felt sick and if he didn't come with us, I would leave him there, and he could make his own way back to Richmond, never mind getting home."

"Bloody hell, and it worked?"

"We're here aren't we?"

I nodded and looked at Jo who was merrily dancing in his own world next to the trees.

Grace and I sat people watching under the trees, while Jo danced for long enough for our feet to recover. I was in the middle of a conversation with Grace about whether it would be ok to put my signed photo of Vince from *Queer as Folk* up in my bedroom at my house or whether to wait until I went to uni, and Jo interrupted us.

"Let's go to the stage, I really want to see *Martine McCutcheon*, she's on now. Come on, you've had time for your feet and ears to recover. I did your things with you two earlier today, it's just this one little thing. It would mean so much to me." Jo looked straight into my and then Grace's eyes, holding up his finger in case we'd forgotten what one meant.

Jo quickly took us by the hand to the main stage, dragging us past a long bar queue as he wanted another drink, then through crowds to reach an appropriate vantage point. He stopped, looked at the stage and then took our hands again and began walking through the crowds nearer the stage. He repeated this another three times, each time dismissing a spot in the crowd as it didn't have a good enough view of the stage, each time dragging us through thickening crowds nearer the loud music.

"Just a bit nearer, I can see a gap over there, come on you two, just a little bit more," Jo said, grabbing our hands once again.

Grace stood still. "No, that's enough, I'm not moving any more. This is it. My feet hurt, my ears hurt and I've had enough. No more." She looked at me expectantly. "You can go nearer but I'm staying here and I expect Kieran is too."

I looked at Jo. "Grace isn't good with crowds like this, and neither am I to be honest." I turned to Grace. "We're staying here aren't we?"

178

Grace nodded once and folded her arms, still clutching onto her camp paraphernalia. I stood still with my hands on my hips and stared at Jo. He knew the game was up, we were not moving anymore. He looked at each of us in turn, slowly making eye contact, began to say something, which was met with a shaken head from Grace. Jo stood next to us, slowly folded his arms and looked towards the stage where Martine was about to start her performance. We'd put up with his moves for the last three times, and enough was enough, we were staying put, and Jo knew it.

Jo remained pretty quiet for the rest of the day, only responding to questions when asked, and volunteering no new information otherwise.

We all slept on the journey back to Salisbury, Grace's head leaning against me as I rested mine on the mini bus window. Jo sat towards the back of the minibus on the way home, he wanted to catch up with Tony, Donna and Kev after we'd separated earlier that day. I looked back to them, sat further back and they were all sleeping, Jo leaning his head against the window.

I drove Grace and Jo back to my house in near silence. He wasn't in any fit state to drive. Jo got in the back of Priscilla, his head lolling about and lay across the back seat. Grace sat next to me to keep me company on the way back.

She commented on how quiet Jo had been since Martine's performance. "Is he usually like this?"

"Never seen him like this. I expect he's just tired."

"Still, this means I can keep you company and show my ignorance of all things car related, by asking questions every time you change gear and things like that." She tapped the gear stick then one of the buttons on the dashboard, starting the windscreen wipers.

During the whole time I'd known Jo, he'd never sat in the back of my car. Even if I was giving other friends a lift too, he'd always insisted on sitting in the front next to me. He said it was for medical reasons as he got travel sick if he couldn't sit in the front. None of my other passengers had wanted to, or felt the need to argue over this clear medical reason, and so Jo had always sat up front with me.

Now, he was laying across the back seat, eyes closed, completely oblivious to the movements of the car. I knew I was seven years shy of a medical degree, however I did know travel sickness had something to do with movement, which was improved by being able to see where you were going, helped by sitting in the front of the vehicle in question. It didn't take a rocket scientist, never mind a doctor, to work out that laying asleep across the back seat of a car wouldn't do you any favours if you suffered from travel sickness.

As I pulled into my drive, Jo slowly sat up. I turned off the engine and he opened the back door, grabbed his bag and waited by the front door as I collected my things. Grace silently followed me and waited while I opened the front door. I showed them to their rooms, Grace to Dad's study which Mum had made up with a inflatable mattress on the floor, and Jo to the room Paul and I referred to as 'the playroom' due to its previous use.

"Thanks for driving," Grace said, tired, but smiling. "I had a top flight time. I learned such a lot about the whole gay thing."

"Night." We hugged and kissed each other's cheeks.

Jo closed his bedroom door and mumbled what I took to be, night, as it closed in my face.

I was too tired to deal with this at gone midnight. *Grace's* words with him earlier wouldn't have pissed him off like this. No, he was just tired, and it would pass by morning. Everyone gets a bit ratty when they're tired.

Twelve

Chapter 12

⚜

I was woken the following morning by the sound of Mum banging about in the kitchen below my bedroom, making a cooked breakfast and watching *Kilroy* on the kitchen TV. I put my dressing gown on and walked downstairs.

She looked up from the frying pan. "Good afternoon! Hannah's at work, how much longer's she staying here? It's a tiny room she's in, full of my sewing stuff, is she alright in there? I've done you and your friends a fry up, hope that's ok. If not I've got cereals and some cheese if they want a foreign breakfast. What do you think they'll like, these friends of yours?"

"It's only half ten, so it's hardly the afternoon. What's this you're watching?" I rubbed my eyes and yawned as a group of people shouted at one another on the TV.

"She's split up with her husband, but her mum's now going out with him, and wants to marry him. So the daughter's not speaking to her mum anymore." Mum paused. "Cuppa tea?"

I nodded, then thought better of it, as I surveyed the scene before me: three pans full of food, a sink full of washing up and my Mum all alone with no help from my brother, or Dad.

"Actually Mum, I'll help you make it."

"They're not veggie are they, your friends? I don't think much of this is veggie is it?" She asked, gesturing towards the frying pan of bacon, sausages, and black pudding.

"They're not veggie, this'll be fine for them. Thanks Mum."

"Do I need to nip out, get a bit more cheese and fruit, just in case?" She paused as she looked at me. "Will they want the foreign?"

"This'll be fine, don't worry. You have met them before, they're not just random people I've picked up at the festival. I've known them for ages."

Some for longer than others.

I made four cups of tea, asked Mum if Paul and Dad were around for tea, and then added another cup for Dad. Apparently Paul was round a friend's house, so wouldn't be requiring my tea making or Mum's breakfast making skills.

I took the tea to Grace's room first, waiting at the door after I'd knocked.

"Come in, but only if you can offer me some top flight man action," Grace shouted.

I pushed the door, handed her the mug and knelt next to the bed.

"Whose is the other one?" she asked, looking at the mug of tea in my hand.

"Jo. I've not seen him yet this morning."

"You're not scared of him, after his strop last night, are you?"

"No, no, he's not really a morning person, so I wanted to

leave him as long as I could. Thought I'd come and see you first." I looked around the room, which hadn't been decorated since the mid eighties, when the house was built. A variety of flowery wallpapers and borders competed for attention on the walls. An old wooden desk was strewn with Dad's papers, computer and enormous dot matrix printer. Grace's clothes hung over Dad's twirley leather office chair. "Vile, I don't know how people live like this. I'd have it all gone, a few trips to the DIY shop and it'd be modern and fresh again."

"You wouldn't even know where the nearest DIY shop is, never mind how to put up the wallpaper. I'm sure it's fine for your dad. And don't change the subject. Is he prone to the odd strop, or has he never done anything like this before?"

I thought back to Australia, debated whether to edit my response to Grace, then remembered my emails to her during the trip. Apart from the last one, when I'd been very honest about what Jo had done with Duncan, I'd always played things down, made a joke of it. Now, I'd have to tell her the truth. But what a shame, what a waste of yesterday's fun. It was so important for Grace to like Jo, I wanted her to understand why we were such good friends. I could still hear her voice when I'd cancelled our date to see Jo.

"Earth to Kieran! Hello Kieran. I asked you a question. You were miles away then. Anywhere nice?"

"Just thinking."

Grace sipped her tea. "He'll be fine. Give him his tea, kiss and make up, it'll be fine. And if that fails, tell him we'll all watch *The Sound of Music* together after breakfast, if that doesn't bring a smile to his miserable gay face, nothing will. Never fails. Trust me, they don't call me the best alternative to the real Claire Rayner for nothing do they?"

"Who calls you that?"

"Never you mind."

"Are you going or just hanging around here all morning?" Grace paused. "You *are* afraid of him aren't you? You're shit scared he's going to have another dramatic strop right here in your house in front of your parents and you don't want to make a scene, so you're going to apologise."

"It was his favourite band. Maybe you were a *bit* harsh."

Grace sat up in bed. "It was *Martine McCutcheon*. He dragged us to three different places, each one closer and closer through the crowd. We'd humoured him enough. We put up with more than enough. Don't you apologise on my behalf. I didn't do anything wrong. I stand by what I said, and I'd tell him the same again. Don't let him walk over you. Stand up to him. Do you want me to speak to him? I'll put something on and come with you."

"No, I'm fine. I'm going to speak to him now." I closed Grace's door behind me and walked slowly upstairs to Jo's room, took a deep breath and knocked.

There was no answer, so I knocked again. After a short pause I heard Jo's voice through the door saying yes. I took this as an invitation to enter, so opened the door, and walked in, holding the tea. "Morning, I made you this. Mum's making us a fry up now. It'll be ready in a bit. She was worried you and Grace might be veggie." I handed Jo the tea and looked around the room. "It's not too bad in here. Black walls—Paul wanted this as a room for his clothes when he was going through a heavy metal phase. Better than Grace's room, it looks like a branch of Laura Ashley's exploded in there with the remnants of PC World."

Jo took a sip of the tea, put the mug on the floor next to the bed and slipped down under the duvet again.

"Did you sleep alright? It's pretty quiet in here isn't it? At least you're not above the kitchen, Mum woke me up this morning. Just the study beneath you." I looked for inspiration around the room, running out of things to say in this one-sided conversation. "Come on. You can't still be pissed off about yesterday, the Martine McCutcheon song? I thought we had such a good time, you can't tell me this is going to spoil it all. You saw them didn't you? You had a dance in those tents, didn't you? We spent the day together buying rainbow coloured tat, you finally got to meet Grace, and liked her didn't you?"

Jo looked away as I mentioned Grace's name. I wished I'd brought my tea upstairs, this was going to be harder than I'd thought.

"It's Grace is it? Now we're making progress. What's wrong with her? Ok, so she was a bit harsh, but nothing I wouldn't have said if she wasn't there. You dragged us through that crowd like we were a couple of dolls. Grace had had enough. She's allowed to tell you that isn't she? Look, she suggested we all watch "The Sound of Music" after breakfast—unless you've got to get home."

I noticed Jo sit up in bed at the mention of the musical. We had movement, but still no sound though.

"Grace said she's sorry if she upset you. She asked me to tell you. Now can we make up and move on. *Climb every mountain* isn't that what Julie Andrews says?"

"*Ford every stream* too. Cooked breakfast you say? And Julie Andrews, in her award winning performance?"

I nodded.

"Fabulous darling. I'll jump in the shower, and be down in a bit." Jo jumped out of bed, kissed me on the cheek and walked towards the door.

"Oh, and Jo, probably best not to mention anything about this to Grace. I think she's a bit embarrassed about the whole thing, she wants to put it behind her. It'll be best if we don't say anything to her about this. Make it easier to continue with this *getting to know all about* each other phase of your friendship."

"Debora Kerr couldn't have said it better. I'm glad it's all sorted. I understand that Grace is quite outspoken, and that's fine, but I didn't think I'd really done anything wrong. Surely you wanted to get a better view of the band too? Well, all I did was help you with that, very reasonable and helpful if you ask me. It's a shame she got herself in such a state. Still, it's all done now. Just a little blip. I'm looking forward to getting to know her more. Anything else, or shall I see you downstairs?"

"No, nothing else." I walked downstairs empty handed. Never mind a cup of tea, I could have done with something much stronger for *that* conversation. *What sort of tug of war was I getting myself into between two of my best friends? And why?*

I walked to my bedroom, collected my video of *The Sound of Music*, which Jo had bought me, and continued downstairs to find Mum in the kitchen putting the finishing touches to a breakfast spread which would have made most medium priced hotel chains jealous.

"Mum, you didn't need to go to all this trouble."

"I've told you before, I'm not having your friends coming round here thinking we're tight or not looking after them. Whenever I went round Dad's parents' house when we was courting, they put on a good spread. These things count. People remember them. They might not say they do, but I know they do. I can still remember the first meal Dad's mum made me when we were courting. Shepherd's pie, with grated cheese on top. They also had two gravy boats one of cheese sauce and one of gravy. It was *to die for*. So no, I'm not having your friends casting *inspersions* on this family when they go home." Mum paused, surveyed the table. "Can you call them, tell them it's ready?"

I shouted from the bottom of the stairs that it was ready, in true family tradition.

Until I met Grace, I'd believed all families communicated like this: standing in separate rooms, shouting to each other, in a well-meaning way, but all the same, shouting. Dad stayed in his study, Mum shouted from her kitchen, I stayed in my bedroom, and Paul sat in the living room. It was only when I went round to Grace's house I realised we were the exception to the rule. Each member of her family walked around the house to talk to each other. Grace's mother gently walked upstairs and knocked on her bedroom door to announce that dinner was served. I felt like I was in a costume drama from the eighteen hundreds, expecting a cook to bang a dinner gong and a butler to usher us to the table.

Now, Jo arrived in the kitchen first and sat at the table. Grace joined us a few minutes later and took the last free seat, opposite Jo. I noticed Jo smile at Grace, who replied with a smile which I noted didn't reach her eyes. *Fasten your seatbelts.*

"Before we start, I'd like to propose a toast to our lovely host, Mrs D," Jo said as he raised his cup of tea to the centre of the table. "Mrs D, for the breakfast to end all breakfasts."

Everyone joined in the toast, raising their glasses of orange juice or cups of tea and repeating Jo's slightly over the top toast.

"That's very kind of you Jo, haven't you got such good

manners." Mum blushed. "Are you listening to this Kieran? You could learn a thing or two from your friend here. Come on everyone start eating, it'll get cold, don't stand on ceremony."

We all started to eat, and not to be out-done, as Grace took a bite of her sausage she said, "This certainly is the nicest sausage I've had in a long time Mrs Donovan. Where did you get it from?" Grace shot Jo a look as she finished her sentence.

"Thank you Grace. Waitrose, they were on offer, two packs for a fiver, so I bought four," Mum replied. "You two can come again any time. Kieran, I could get used to this. Normally no-one says a word when I put the food on the table. All I get is a grunt, and that's it. Nothing. But with you two, it's a bit different."

We finished breakfast and keen to avoid any more of this impromptu best friend show, I left the table. "I'm going to set up the film, so it's ready for us in a bit. Come upstairs when you've finished." I looked at Grace and Jo as they chewed their meals.

"See you soon" Grace replied.

"I'll be up in a bit, but I'm going to help your Mum with the plates first," Jo replied, not wishing to miss this opportunity to shine in front of Grace.

"Me too, that way it'll be quicker, see you soon," Grace added quickly, giving Jo a look across the table.

"I'm spoilt for choice here," Mum replied, looking at my two friends as they glared at each other across the table. "I could get used to this."

I left the room and went up to my bedroom to sort out the video. I arranged a seat either side of my bed, and sat on my bed once the video was in the player. I didn't want Grace and Jo sitting next to each other, who knew what could happen with them both behaving like this? Hannah would sort them both out, but she still wasn't back from work.

Grace was first to arrive.

"What the hell do you think you're playing at?" I hissed.

"Nothing. I can't bear to sit back and watch him charming your Mum like he's charmed everyone else. I know what he's really like, and I'm not being taken in by his crap. All this 'can I help with the plates Mrs D, here's a toast to the best breakfast maker, Mrs D' crap, it's all just for show."

"That's a bit harsh. He's just being nice to Mum, he wants to help her."

"Why wasn't he nice like that yesterday with me and you at Pride, why did he behave like a celebrity who hadn't been given their rider correctly? Why did he drag us through the crowds like a pair of dolls until I told him to stop?"

Grace's question hung in the room, like a cobweb which you've meant to dust away for a while, but which has ultimately been ignored by your laziness and ignorance.

I spoke first to fill the silence, "Please, for me, can you play nicely with him? I can't bear all this tension, I feel like I'm being torn apart between the two of you."

"Ok, but what happened to his mood this morning after I spoke to him at Pride yesterday? What was all that performance about?"

"No performance. He was just tired, and wanted to leave us some space together after you told him you didn't like crowds. He was being considerate actually."

"Right, I can see what he did there. Ok. For you. I'll be nice, for you. I mean, two hours of a musical, how wrong can it really go?"

"Exactly. Thank you. I appreciate it."

Jo bounded into my room like an excited puppy. "Appreciate what? What has Grace done now, pray tell?" He cupped a hand behind his ear in an exaggeratedly camp way.

"We were talking about how she'd helped Mum clear the breakfast things," I replied. "That was all."

"I see," Jo said. "It was a good idea of mine wasn't it? I thought it would be nice to show her how much I appreciated her cooking. It was good of Grace to join in too."

Grace nodded and smiled, again it didn't reach the eyes. "Are we watching this, or are we sitting about mincing all morning? I don't know about you two poofs, but I've got things to do, people to see, and I've got to get back home by four-of-the-early-afternoon-o'clock if that's Ok, Kieran?"

"Of course, I can definitely get you home by then. Let's get on with it."

"You know why we're watching this do you Grace?" Jo looked at her; all puffed up like a pigeon.

"I thought if you put more than two gay men together in a room, without dance music, *The Sound of Music* just started to play in the background," she replied then laughed nervously.

Nothing from Jo.

She took a breath. "No, but I'd love to hear why."

"I directed a production of *Beautiful Thing* at college recently and there's a scene where the mum and her boyfriend watch *The Sound of Music* while the two boys share a bed, and discover they both fancy each other. The scene with the two boys has *Doe a Deer* playing in the background."

"I see," Grace replied, pursing her lips. "I thought it had *Sixteen going on Seventeen* in the background, but maybe I'm wrong."

"I think you're right Grace," I said, looking at them both.

"That's the song I remember playing in the background."

Jo frowned, looked at me and replied, "I think we're both right. Are we watching this then?"

I pressed play and we watched Julie Andrews running across fields in the Austrian countryside wearing a nun's habit. Never before in the course of gay campness, had something so camp, been watched so many times, by so many people.

We slowly became absorbed in the plot, occasionally making comments on the characters and music. Jo thought Ralph looked similar to a friend we knew from The Duke.

When the Baroness appeared for the first time Grace commented, "I bet she doesn't suffer fools gladly does she, just look at her clothes, she's like a pre-war Cruella De Ville, not in cartoon obviously."

We laughed and the tension was finally broken, I'd brushed away the lingering cobweb.

I took Grace home, allowing plenty of time for her 'people to see and things to do'. She was quiet in the car on the journey.

"Who are these people you've got to see, and what are these things you're doing this afternoon?" I asked, after a particularly long silence.

"Nothing much. I'm starting the next edition of Grace Times and need to get ready for some work experience at The News next week. I'm gathering in my previous articles to show them how talented and worthy of a proper journalistic story I am, rather than endless "Not much happens in Gosport" and "Dog found tied to lamp post in Cosham" type stories. Imagine if I write the next story about a murder in Paulsgrove? That would be great." She paused. "Obviously, not for the person who'd been murdered, but you know what I mean."

I nodded, pleased we were back to our usual form.

Chapter 12

Grace hugged me in the car as she said goodbye. I watched her as she walked to her front door, she didn't turn around and wave like she usually did. She walked straight into the house carrying her bag and closed the door behind her.

I drove home, ready to drop Jo back in the other direction to his car in Salisbury. As far as he was concerned, Pride had been a complete success and he looked forward to the next time he could meet Grace.

***

The summer passed and I attended a variety of youth group and friends' parties and BBQs across Hampshire, each time carefully coordinating the use of my combat trousers with Jo. I saw Grace a few more times as she prepared to go to university like me, each time she was more nervous about leaving home and the security she'd built herself. Hannah and I worked hard at the hospital, me frantically saving for university, and Hannah spending every spare penny on music, clothes and drink. Hannah eventually moved back home after her mum's peace-making efforts, no apology from Himself, but now Hannah spent as little time as possible at home, which wasn't too hard between her 60 hour week at the hospital and going out four or five nights a week. She had managed to take burning the candle at both ends to a whole new level.

"Never mind burning it at both ends, I've snapped the candle in half and lit all four ends" Hannah explained when I visited her one evening between long days at the hospital, as we were about to meet Jo in town for the third night running.

Despite my initial worries about Hannah speaking a bit too plainly to Jo, they got on like the proverbial house on fire. It was the perfect bit of friends combining for me—I saw two of my best friends at the same time. On reflection this was probably due to the fact that they only ever met in the various gay pubs and clubs in Southampton, and had to speak over the noise of the latest dance version of *Kylie* or *Steps*. This meant it was quite hard to get into a deep and meaningful, and as such there wasn't really much to disagree with on either side. Both were getting what they wanted: time out with me, dancing and drinking. "Happy days" as Hannah often said.

Once I tried to broach the subject of Jo's behaviour at Pride with Hannah. She'd looked at me and said, "You can't seriously tell me you're surprised at what he did can you? Look, as long as he stands his rounds, I'm not arsed," Hannah summarised, while Jo was at the bar. "He seems a good laugh to me, a bit full of himself, but that's not a crime is it?"

My parents gradually grew to know Jo and Kev, each time asking them more questions, conversations becoming easier, getting used to their presence as we met at my house before our next adventure. Kev brought his car round one Saturday and as promised, under Dad's watchful eye we set to work: Dad stuck under the bonnet while Kev and I cleaned it inside and out until its original colour shone through—light brown as it turned out! "If you want help buying a new one, you know where I am," Dad said over dinner afterwards. Kev replied how much it meant to him, since his Mum was as useless at cars as him, so they never knew where to start.

Jo soon learned which topics impressed my parents, and merrily wheeled them out each time he visited. I'd walk into the kitchen to find him and Mum deep in conversation about what his next hairstyle should be, as Mum showed him the latest cuts from her *Hair* magazine. Each time Jo turned up in a different old car—"She's gone, gone to the great scrap yard in the sky, poor thing"—he asked Dad to give it the once over, and they talked easily about the new car while I finished getting ready. I overheard Dad talking to Mum about my new friends, "Bit arty farty sometimes, nice boys once you get to know them", and my chest puffed up with pride, *proper gay pride* this time.

As the summer flew by I found it harder to fit Grace into my diary. Since *The Sound of Music* morning I'd not friends combined Grace and Jo again. I couldn't bear the feeling of tension between them, and the feeling I had of being pulled apart by both their different needs and requests. They seemed to bring the worst out in each other, so I resolved to keep them apart at least for the time being. I agreed with what Grace had done at Pride, but wasn't sure if it was worth the fallout from Jo afterwards. Surely, it was easier to go along with Jo if it meant avoiding repeats of his Pride performance? That seemed like a small price to pay for the fun I was having with Jo for the rest of the time. I trusted Hannah's judgement of people and she thought Jo was a good laugh, and that was good enough for me.

Thirteen

Late September 1999

Although Jo was in proud possession of a letter confirming he could defer his place at Central School of Speech and Drama for a year, he'd done nothing to prepare for the ever approaching September when he was due to start. I later learned that his mum had called while he was in Australia to confirm his place, but Jo hadn't read any of the paperwork and simply got into his mum's car—which unlike his was strong enough and large enough for the trip to London. He took two suitcases of clothes, four bin bags of shoes and a cardboard box of CDs and videos and was driven to north London. He was very pleased about getting into such a prestigious university to study his dream subject—drama—and enjoyed telling our friends from The Duke, Out! and anyone else who would listen about it.

I had checked with Kings College about my deferred place once a month during summer and had started packing my things pretty much as soon as I got back from Australia. I had a pile in the corner of my bedroom mentally marked 'university', into which I placed various items of clothing, CDs, videos and other essential items—including a complete set of *Teletubbies*, a poster of *Steps* (which Hannah had bought me while at one of her many concerts), and a variety of framed pictures of me with my friends, new and old. All of which I knew I couldn't live without when I was away from home.

After much deliberation I'd settled on English and cultural studies. For a short while I had toyed with the idea of European Studies at a far flung university in the north east. This was quickly deleted off the list of options as soon as Hannah pointed out to me that it was far too far away. "You've lived your whole live in the south, you've never even been further north than Essex, to visit family, and now you're thinking of going to the north east for uni? Are you mad? You won't be able to come back and visit home at the weekends. And it's really cold up there, *see that later*." Hannah's damming phrase for something you'd never want to think about again, never mind later, told me exactly how foolish I would have been to ignore her advice.

The European Studies part had been knocked on the head after talking to Grace. A bit of research had uncovered the fact that the course would not involve learning about the culture of European countries, which I would have found interesting, but in fact revolved around politics and the history of Europe. Neither of which were subjects I'd had much contact with so far. Grace's questioning helped make my mind up when she asked me a few select questions. "Ok, Mister History and Politics, do you know who Bismarck was?"

"I've heard people talking about sinking the Bismarck, so I'd assume it was a ship, something which probably sank in the war," I replied proud of my skills of deduction.

"Not quite."

"Ok, so maybe it was a boat before the war?"

"He was the leader of Germany in the nineteenth century."

"Nothing to do with a boat?"

"They named a boat after him yes, but rest assured you won't be learning about the boat if you go to that uni."

So my mind was made up, English and Cultural Studies at Kings College in London. I would be able to come home at weekends, back to my very own Porpoise Spit, to see Mum and Dad, Hannah, Kev and others who hadn't left Hampshire.

Now, Mum dropped me off at my halls of residence and helped me settle into my small room, with an en-suite bathroom no less! She took me to the local supermarket to stock my cupboard with pasta and tins of beans before reluctantly hugging me goodbye and walking slowly to her car. I'd debated taking Priscilla, but realised I'd have no use for her once I was in London and feared for her safety as much as my own.

Mum's relief to find her car still in one piece, despite being parked in a not too nice corner of south east London, was masked by her sadness and reluctance to leave me again.

"If you need anything, just ring me. Are you sure you've got enough food? I can easily nip back and get you some more pasta, or would you like a curry or something? Do you know how to make things from the little cook book I bought you? I can show you the macaroni cheese recipe if you want—it's dead simple, but you have to remember to buy the strong cheddar, and I sometimes stir in a bit of Dairylea. Did we get you enough cheese?" She paused and looked at me stood on the pavement waving her off.

"I'll be fine. Mum, I travelled round Australia for months, I think I'll be alright in London. It's only two hours if I want to come home. It's not like it's a different culture is it?"

She looked at a group of students walking past me to their halls of residence. "Yes but you never know. I'm not being funny, but you can't be too careful, and it's not about skin colour though is it. It's a big place, London, isn't it, and you've got to look after yourself. Keep your things safe and look after yourself."

"I'll make friends soon. And in the meantime I've got Jo, I told you he's in London too, so we can look after each other."

"Yes you did. Well just make sure you do—look after each other. If not I'll be having words with his mum." She wiped her eyes with a tissue from the car. "Must be the dust, I'm not used to all this traffic and dust."

"Bye Mum, I'll call you in a few days. You'd better go before the traffic gets worse."

"You've definitely got the new mobile phone haven't you? So you can use it for emergencies to call us."

"Yes, I've put your number into it already."

She started her car, then wiped her eyes again. "You gave me the number for the phone in your room didn't you?"

"On that bit of paper in your handbag."

"Silly me. I remember." Her car pulled out of the cul-de-sac onto the main road full of south east London traffic fighting its way across London. I watched her car as it disappeared into the traffic.

I smiled as I thought about Dad helping me get there, in his own way. He couldn't settle me in with Mum, as he was working and couldn't get the time off. Instead, he'd helped me choose the course: "Think about what you're really interested in, and what you want to do when you're older. Nowadays there's all sorts of courses, it's not just maths and English." Together we looked through the university prospectuses, studying the course content in detail. Gradually I narrowed it down to a shortlist of three: Kings College, Cardiff and Sussex. Once, I strayed from his area of expertise, and asked him which of the three had the best social scenes: he'd shrugged, and instead replied that was up to me, but they all had good rankings in the *Times Good University Guide* he'd recently read. Eventually together, we'd arrived at my final choice, and now I was stood there, in front of that choice, ready to start a new part of my life. Dad's universal advice ran through my head: *the more you put into it, the more you'll get out.*

I was just me, Jo and London, and three years of university together, and I couldn't wait for it to start.

After a few days of meet and greet events at Kings, I felt if I had to tell one more person which A levels I'd studied, and where I grew up, I would run away screaming from the daintily arranged nibbles. I hadn't heard much from Jo since we moved to London, apart from the odd text message. His parents had bought him a newer mobile phone for university and agreed to continue paying the bill. Dad, for the sake of technology and Mum for the sake of missing me, had bought me my first mobile phone.

Dad had said, "If you think I'm paying for Kieran to chat to his mates all day and facing a hundred quid bill, you can think again. Even mine's got a cap on it, and I use it for work. You're not going to use it like that. It's very easy, one call to the mobile company and it's done."

Mum, excited about being able to reach me whenever and wherever I was, had taped my mobile number to the front of the phone book, next to the house phone.

Now, I was lying on my bed, watching a video of The Creek as respite from the recent series of meet and greets. I wanted to spend time with people I knew well. My mobile phone bleeped indicating I'd received a text message.

Hi, missing you, fancy going to Uni of London Union for lgbtsoc tonight at 8? Love Jo xx

I dialled Jo's number. "Where's this then?"

"Russell Square or something, there's a Tube station right next to it. Come on, let's see what London has to offer in comparison to Southampton!"

"As long as it's not full of, what were they called, when we went to that pub in Soho for Pride?" I looked at the single bed by the window, desk with my TV and video recorder and a little door which led to my very own ensuite bathroom.

"Bears. No Kieran it's not another bear bar, it's just some gay students, just like us, trying to make some friends. And who knows you may even meet your Prince Charming. And if it's shit we'll go somewhere else, I'm sure Soho can't be that far away, and we can catch up on our first few days here."

"Ok."

We made arrangements for where and when to meet and I put the phone down. My stomach immediately felt like a tight knot and I felt sick. I put up some posters of *Depeche Mode* and my favourite boyband of the moment, *A1*, which I'd taken from home.

I waited outside the front of the University of London building, which was a large art deco structure near to Russell Square station. Art deco—my mind immediately returned to Brad and I was flooded with a mixture of emotions from sadness to lust, all at once. I had allowed plenty of time to find it, and negotiate the Tube, so arrived early, more time to think about Brad. Jo turned up fifteen minutes *after* our meeting time, smiling, dressed in a shiny purple shirt, baggy grey combat trousers and medium high platform trainers. I immediately felt under-dressed in my orange t shirt, black leather jacket and jeans.

We linked arms and walked through the door. I looked around to check no-one had seen us as we left the pavement.

"Kieran, don't worry, it's London, everyone's gay anyway." He put on a girlie American voice. "We're not in Kansas now Toto."

The hall was filled with LGB, and don't forget T, students from all the University of London's colleges, and a few more besides. Strictly speaking Jo didn't attend the University of London, and I hadn't bothered to ask him how he'd wangled us invites to this. I knew what his response would be, something involving a borrowed student ID card from a new friend, or the catch all, "It'll be fine" with a wave of his hand, which seemed to get him out of most situations.

We stood by the bar and Jo ordered us drinks. He handed me mine and I took a nervous and deliberately slow sip, looking around the large wood panelled room at the same time. Everyone seemed to be in little cliques, small groups of three to five students gathered in circles. They all seemed to be talking about the same hilarious thing, as every now and then the whole group laughed as someone reached a punch line. Jo stood next to me sipping his cocktail—he'd read in Attitude that cocktails were the sign of a sophisticated man, so from now on he said he'd always drink cocktails.

"What's that?" I asked, nodding to his blue firework of a drink, adorned with small umbrellas, fruit and twirls of fruit peel.

"It's a Blue Lagoon. Fabulous isn't it? Everyone who sees me will know that I'm sophisticated and mature. I'll have a few more sips and we can agree a plan of attack."

"What's it like?"

"Vile."

After a few minutes of quietly sipping our drinks Jo looked at me and asked, "Right, what are we going to do? I'm not sitting here all night. I want to meet some new people. No-one's coming up to us here, we'll just have to go to them."

"But they're all in groups, we can't just…"

"Bollocks, follow me, we'll find a group which has the highest number of cute guys and just take it from there."

"But what will we say?"

Jo was gone, so I quickly grabbed my drink and followed him as he cut through the crowd. He dismissed groups as we walked by with a "nah" or "too many girls" or "I didn't know it was fancy dress!" Eventually we stopped at a group of two men, a few years older than us, both drinking bottles of beer, not touching each other, talking quietly and looking around the room to see who else was having more fun than them. Jo leant in between them and said, "Excuse me, but don't I know you?"

They both shook their heads replying that they weren't sure. Both had strong southern Irish accents, which immediately made me think of having sex with a farm hand in a barn. *I really did need to get 'some' and quick.*

"I'm sure I've seen you before. Do you live near Southampton?" Jo stood between them now, pointing at their faces.

They shook their heads.

"Have you ever been to The Duke, in Salisbury?"

More shaking heads.

"Were you in that film…what's it called?" He snapped his fingers and closed his eyes, in mock concentration. "The one with the man, and his friend. And they live in the house…"

"With the blue door?" I finished, starting to enjoy myself.

"Yes, on the corner. And they live there, and there's something about a war they go away to, or maybe it was a piano."

The guy who looked like he'd just run through Cyber Dog with glue on his body turned to Jo and smiled, understanding where this was going. "Sure, that was us, wasn't it Sean? Always there for a laugh. Fabulous so we were. Do you want our autographs?"

Without missing a beat Jo replied, "I don't collect autographs, but a kiss would be a good start, unless you two are together."

Cyber Dog looked at the other man, and moved one step away. "Together, I don't think so, we're just friends."

Jo looked at Cyber Dog, his eyes glinting. "So, how about a kiss? Or if you're shy you could buy us drink if you like. You looked like you could do with some company, stood there looking around the room to see who else was worth talking to. Well now you've found them, we've rescued you."

Cyber Dog leant over to kiss Jo's cheek.

"Now that we're intimately acquainted, I feel like I should know your name." He shook first Cyber Dog's hand, then his friend's. "So come on. I'm Jo, this is my friend Kieran—no we're not together, *eugh* the thought of it, it'd be like shagging your brother. What's your name?"

"I'm Andrew O'Shea, and this is Sean Hughes."

"Alright?" Sean said and put his hand out for me to shake. I stared into his deep blue eyes, looked down at his square jaw covered in a few days of stubble and noticed a torso and arms which only come from physical work rather than obsessively pumping iron in the gym, and I immediately and totally fell in love.

I took Sean's hand and shook it, something I wasn't used to doing with other gay friends. All my friends kissed on at least one, if not two cheeks to greet, but this somehow made him more exciting.

Andrew was studying hospitality at a former polytechnic in north London. Sean was studying to be a vet at one of the colleges in London.

Andrew explained they'd known each other since the start of secondary school at eleven. They'd grown up in a little village an hour or so from Dublin, before moving to somewhere north of north London at fourteen. Their dads came to London (for as far as they were concerned north of north London was still London) for building work, and never went back. "I thought we'd out grow each other when we got older. Turns out, we were both a couple of queers, so we just stuck together. So here we are. Our da's did us a favour, moving to London, soon as we realised we were gay, we had it all on our doorsteps. Imagine if we'd told them that, when they came home, dirty boots and hard hats an all!"

I looked at Andrew and quickly allowed myself another glance at Sean's arms. "Did you decide to both come to London together to study, or did it just happen?"

"Once we realised we were gay, we were always on trains to London and in the Nellie pubs and clubs. Going to uni here's like coming home!"

"After what we'd been through together," Sean said, staring at me with those beautiful blue eyes. "I couldn't imagine doing it without him." He looked into the distance and I noticed a sadness in his eyes. He took a sip of his beer. "Who wants a drink?"

Sean went to the bar and Andrew leant in towards us as if he was going to tell us a terrible dark secret about Sean. I braced myself for the worst.

"Poor soul, he's after having his heart broken. His man of two years dumped him at the beginning of the summer, so I've been looking after him a bit. And he wouldn't admit to me looking after him, it's normally Sean who does the looking after. Likes to protect you see. Don't tell him I've told you. He's not normally this shy, but as he's been burned he's keeping a distance from men for the moment." He paused, obviously thinking about what he'd said and checking to see if Sean was back from the bar yet. "Anyway, shall we go somewhere else after this round, I'm a bit bored of this, London's got a lot more to offer than this old place."

"Exactly what I said to Kieran. And he didn't even want to come out tonight. Did you know what I was doing when I said I thought I knew you?"

"I was just glad to talk to someone else," Andrew replied. "I thought we'd been here hours, but when I checked my watch it was only twenty minutes. Sean was just looking around and didn't have much to say. It was a miracle I got him to come out at all really. Your mate seems to like him."

"Maybe a bit yeah." Jo winked at me.

My heart leaped for joy. This was it, this was my Prince Charming. I actually thought I could hear church bells ringing and had to stop myself asking him what colour he wanted the bedroom to be. *Deep breath.*

Sean returned with our drinks. "I got you some crisps in

case you're hungry and I hope Archers and lemonade's ok. It was either that, or fifteen kinds of glow in the dark alcopop, and I couldn't call you, so I thought…"

You thought I was butch enough for Archer s and lemonade, but not alcopops—should I feel offended? "That's fine, thanks." I paused, thinking about what he'd just said, immediately getting over the campness slight. "Are you asking me for my phone number?" I took the drink from Sean.

"Only so I can check what drinks are on offer at the bar. Make sure I get you the right one."

"I see."

Bingo!

We went on to Heaven, a nightclub under some railway arches near Charing Cross station. Sean sat next to me and was in the middle of telling me about his ex-boyfriend:

"We'd been together about two years, and I'd always been there for him. His parents split up, and I was there. His brother sending him abusive texts, I told him to ignore them. The whole time. Don't get me wrong, we had good times too—we used to laugh so much my cheeks ached. When we went out people used to say we were like a comedy double act. So it wasn't all bad no?" He shrugged and looked up at me, from where he'd been staring at the ground. "Then my auntie dies of cancer. Just like that, suddenly out of the blue. One minute she's going to the shop to order a set of curtains for her living room, next thing my cousin's picking them up and her mum's dead. I didn't know what to do. No one had died in my family before. Well they had, but not since I'd been alive." He laughed nervously.

"I went to bits. Couldn't go to college. Stopped sleeping at night, stayed up watching TV. Wanted to go out all the time.

Me and my auntie were really close you see. She used to come round all the time. She came over to visit me mum and didn't want to go back. In the end she got her own place near us in north London. She didn't have any sons, just two daughters, and they'd told her she couldn't have any more children. Don't get me wrong, I love my mum, but this auntie and me, we had something special. I used to take her with me and the ex to gay pubs and bars in London. Loved a bit of cabaret did Auntie Lynne. Mum was interested, listened to our stories when we saw her for Sunday lunch, but I'd never ask her to come out with us. Never. Most of the time Auntie Lynne wouldn't let us go out without taking her along too." He laughed again, this time allowing himself a smile.

"Suddenly that was all over. No more nights out, no more laughing at the drag queens and saying she could do better. No more singing karaoke to *I've Never Been To Me* by *Charlene*. Cos she was gone, in a box, dead. With her curtains from Marks and Spencer waiting to be collected by my cousin.

"My ex didn't know what to do. He just let me go out all the time. He didn't call me to ask how I was, didn't come round to my parents to see me. Andrew did all that. Everything my ex should have done." He looked up at Andrew who was sat getting intimately acquainted with Jo.

"And that was when I realised—it had all been one way. You're supposed to be there for each other, not just one propping up the other one. All the laughs, all the comedy double act, it was all because I was there for him. He didn't really give me anything back. Shame it took me two years to realise. Suppose that's when you realise who your friends are. That's when me and Andrew got really close. Not like *that*, never—it would be like sleeping with my brother. No, just there for each other. He was there calling me, coming round, checking I didn't lose it. My ex just drifted away, I suppose I was too much of a mess, too hard to deal with. He stopped calling me, stopped coming round. Soon it had been a few months and I'd not heard from him. So I didn't bother calling him. I'd managed without him up to then, so why bother? No big fireworks, no big row, the relationship just died. Jesus, Mary and Joseph, sorry, that was a bit heavy, sorry Kieran. I've only just met you and I've told you all this. You must think I'm a right mess. Do you want a drink?"

I looked into his deep blue eyes, glanced at his jaw, covered in stubble and wrote myself a strong internal memo to not lean forward and touch his face. I wiped something wet from my eyes—obviously the smoke from the club, definitely not his story.

"Kieran, hello, do you want a drink? Are you ok? Do you want to go outside for some fresh air?"

"Yes, same again. That sounds nice, if you know where to go for some air, I think the smoke's affecting my eyes."

"Ok, follow me." Sean stood and took my hand.

I looked at Jo and Andrew who were snogging each other's faces off, tapped Jo's shoulder so he saw I was leaving and followed Sean.

A few hours later we left Heaven, holding hands with our respective partners. Jo and Andrew enthusiastically kissing each other at every opportunity while Sean and I gently held hands like extras in a costume drama. I much preferred my version to Jo's alternative.

We worked out we had to wait at different corners of Trafalgar Square for our respective night buses.

"I've got to go over there," I said pointing to the far corner of the square.

"This is me," Sean replied looking at the bus stop where we stood, surrounded by a crowd of people in different states of messiness waiting to be ferried back to their corner of London.

"You've got my number…" I felt my mobile phone in my pocket.

"So I can check which drink you want at the bar." Sean held my hands.

"So, I'll see you then."

"I'll give you a call, take care, Kieran, I've had a grand time. Sorry if it got a bit heavy back there. You're so easy to talk to, and it just…"

I leant to hug him and felt him kiss my cheek, so I responded with a kiss on his cheek. "Right, bye, Sean. Jo, are you ready?"

Jo came up for air, looked at me and said, "Ready when you are."

We walked towards our bus stop, waving as we left. I sat on the night bus and checked Sean's mobile number in my phone, treasuring it like a diamond ring.

"Don't even think about texting him tonight" Jo said, looking at me staring at my phone.

"I wasn't going to, I'm just looking."

"Liar! I know you. Soon that familiar scent of Obsession by Disco Kieran will be making a comeback. And I'll be ready for it."

I knew I had to build some bridges with Grace, I just wasn't sure where to start. I wondered how she was settling into her university life. I waited for Grace's email in response to my latest dramatic episode. She replied the next day.

From: g.465.english-ugrads@cambs.ac.uk

Late September 1999

To: k.donovan.901@kings.ac.uk

Dear Disco Kieran,

Sounds like you're having a great time in that London with Jo. This Sean sounds gorgeous, you must let me know if anything progresses with him. In the absence of me getting any, I'm happy to take what crumbs (even if they are vicarious gay crumbs) are thrown at me. If there is any knee trembling man on man action, I want to hear about it—ok?

How are you finding getting around in London? I've always found the Tube a bit of a mystery especially the way that the tube map doesn't show where the stations really are. I went to London with a school trip years ago and we spent half an hour getting from one station to somewhere else, and it was only after speaking to a proper Londoner (and before you ask, he wasn't dressed as a Pearly King or Queen and necking jellied eels by the bucket load, but I did know he was local) he told me that I could have walked between the two stations in less than five minutes.

I've settled into my room in halls—I can't help thinking I'm in a posh hotel as I have an en-suite bathroom. I keep expecting someone to bring round room service for dinner. Sadly they don't and I am working my way through the student cook book which Mother bought me. So far it seems to consist of a lot of pasta and potatoes, which is fine by me.

Cambridge seems pretty good as far as cities go I suppose. My halls are about twenty minutes walk from the city centre, which is perfect for me as it's too short to get a bus, and makes me walk, hence fulfilling one of my new year's resolutions (albeit nine months late, but who's counting!) Cambridge seems large enough to have an interesting variety of places to visit (so far I've concentrated on the local pubs and am getting quite well versed with various ales in half pints, which I find much easier to manage and less likely to result in me wiping sick off my boots than when drinking spirits). Turns out that working in the pub as a "hostess" was the perfect training for my new found hobby of drinking! It's also small enough as a city to walk (or stagger) around quite easily—hence the question about the Tube.

I introduced myself to my flat mates on the first night. We were all telling each other what we'd done before coming to uni. This one girl, who looked like she could be a good prop in a rugby match, said she'd helped to build a well and irrigation system for a village in Africa during her gap year. She politely asked what I'd done in my gap year and my response that I'd worked as a hostess in a pub, done some shifts in my local library and volunteered on the local newspaper made me want to end it with "I'll get my coat" a la Fast Show. *Instead I offered to make a round of tea (I find being able to make a good round of it often dissipates tension and kills time when a conversation is flagging a bit, allowing it to breathe new life and regain focus).*

On the second day I marched up to the Students Union and demanded to speak to someone who worked on the uni paper. It felt like that scene in Withnail and I, *when he says he demands to have some booze. Unfortunately, I didn't have the lovely Richard E Grant next to me...sigh...but these are the crosses we have to bear. I spoke to someone called Stu, who's given me a try out slot on the next edition of* The Cambridge News. *If I'm not good they don't publish it and that's it, if they like what I do and I don't get too much red pen on my article, I'm allowed back for the next edition.*

I felt it was a bit too early to point out that the name of the paper was more than just a bit crap, but think I'll save that for a conversation later with said Stu.

Before you ask, no, Stu's not cute or grrr in any way shape or form. Imagine Penfold *from* Danger Mouse *and you're there.*

So I've got to write an article about how the Student Union is having a re-furb and interview some students about what they'd like from the new building. A few vox pops and some blurb about why it's being done and Bob's your Uncle and Fanny's your Aunt, as some cockneys say (I believe).

I'm not sure why I've come across all faux cockney in this letter, perhaps it's thinking of you up in the big smoke.

Anyway, must go, I've got to iron my Wonder Woman *T shirt for an evening of disco music at the union tonight.*

Keep polishing those disco tits

Lots of love Grace xx

Fourteen

October 1999

*I*soon settled into a new rhythm since moving to London. It's amazing how quickly you settle into a new routine, as if the old one never existed. I noticed this on family holidays as a child: soon we got up at a similar time every day, sat around reading or sun bathing, ready for lunch or a trip out in the car. Afternoons of tea and cakes followed the mornings, before an evening of TV together, while I tried to read more of my book. This new routine wasn't quite as relaxed as that, but I was grateful for the distraction from the large empty spaces in my schedule since Sean hadn't called.

I got up at nine-of-the-early-morning-and-nothing-to-do-all-day-o'clock, dressed and had a cup of tea. Took my CV to all the nearest places I thought I stood a chance of getting a job—pubs, shops and a few hospitals. Returned to my halls of residence for some pasta and sauce and another tea, before going to the library to check my emails. As Grace was at university too, we were both enjoying the novelty of free internet access and hence unlimited emails. Most days Grace had replied to my missives, and if not, I sent her a detailed update about my situation. I printed out the emails, so I could read them in a more relaxed fashion back at my halls, sipping another cup of tea, listening to the latest *B*Witched* or *Steps* album in the background. I went to the few lectures and seminars I had—which shockingly only added up to a total of eight hours a week—equivalent to one shift at the hospital. Some days I'd treat myself with a trip into central London, every time marvelling at the 20 minute train journey to reach what had previously seemed such a distant and unattainable concept. I discovered H&M and the biggest Topman I'd ever seen, gradually buying myself a new item of clothing to add to my wardrobe each time I went there. I'd never seen an *H&M* before, so enjoyed wearing my new 'exotic' clothes around uni. I soon realised really how 'exotic' when I turned up in a long sleeved red T shirt with dragon patterns down each arm one morning to find half the other men in my lecture wearing the same.

Another 20 minutes and I was back in my little corner of south east London, where I made myself an evening meal of something involving pasta and tomatoes with perhaps a touch of garlic (Janice, one of the students I was sharing a kitchen with had begun to introduce me to the whole new world which was herbs and spices).

Janice Cohen, (of the New York city Cohens) regularly returned late at night, slightly drunk and began to forage in other people's cupboards for food. "I'm all about stealing other people's food, but I'll replace it tomorrow morning, definitely," she said in a strong New York city accent, pushing her sleek black bobbed hair behind her ear and looking out of the corner of her eye in case anyone else entered the kitchen.

I went to the meet and mingle events the university put on in the first few weeks, in an attempt to make a group of displaced people suddenly feel like they had friends instantly. This didn't work with me. Apart from the odd girl I clicked with on a basic level, like Janice, I didn't find myself drawn to anyone else. I'd seen enough people during my travels and work at the hospital to be wary of people who best-friended me within five minutes of meeting. I watched this happen with groups of Sloaney girls who claimed to have been separated at birth when they bumped into each other at the meet and mingles, and then weeks later had stopped speaking and blanked each other in the uni corridors. I noticed a few other men who were probably 'specialists' as Grace referred to us—the pierced eyebrows and Mohican hair gave the game away somewhat. I just stared at them as they paraded around college looking like gay peacocks, not daring to speak to them in case they weren't actually 'specialists' but just a bit more unconventional than the average man I'd seen back home.

I longed to show Jo these new gay peacocks and the Sloaney girls, knowing how much he'd enjoy striding up to them and introducing himself as a famous actor, or claiming to have seen them already. Each time I invited him over he said he was too busy to cross London to see me. Instead I told him my stories on the phone most evenings from my small en-suited room.

Sometimes he answered and I rushed through my news as he got ready to go out with some friends to, "Just go through aspects of characterisation" or to follow some "gay best friend gorgeous" guy he'd met at the LGBT soc.

Sometimes he was rushing out to meet Andrew, so I asked him if he'd heard from Sean, or whether I should call him.

"Is that a whiff of Obsession, by Disco Kieran I'm getting there? Listen sweetie, if he wants to call you he will, but don't spoil it by chasing him."

"Can you ask Andrew if he's seen Sean lately?"

The line was already dead.

The first month of university was turning out to be a very busy time, for some more than others. Understandably I didn't see much of Jo for the next few weeks.

"I'm getting deeper and deeper into Andrew's pants, so I may be gone some time! Isn't he fabulous. At last I've met someone who's as dirty as I am," Jo replied when I asked him when we could next see each other.

"What about a double date with us two and Andrew and Sean?" I tried, staring at my empty diary next to the phone in my room.

"Let me know when he calls and we'll do it." He put the phone down.

I wasn't used to having all this time to myself, so was unbelievably relieved when one of the local hospitals called me for an interview as a health care assistant. Ursula from Nursing Admin offered me the job on the spot and I couldn't believe my luck when she explained how much I'd earn per hour, including a magical and unexpected thing called London Weighting.

"Is that London Weighting per shift?" I looked around Ursula's office: four desks with women wearing head phones and microphones, typing madly and staring at the screens.

"Per hour."

I felt like I'd won the National Lottery and immediately

signed up for a smorgasbord of shifts over the next few weeks, allowing me to try most wards on for size. Ursula flipped through a lever arch folder of shifts while I read the various notices and posters on the walls about hand washing, nursing pay rates from my A grade to top sister of the ward I grade. Pleased with this new distraction I suddenly felt at home again. My weekly schedule was gradually filling up to a level I was used to. The large empty spaces left by my lack of friends were gradually closing up as I spent more time at university as I started work on my assignments and the hospital as I signed up for more shifts to fund my growing *H&M* habit.

The loneliness and sadness had crept up on me slowly: one hour of each day at a time. At first, I told myself I was blissfully happy there, throwing myself into everything to fill in the huge blanks of time during each day. Going to London was meant to broaden my horizons, not make them smaller. My world now consisted of the hospital, my lectures and my small en-suite bedroom. I knew some students on my course, but they weren't what I'd call friends, just filler really—people to make small talk with before lessons and if I bumped into them in the library. I had started to work nights at the hospital, if I wasn't going out on a Friday and Saturday night, I might as well work—and it was more money. I slept during the day between lectures which killed more time. I'd stopped calling Jo as I couldn't stand the different excuses each time. He had his own life to start in London and I had mine. I reasoned it was a bit unreasonable of me to ask him to break off from making new friends to check on one of his older friends. *I'd travelled around Australia, so moving to London would be easy, right?*

I looked at the bedside alarm clock glowing next to my

portable TV, 19.21. Another episode of *The Creek*, or I could switch the lights off and go to bed. I listened to the noise of South East London just outside my window: ambulance sirens, police cars, buses swooshing past, groups of people laughing, dogs barking. Everything close enough to touch, yet all I wanted to do was go to sleep.

Bloody hell, what's wrong with me? "The more you put into it, the more you'll get out," Dad always said. He'd be proud of what I was putting in *academically*, and of what I was putting in *work-wise*, but he wouldn't be pleased with my efforts *socially*—even if he wasn't the most sociable person, he knew I was, and had seen how important friends were to me.

I thought about Disco Kieran and immediately Grace.

I climbed into bed and noticed an email Grace had sent me a few days ago, as yet unread. I began to read it, slowly sitting up in bed as I committed myself to reading the whole thing.

From: g.465.english-ugrads@cambs.ac.uk

To: k.donovan.901@kings.ac.uk

Dear Disco Kieran,

Hiya!!!: throws hands in air in a my life how busy have I been lately gesture: Sorry for not replying to you sooner, but I've been on deadline again. It's ironic that I've been too busy doing lots of interesting things, to write to you about how I've been doing lots of interesting things.

By the way, Stu loved my article about the Student Union refurb, thanks for asking. He said he liked my "style" throughout. I kept expecting him to pull out a copy of the article with red ticks at various points throughout so he could say "I like what you did there".

Sadly, he didn't do this, but all the same he was pleased.

You did sound a bit low in the last email, so I hope you've heard from your platonic other half by the time you receive this. A month in, and he's still not had chance to meet yet? He must have been even busier than me, and I have been about seven kinds of busy lately. Give me Jo's address and I'll write him a strongly worded letter (or email as you can see I'm well versed in the use of email now) reminding him about your existence. You said you've told him you miss him and want to meet, but he's still not had time to see you? It sounds to me like he's got his own brand of Obsession going on, but luckily for him it sounds like it's being reciprocated by this new (and by all accounts a bit filthy) Andrew. I like a bit of 'action' as much as the next man or woman, but surely he needs to come up for air (if you excuse the pun) and at least share some of the edited highlights with you? That's certainly what I'd do. If you don't see him by next week ring me and I'll bring emergency Auntie Claire Rayner supplies and will visit you for a few days. Think of me as a Mary Poppins *crossed with Claire Rayner—I'll sweep into London on the train and cheer you up.*

In the meantime, you know where I am if you want to chat—I gave you my halls number and my wizzy new mobile phone number too. I'm also 'online' as I believe it's called, most days so will endeavour to send pishy news soonest. Still no sign of the dishy Sean then? As unlikely as this may seem, I am inclined to agree with Jo on this one. If he's not called and he said he would, then try to keep your dignity and leave it. Yes, I know how hard that is, particularly when you're sans best friend to vent to, but trust me it's the best path in the long run. (Remind me that I told you that when I see you and tell you all about this guy on the student paper for whom I've built a perfume factory selling bottles and bottles of Obsession by Disco Grace). Which neatly segues me to invite you to Cambridge for a weekend. Let me know when works for you and we can pencil and then pen in our respective diaries. It's only an hour from London, so it's not like going up north or anything like that...shudder.

Well done on the job front—transferrable skills aren't they so, well, transferrable! Is it much different working in a hospital in London than in the New Forest, or is the main difference you've so far noticed the fact that you get 'London Weighting' for every hour. I must say I nearly fell off my swivelly chair in the library when I read how much you'd be earning with this 'London Weighting' yoke too. Certainly *adopts deep voice* a lot more, then I've ever earned. However, you are looking after the sick and needy of South East London, where as I was just serving food to the already slightly over-weight and not particularly grateful of south Hampshire. I haven't looked into getting gainful employment here yet, between the uni paper and that other thing I'm here for...what's it called...oh yes, my English degree, there's not much time left. I suppose I could always adopt the Hannah method and just not sleep more than a few hours a night. Based on recent experience that isn't a good idea for me, as I fell asleep in a lecture on Monday after being out until far-too-late-on-a-school-night-o'clock Sunday night. I went to a pub quiz with Stu and the other uni paper guys and it all got a bit hazy after last orders.

Monday morning I noticed a VERY dubious stain on my black suede boots, and a complete absence of the Aerosmith T shirt I was wearing that night. The black leather coat, all present and correct, but the T shirt—no idea. Stu is 'putting out feelers' in the local area (he's very big in the Cambridge area, having been here for a few years) and so hopefully I'll be reunited with Aerosmith soon. I'll keep you posted. It's all most vexing as I bought that on a particularly fruitful charity shop trawl with you last summer and I'd grown very attached to said T shirt. (Not physically attached, as that's *revolting, but mentally attached).*

Anyway, that's enough rabbiting on, I'm off out again to do a bit of low level stalking for the mystery boy on the paper. Now where did I leave those binoculars...?

Lots of love
Keep dancing
Disco Grace xxx

I put the email down and noticed I was smiling for the first time in recent memory. Never mind going to bed at half seven, I'm Disco Kieran, I'm in London, I have a pair of black and white combat trousers which are rota'd with one of my best friends, who the hell did I think I was becoming? I'm not just sitting around here all night on my own.

I put on my shoes, threw on my new *H&M* dark blue velvet jacket and walked to the university library. I saw an email from Hannah unopened in my inbox. I printed it off, only reading the first paragraph to whet my appetite.

From: hannahgreeneloves-steps@hotmail.co.uk

To: k.donovan.901@kings.ac.uk

Hiya!!

Get me, sending you another email, it's so much more fun than college work. It's going to take a while to get used to this, I'm so used to you being just around the corner. But you're right, it's much easier this way, long newsy emails (longer than most of my college work, but more of that later).

We don't have internet at home so I can only use it at college, I'm still not that arsed about it all. Back to emails though, I am all about the fact that it's free though, and there's no having to remember to buy a bloody stamp. I've had letters sitting in my bag for months before I got round to buying a bloody stamp. See stamps later!

I folded the email and put it into my new *H&M* record bag and walked back to my room.

I made myself a cup of tea, lay on the single bed in my room, (always a bit of a worry if I were to ever get some 'action', but I reflected that a single bed would mean more snuggling with said perfect husband/boyfriend, so not to worry), put on my *The Creek Soundtrack* and settled down to Hannah's email:

From: hannahgreeneloves-steps@hotmail.co.uk

To: k.donovan.901@kings.ac.uk

Sounds like you're settling in well. I'm so jealous of your new job. I'm still stuck here, washing plates in the kitchen. Mind you the new matron reckons I'd make a good care assistant so we're working out what I can and can't do at the moment. Ok, so I won't get your fancy 'London Weighting' but also I don't have to pay stupid money for a Bacardi and Coke, like you do in London, so it all evens out I suppose!

Can't remember if I told you this before you went to London, but since I got my A level results back and they weren't exactly what I thought I'd get, I'm staying here at college another year to re-take some of them, and take some different ones I'm more arsed about. In the mean time, I'm going to carry on working at the hospital, but hopefully as a carer.

I say the results weren't what I thought I'd get, but in actual fact, they were pretty much exactly what I thought I'd get being as I'd not done any real work for them, it's just they weren't exactly what Mum and Himself expected. As you can imagine, Mum went doo lally tat when I read out the results to her, screaming that she wanted me to do better than her, and how was I supposed to do that with these grades. Himself just grunted something about spending time in "bloody queer bars in town" so rather than have another full-blown row with him (where I would have probably broken the telly or something), I got in my new car and drove to the forest to calm down. I can't remember if you've seen my new car, or was I still on the moped when you left? Seems like you've been gone ages. Anyway, I've got a car now, see helmets and waterproofs later—it's a Renault something or other. And it's metallic blue.

Leaving rather than shouting turned out to be a good choice, Himself hasn't mentioned anything again about it (not in front of me anyway). I think Mum's spoken to him about his stupid homophobic comments. That's enough of that, moving on...

Sean sounds delicious—if I wasn't a big ol' lesbian, I'd snatch him off you! You said you'd not heard from him yet, it's been weeks, any news? I'd just send him a text message, or you could "missed call" him. That's where you call his mobile, but don't wait for him to answer, that way he gets a little message saying you've called, and hopefully calls you back to say "you've just called me". This girl at college does it all the time. Sneaky bitch, but I love it.

How's Jo finding London? Have you seen him yet? I bet he's too busy dancing to see you eh? It must be all a bit too much moving to London together for you two. I'd have thought he'd have wanted to go to the gay clubs together. Maybe he's checking them out with his new drama friends (like Jo needs more drama in his life!) and then he'll go back with you once he knows which ones are the best. Or maybe he's just lashed you cos he's met this Andrew bloke and he can't walk straight for all the sex he's been having. Dirty bitch!

If you don't see him soon tell him from me he's a shit friend and if he's not careful I'll lash him! Seriously though, if you're lonely, call me, I could come up for a weekend if you give me a bit of notice. If not, let me know when you're next coming down to Hampshire and we can have a proper mince and catch up. I want photos, stories, gossip, the lot. Even if all it does it make me glad I don't live in London, I want to hear it all.

Lots of love
Hannah xx

I put the email next to Grace's and smiled to myself, noticing a tear had formed in each eye, I wiped them off my cheek. *The Soundtrack of The Creek* had reached a crescendo, which took schmaltz and teenaged angst to a whole new level. This, combined with Hannah and Grace's messages meant my eyes were now leaking quite significantly. They had reminded me I wasn't alone, but at the same time they had reminded me how lonely I had felt over the last few weeks since going to the University of London Union LGBT event.

It had been over two weeks since I'd called Jo and since then I'd heard nothing from him.

I picked up my mobile phone, re-read Hannah's email and then missed called Sean. I willed my phone to ring, but instead fell into a deep exhausted sleep.

Fifteen

Chapter 15

It had taken a long campaign of persuasion for Kev to visit me in London: phone calls, texts and even the odd email. Not really one for technology Kev never replied to any of the emails, but I thought it important to maintain a multi-pronged approach. Jo would have pulled out the 'best friends' card, but I preferred to entice with interest, rather than guilt. Normally not one to shy away from new experiences, and I'd have thought very keen to sample the bright lights of London, Kev eventually gave in and agreed to visit, but only when I told him about the total radio silence from Jo.

"Well in that case we'll go to the Black Cap, it's somewhere in London, starts with a C."

"Camden?"

"Sounds about right, and I want to see this drag queen, Sandra she's called. Meant to be filthy, racist, sexist, everything. It'll be amazing, can't wait."

My face said it all, I was pleased he couldn't see it over the phone.

"I know what you're like, it's ok, cos she's black. She's taking the piss out of herself. You'll have to see it to see how she gets away with it. She's well renowned in performing artiste circles, shame is she doesn't really go outside the M25, so Hampshire, you've got no chance. Might as well make the most of the trip, steal some of her ideas. No one's going to tell down in Southampton and suddenly I'm all cutting edge and risqué. I'm a genius."

I closed my mouth. "Don't you think Jo would like it?" I was keen to understand why he didn't want to see Jo.

"Don't think he'll be up for the dress shopping either."

"For you?"

"Unless you've suddenly developed an interest in being a drag queen, yes, me. Who else? Which reminded me, I still need a stage name, I'll ask Sandra, someone told me she's really called Dale, quiet as a mouse without his wig and dress I've heard. Read something in *Boyz* about her. Fascinating."

Jo's disappearance had reminded me how much I missed Kev, how much I missed how he was completely unlike Jo in so many ways I'd never really appreciated until now. For so long, Kev wasn't stood next to me, arm looped through mine, or shouting at the bar for a vodka and coke. So when I saw him tottering on his heels through the ticket barrier at Waterloo station relief flooded through my body. I'd noticed him miles off, as he teetered off the train, carrying his suitcases, who else could it be? He wore a bright red spiky wig, pink angora jumper which hung off one shoulder and came down to his knees, his legs covered in yellow tights and finished with shiny blue stilettos.

He ran towards me and hugged me tight, knocking me with two of his bags.

He stopped the hug and stood back. "What do you think?" He put the cases down and held his arms out either side of his body. I noticed a little handbag in the shape of a Rubiks Cube hanging off one shoulder.

"For tonight?"

"No, you twat, this was just for the journey, I've got more where that came from."

"Eighties?"

"I know that, but what else?"

Confused, and not wanting to offend, I persevered. I noticed a few people passing us with their luggage and pausing to take in our floor show. "What look were you going for?"

"Every-day-eighties, is the wig too much?" He pulled at the red hair.

"I never expected anything less of you, it's perfect. No one will even notice."

Kev smiled. "That's what I was hoping, I wouldn't do this back home, but I thought, on holiday in London—why not?"

"Exactly. We did say just this weekend didn't we?"

"Yes, why?"

I gestured to his pile of bags on the platform as people picked their way around them.

"This little lot, I tell you Kieran, I wanted to take a lot more, and I had Mum helping me slim it all down, so this, it's practically a capsule wardrobe. That's why I wanted to come in the car, but someone insisted I get the train."

I'd insisted he get the train for fear of him being let loose in his car anywhere near London. From when the date was set for his visit I'd had visions of him getting stuck on the hinterlands between the M25 and my little corner of south east London: Bromley, Orpington, that sort of place. Stuck on the hard shoulder with his hazard lights on, dressed head to toe in leopard print with two big red hatboxes. In my mind it was like the *Shania Twain* video for *That Don't Impress Me Much* only this time I'd have to leap in and convey him to my halls of residence, and *Shania* wouldn't be there to help. After three nights of cold sweats I had explained it wasn't like driving round Southampton and I couldn't cope with the stress if anything went wrong, so we agreed on a train, with a compromise of taxis for emergencies.

Now, Kev leant against a leopard print suitcase. "Can't remember the last time I travelled on the train. In fact, it might have been the last time I went to London, school trip, something about a museum."

"Science museum?"

"Do you remember?"

"How could I forget. I spent the whole time having paper balls spat at me, and you were late."

"I thought if I minced about at home enough we'd miss the train and I wouldn't have to go. Instead I spent the whole day being shouted at by the usuals."

"Same lot who were spitting at me." I felt my face, suddenly the memory of their spit on it came back to me.

Kev nodded and we caught each other's eyes, sharing a moment of relief that we'd passed that stage in our lives.

"And look at us now? Ready to go to a drag show in London, and me, with a suitcase of dresses!"

"Just the one?" I pointed to the pile of suitcases on the platform.

"Ok, a few suitcases, but anyway, fuck 'em."

"Fuck 'em," I replied. "Never mind all that, can you imagine what you'd have been like, driving in London? In those heels!"

"While we're on that, emergency taxi to yours? I don't think my legs will hold out on the Tube."

We got out of the taxi—the first and only time I'd been in one since moving to London, which I had pointed out to Kev a number of times throughout the journey. Kev handed over some notes, "Keep the change," he said, grabbing his things and stumbling out of the door.

"Get you, big spender?" I smiled.

"I've always wanted to say that to a taxi driver. That and, 'follow that car', do you reckon we'll have a chance this weekend?" Kev pulled out a long black cigarette holder from his Rubiks Cube handbag, put a Marlboro Light in the end and lit it.

"Get her, Marlene Dietrich." I laughed, holding the gate to my halls of residence and looking back as Kev gathered up his bags and followed me.

"If you can't have fun when you're on holiday, when can you?"

I settled him into my room, and started to make us dinner. Mid-mince-browning Janice walked into the kitchen, jar of Nutella and spoon in hand.

"What's that?" she asked, mouth-full of Nutella. "Can I steal some? I guess it's not stealing if I ask is it really?"

"It's a ragu sauce, for spag bol." I looked away from the frying pan and smiled at Janice.

"So you'll have heaps for just you, I'm *so* having some when it's ready. I guess I'll have to buy some food of my own soon. Just not today. I'm busy with a paper." She lay down on a row of soft chairs next to the wall in the corner of the kitchen, dripping Nutella into her mouth.

"How's that going for you?"

She wiped a blob of Nutella from her chin and pulled her hair from her eyes. "So far, I've got the title, and some books from the library. I'd have thought my shiny new Apple laptop would do a bit more than just sit there with a cursor flashing at me accusingly, but no, it's not started the paper for me yet, and I don't think it will."

I turned back to tend my mince and added some tinned tomatoes.

"I heard someone in your room, get lucky did you?"

"I wish! My friend Kev's staying for the weekend."

"What you got planned?" Janice started fishing for an opportunity of a good time.

"This tonight, dress shopping tomorrow, there's some special shop he wants to see. Don't get much chance of that back home, then out to see this drag queen he's been going on about tomorrow night. Sunday, probably just Hollyoaks omnibus in bed." I paused for effect. "Why, what you up to?"

"There's the paper…" Another blob of Nutella into her gaping mouth, still laying across the chairs.

"Hmm, you mentioned that…"

"And I'm *so not doing it* this weekend, am I? How about making it a threesome?"

I stirred the sauce and before I could answer Kev walked in, looking like *Shirley Bassey*, floor length red sequinned evening gown, gloves up to his elbows and a large black wig. "Did someone say something about a threesome?" he asked, pausing at the door to hold both arms out then walking towards Janice where he held his hand out for her to kiss it.

Janice sat up, put down the jar of Nutella and spoon,

shook out her sleek black bob then took his hand and after considering what to do, eventually shook it in a semi formal, semi friendly way. "Janice," she added.

"Kev." And he curtseyed.

Janice's eyes lit up, immediately seeing much more potential for fun, she squinted her eyes then looked at me. "This is Kev? Well, it's lovely to meet you. I've heard all about your plans, just wondered if you could do with someone to make it up to a threesome?"

"Sweetie, any friend of Kieran's is a friend of mine. When's dinner ready, I'm starved." He sashayed over to a chair next to the table in the corner.

Kev had explained the oft fabled drag queen, Sandra, we were seeing the following night, and Janice listened in horror as he explained her act.

"Oh, my, God, there's like, no way you could do that in the States, not even in New York. That's like, so rude." Her mouth stayed open as wide as her eyes.

Kev caught my eye as I stood at the sink. "That's like, the whole point, sweetie." He aped her accent, badly.

"Now this I've got to see!" Janice put a spoonful of Nutella into her mouth and chewed thoughtfully.

Somehow Janice managed to get Kev to talk about his ex boyfriend, something I'd not yet managed. All I had were glimpses into their relationship from odd phrases he'd drop into the conversation since they split up, normally accompanied by lots of vodka and run mascara. I sat at the table, listening to their conversation, impressed at the details Janice was gently teasing from Kev.

"At first he was so kind, I couldn't believe how lucky I was, holding doors for me, always offering to pay, but gradually it all fades. You don't notice it at first do you? It sort of creeps up on you. One moment he's telling your mum how much he loves you, next you're waiting in a pub for him to arrive all night, then he's borrowing money off you. And you give it to him don't you, cos he loves you and you do things for the people you love. Then you're afraid of asking him for it back, 'case he does it again." Kev looked out the window.

Janice touched his arm and asked gently, "What?"

"I'm so stupid. You can't tell people." He looked at Janice and me through teary eyes. "Cos they don't understand why you don't just leave, but it's not that simple is it? Every time he says how much he loves you and you believe him. Believe him he'll never do it again, but he does. Next time you ask him for the money, or say 'where have you been?' when he's late. Not always straight away, he never did it in public. Didn't want anyone to think different of him. He'd wait until we were alone, back at his flat or in my car, then it would come, out of the blue, couldn't remember what you'd said or done, but it was there, came back to bite me.

"'Course, for ages I thought it was my fault, shouldn't push his buttons, shouldn't pester him for stuff, asking for money, it's rude isn't it? I deserved it, didn't I, silly old Kev, no one else would have me, who else would want this?" He gestured to himself with his long red gloved hands. "Not knowing if they're going to pick up a man or a man in a dress every time they go out. Arthur or Martha. Thought it was just a joke, bit of banter, but that's not a joke is it?"

"How many times did it happen?" Janice leant across the table, towards Kev, quickly shooting me a look of sadness.

"Lost count, you sort of get used to it, get used to telling lies to your friends, they must have thought I was the clumsiest person they knew, falling down the stairs, walking into doors, all the time. Course, I used the heels as a good excuse, but that can only take you so far. The makeup helped, covered the marks he made, which made it worse, made him do it more, why was I wasting money on makeup when I could give it to him? I never did get that money back."

I looked at Janice.

She wiped a tear from her face, looking away from Kev so he wouldn't notice. "Money well spent, it taught you how much of a user he was, and now he's gone."

Kev sniffed. "Took me long enough to realise though. He pushed me so many times before I'd had enough. 'You'll be lucky to get anyone else, anyone who will put up with this shit! Can't you make up your mind what you are, instead of all this messing about?' he'd say." Kev wiped his eyes with a tissue Janice handed him, taking a deep breath to compose himself. "So, when's this food ready, I'm starving, Kieran, are you still mincing about with that mince?"

I smiled and Kev smiled back at me with red eyes, a weak smile and a deep breath.

What a wonderful, brave friend he was. I wanted to hug him but sensed the subject was closed and he didn't want to prolong it with hugs and more tears.

By the time we'd finished our spag bol, Kev and Janice had firmly best-friended each other. I collected the plates and watched them laughing together.

Kev stood up. "You don't have to do that, leave it." He walked over to the sink and pushed me away from the washing up.

"You're going to wash up, dressed like that?" I asked, taking in the floor length dressed, wigged, gloved sequinned Kev in front of me.

Janice swivelled round on her chair, ready for a front row seat.

Kev stood, hands on hips, giving it the full *Shirley*: "I've done a lot worse than *that* in a lot more than *this*, stand aside, I'm going to wash up." He took off his elbow length gloves, replaced them with yellow Marigolds and started to wash up.

Sixteen

Chapter 16

*J*anice decided to leave us to shop alone, and at least *attempt* to work on her paper, leaving her free to join us for the evening of non-PC fun in Camden.

"So where's this special dress shop you want to see?" I asked as we walked to the Tube station.

"What do you mean?" Kev replied, dressed down in flared jeans, trainers, a blue T shirt and black hoodie.

"You've come to London to buy some dresses, not that you need many more, but we'll leave that for the moment. I thought you'd planned to visit some special drag queen shop."

"I've got loads of drag queen dresses, I want normal, everyday stuff, you know so I can just blend in."

Pausing before I opened my mouth, I replied, "So where do we get stuff like that?"

"Topshop, Dorothy Perkins, Pilot, H&M, have you heard of these places?"

I nodded slowly, my mouth stayed open

Kev closed my mouth for me. "I know what you're thinking, but trust me, it'll be fine, it's London. I read all about it in Boyz. Top tips for buying a new wardrobe. Come along, follow me."

Falling behind slightly I thought about what he'd just said.

"Actually, I don't know where I'm going, where's this bloody Tube station anyway?"

I caught up with Kev, looped my arm through his and strode off to the Tube.

Three shops later, surrounded by bags, I sat outside the men's changing rooms of H&M Oxford Circus, their flagship store. Women waited patiently for their boyfriends and husbands to leave the cubicles in the new clothes, waiting for kind word of encouragement to persuade them to buy the clothes.

Kev left the cubicle in a red and white spotty dress with puff ball sleeves and red heels. He held the fish net tights in his hand, still wrapped. "I thought these would go with it too? Didn't try them on cos they're non-refundable, hygiene or something." He smiled, held out his arms, and did a theatrical twirl.

"Very nice, goes with the cardigan from Topshop. What else is there left?"

"Two more dresses, a couple of skirts and I've asked the shop assistant to find me a pair of leather boots in a nine, and some more of the cotton dresses. Versatile see!"

"Perfect, I'll tell her you're in there when she brings them."

Kev disappeared into the cubicle.

Women all around me who had previously stopped to stare at Kev were now deeply immersed in their own boyfriend/husband sartorial dramas. Jo would hate this. Jo would rather *die* than be here now, with Kev and me in this shop. Jo wouldn't have had any part in this at all. Jo seemed a bit dismissive of Kev and his cross-dressing, explaining that he didn't really understand the attraction in dressing up like that all the time, when he was a man. It was only after he'd told me this I reflected that was a bit much from someone so into drama, and dressing up, in particular in female characters' clothes. But I hadn't pursued that particular line of questioning with Jo.

The shop assistant walked to me, carrying a box of brown platform leather boots. She held out the box of boots. "Hello, sir, was it your…friend who wanted these in a nine?"

I nodded, grabbing the box of boots. "He's in there, I'll give them to him, he's just trying on one of your new dresses. He mentioned something about cotton dresses."

"What size?"

I shouted, "Kev, what size dresses are you after, the lady's going to get you some more to try on?"

"Twelve, thanks," came the reply from the other side of the cubicle door.

The shop assistant left me the boots and disappeared.

Kev appeared in another cotton dress, this time looking a bit more like one of Little Bo Peep's helpers.

I screwed up my face.

"It's gypsy, it's very in at the moment, in case you didn't know." Kev held out his arms either side of his body and spun round as usual.

A woman next to me said, "He's right, it's in all the magazines, they're full of it. Mind you, doesn't suit everyone though." She smiled and turned away.

Crestfallen, Kev returned to the changing room.

I shouted after him, "It's not like you've not bought anything else today."

"I'll be out in a minute, get the bags ready."

As Kev left the changing room, dressed in the jeans ensemble, the shop assistant arrived, carrying an armful of brightly coloured dresses.

"All twelves, do you want to try them on?" she said quietly.

"I'll have one in each colour, follow me, we're going to the till now," Kev replied, striding off in front of us.

At the nearest McDonalds we surveyed our purchases over burgers and fries.

"Not bad for a morning's work." Kev patted the nearest bag and felt the fabric of one of the cotton dresses.

"Can't believe we got away with it."

"Got away with what, we didn't steal anything, I paid for it all, with my hard earned money. Well, Barclaycard's, but let's not split hairs."

"Trying on women's clothes."

"If you just get on with it like it's not an issue, they can't say anything. It's them who've got an issue. If you can't do that in London, where can you?"

"Could you imagine, doing it in Salisbury?"

"That's why we did it here. Where now?" He folded up the burger box and wiped his hands on a napkin.

"Depends what else you want to do before tonight? Don't you want to see any of the touristy things while you're here?"

"With this little lot?" He gestured to the bags.

"One thing, then home, well back to mine, you know what I mean. Otherwise you're going to get back and everyone will ask you what you saw and so far it's my halls of residence, Oxford Street and a cabaret club in Camden."

Kev shrugged. "Ok if we must we must." He picked a

small compact mirror from his jeans pocket and checked his teeth and face. "Nothing in my teeth. Could do with a bit of foundation though. Wanna check?"

I took the mirror and checked my teeth, nodded and handed it back to Kev.

"Can we go to Trafalgar Square, I want to have my picture taken sitting in the paws of the lion, and Big Ben, then I'm done. I can say I've done London."

"Done."

"Can we get a taxi back? Shopping emergency…"

"Done again, but I'll pay this time, you've spent enough already."

Once we got into tourist sightseeing mode, Kev loved it. Fortified with food, we each took half the bags and visited Kev's tourist spots. I took a great picture of him standing in the middle of the lions' paws, then he started doing an impression of the bird lady from *Mary Poppins*, and began feeding the pigeons. I explained they're just rats with wings, and you're not allowed to feed them, pointing to one of the many signs around Trafalgar Square. Kev ignored me and said it was part of the tourist thing. Eventually I dragged him to Parliament Square where I took photos of him in front of Big Ben. He picked up the bags and started running towards the Thames, excited that we'd not yet seen it. I ran after him and showed him the quickest route to the river. Kev saw the boats offering trips down the river and asked if we could join one. I pointed out the time and how long he normally needed to get ready for a night out and he quickly realised it would have to wait until the next time.

He fell asleep on my arm in the taxi home, only waking to put a note into my hand as I paid.

A few hours, and numerous outfit changes later, Kev settled on the head to toe leopard print in a homage to *Shania Twain*, big red lips, pale face makeup and a massive curly red wig finished the look.

"You're not taking a red hat box on the tube, I draw the line at that," I said as Kev strutted into the kitchen, wobbling slightly on his very high leopard print boots.

I wore dark flared jeans, platform Doc Marten trainers and a short sleeved shirt in a swirly blue pattern that had already started sticking to me thanks to its *very* artificial fibres. *If it was good enough for Vince from Queer as Folk, it was good enough for me.*

Janice sat chewing gum dressed in her idea of party clothes: smart jeans with a summery dress worn over the top and blue trainers. "Good Lord, I've never been out-dressed by two guys before!" She exclaimed, taking in both our outfits. "What sort of a place is this we're going to? Will they let me in if they know I'm straight?"

"Just don't rub it in their faces, and you'll be fine," Kev teased, winking as he lit a cigarette he'd just put in its long holder. "Taxi or Tube?"

"Tube, it's not an emergency and we're not in a hurry," I replied immediately.

"In these boots, you must be joking." A cloud of smoke surrounded his head as he looked at his boots.

Janice waved away some of Kev's smoke then looked at him. "Trust me sweetie, no-one will look twice. We'll get a cab home, that counts as an emergency doesn't it Kieran?"

"Ok." I shrugged, clearly I wasn't going to win this one.

Sandra walked on stage an hour after she was billed to, by which point we were all well past our fourth drink, and all feeling the effects.

Kev screamed, almost knocking his cocktail into his lap when Sandra started her act.

Sandra peered through the stage lights to Kev's screams, her emphasised Jamaican accent exactly as Kev had described it: "Wha' she screaming at, me haven't started yet. Oh see, first time is it love? Thought you'd come an' have a laugh at a gay bar?" She stepped off the stage and walked towards us.

I froze, terrified of one of my biggest fears coming true, being locked in a war of words with a drag queen. Sure to lose I stared at the floor and sipped my cocktail through the straw slowly.

Sandra looked us over one at a time. When she reached Kev she smiled, my heart started beating again, we were safe. "Thought you was a girl over there, an that's me saying. Where you get this lot?" She stroked Kev's leopard skin top.

"TK Max." Kev beamed. "It's Shania Twain."

"Wha' you think I's, blind darlin'? So you come here to see how the professionals do it yeah? Wha's your name?"

He nodded. "Kev...I read about you in Boyz and wanted to see my friend at uni in London, so, well, here we are."

"'Ere you are. Well, you just watch an' learn." She wiggled back to the stage.

Kev pulled a notebook from his leopard skin handbag and started scribbling in it, as Sandra worked through her act, ad libbing when anyone dared heckle her from the audience. She dragged one drunken straight man from the corner, who'd made a point of shouting out how un-funny he thought she was, gave him the microphone and told him to show everyone how funny he was. He went bright red and started telling an awful Englishman, Irishman and Scotsman joke which got no laughs at all.

"Me rest me case," Sandra replied, "someone take 'im away." Bouncers removed him from the stage and he wasn't seen again.

Sandra oozed confidence, un-phased by anything. She just dealt with everything and everyone as it came, mixed with some self deprecating humour, all washed down with pitch perfect *Shirley Bassey, Macey Gray* and *Donna Summer* impressions. She only left after two encores, one of which involved telling a black woman in the audience that she didn't believe her name was Gloria, she was sure it was Umbagonkta, but she tells everyone it's Gloria to sound less black.

Janice put her hand over her mouth at this and looked away, as if the PC police were about to arrest them all.

The "Gloria" in question—we never found out if that really was her name—laughed so much she squirted Hooch out of her nostrils all over her top, Sandra took a final curtsey and left through the sparkly curtains stage right.

Janice sat open mouthed, staring at me and Kev. Kev put his notebook, pages full of scribbles, back into his handbag and I finished my cocktail.

"Don't think we can top that do you? Shall we go?" I looked at them both.

Kev replied, a huge smile across his face. "Exactly what I needed, next time you see me it's gonna be fabulous."

"I just, it's just…she…" Janice struggled to string a sentence together. "In New York City she you couldn't get away with that, but here…Good Lord…Have you got Chinese food at home?"

I nodded. "In the freezer, specifically for times like this."

***

The next morning Kev appeared in the kitchen, a blue dressing gown wrapped protectively round him, a blue head scarf and large *Jackie O* sunglasses covering his eyes. He lit a cigarette and slumped in the chair in the corner. We drank vats of sugary tea with the *Hollyoaks* omnibus in the background, Kev smoking *Marlboro Lights* without a holder, just plain old holding the cigarette himself.

Janice appeared, hair huge and dark, not its normal sleek bob, wearing *Friends* pyjamas.

I looked her up and down and before opening my mouth she replied, "They were a present from an aunt, is there any coffee or are you Brits sticking with your tea obsession?"

Kev took a drag on his cigarette. "Make yourself a coffee and join me ogling the cute men in this programme." He patted the seat next to his to confirm he meant it. "I have no idea what's going on at all, but they all look good enough to eat, it's doing wonders for my hangover." He blew smoke away from Janice.

Janice snuggled next to Kev and joined him in his spectator sport, sipping black coffee periodically asking us both whether we fancied the men on screen at that point. I joined them after handing out Kit Kats and smiled as Kev had fallen asleep on Janice's shoulder.

We finally got ourselves together at half-past-two-of-the-morning-after-we-went-to-a-cabaret-bar-and-Kev-found-

244

his-drag-queen-inspiration-and-a-new-best-friend-o'clock and walked around Greenwich Park, taking in the fresh air and feeling of being in the countryside, but pleased we'd only walked 20 minutes from my halls of residence.

"What time's your train, Kev?" I looked at Kev, as we walked past a bench of Chinese tourists laughing at a squirrel as they sat under an enormous oak tree.

"Six, seven, ages yet, I wish I could stay, wish I didn't have to go back to fucking Salisbury. What a dump compared to here."

Janice looped her arm through Kev's and I took his other side. "Sweetie, if you lived here, it wouldn't be like this all the time, it wouldn't be a vacation all the time."

"Suppose," he replied.

"Imagine their faces in The Duke, when you show them your new act," I said.

"And the new dresses," Janice added.

Kev chewed on a Snickers bar I'd just handed him.

"You'll be back soon, especially now there's two of us to visit here," I replied.

"Two?" he asked.

"Me too, dummy," Janice replied. "Well, three if you count Jo."

"*If* you count him," Kev said.

I watched Kev push his suitcases on a trolley as he walked up the platform at Waterloo station; he stopped to wave as I waited on the other side of the ticket barriers. Soon he blended into the crowd, his jeans and hoodie no different from countless others.

Janice put her arm around me as she sensed I was descending into my traditional post-fun low. "He'll be back soon, I promise.

Now, he's more reasons to visit London."

With all this rushing about, shopping, drag shows and Janice avoiding writing her paper, I hadn't thought about calling Jo, or how he'd not been in touch with me either. And more importantly, I'd completely forgotten about Sean. I was so pleased with myself.

Until I sat in my room, later that evening watching The Creek, revelling in how complex their love lives had become, I remembered how sadly simple mine was. I looked at Sean's number, saved safely in my mobile phone as my thumb hovered over the button to write a text message, then I put the phone down. Stcp away from the phone, I'm not this needy single man, I'm a modern gay man at uni from the late nineties, and I don't need any man to define who I am. *What was it Debbie Harry sung about the twenty first century coming? In fairness, she had said how much she wanted that man, and that it would be much better when he came along, even if it was the twenty first century.*

I had a shower, made myself something to eat and after debating what would take my mind off Sean most, settled down to a repeat *Queer As Folk* marathon, again grateful Grace had taped it for me while I'd been in Oz so I could see what all the fuss was about. I compared my shirts with Vince's from the show, enjoyed how Vince and Stuart reminded me of Jo and me. Then, I imagined what it would be like having Vince as a boyfriend. And I was back thinking about Sean again. Bugger. No, not bugger, that was worse, or better, or something. Damn and blast, that's better.

Half way through the *Queer As Folk* episodes I called Grace, and asked her did she mind just you know, chatting for a bit, or I was worried I'd let Obsession by Disco Kieran overtake me, and I would call Sean.

"I am, as they say, all ears." I could hear her smiling on the phone. "Shall we do landline to landline, I sense this isn't a quick five minutes?"

We swapped phones and I told her about Kev's visit, and how there was still nothing from Sean. "What to do?"

"Are you sitting comfortably?"

"Yep." I explained I was leaning on the wall sitting on my bed.

"If he calls he calls. If he doesn't call he doesn't call. You can't make him call. It's Buddhist or something, I read all about it in the library on the quieter days. Basically, long story short—whole spiritual ethos in a nutshell—*the universe will provide, or it won't*, and you must be grateful for that."

I blew a raspberry then sighed.

"Tell me about the people in the shop when you went dress shopping with Kev again? It sounds priceless. I'm sure I could make some sort of story out of it for the uni paper. If not, just tell me again, sounds like we could both do with a laugh."

And so I did, I told her all about Kev, and Janice, and what I'd been learning at uni—nothing about Bismark—and she even allowed me a bit of a post-mortem of meeting Sean and Andrew. When, after over an hour and a half, we both said we loved each other then I put the phone down, my ear warm, I had a big smile on my face. *The universe will provide, or it won't.*

I pressed play and continued the Manchester adventures of Vince, Stuart and Nathan, all bright shirts and dance remixes and felt life had turned out pretty well overall.

***

About the Author

Liam Livings shares his house with his boyfriend and cats. He enjoys baking, cooking, classic cars and socialising with friends. He has a sweet tooth for food and entertainment: loving to escape from real life with a romantic book; enjoying a good cry at a sad, funny and camp film; and listening to musical cheesy pop from the eighties to now. He tirelessly watches an awful lot of Gilmore Girls in the name of writing 'research'.

Published since 2013 by a number of British and American presses, his gay romance and gay fiction focuses on friendships, British humour, romance with plenty of sparkle. He's a member of the Romantic Novelists' Association, and the Chartered Institute of Marketing. With a masters in creative writing from Kingston University, he teaches writing workshops with his partner in sarcasm and humour, Virginia Heath as https://www.realpeoplewritebooks.com/ and has also ghostwritten a client's 5 Star reviewed autobiography.

You can connect with me on:

🇫 https://www.facebook.com/liam.livings

Also by Liam Livings

For chat, early notice of new releases, snippets of works in progress and talking about what we're loving at the moment, join my Facebook group: https://www.facebook.com/groups/LiamTeaAndChat/

Sign up to my newsletter, to hear about my new releases and much more, and you'll get a free copy of A New Life For Christmas https://dl.bookfunnel.com/sj5ko31m2t

A house exchange between two single men leads to a romantic new life for both of them.

Oliver and Kyle live thousands of miles apart, but each needs a break from his current life and love. Enter the Cloud B&B website, a wonderful new way to exchange homes for the holiday. They both muster their courage, and decide to visit another continent for Christmas.

Printed in Great Britain
by Amazon